Dare to Tempt an Earl This Spring

WEDDING FEVER, BOOK 1

SARA ADRIEN & TANYA WILDE

© Copyright 2025 by Sara Adrien & Tanya Wilde
Text by Sara Adrien & Tanya Wilde
Cover by Kim Killion Designs

Dragonblade Publishing, Inc. is an imprint of Kathryn Le Veque Novels, Inc.
P.O. Box 23
Moreno Valley, CA 92556
ceo@dragonbladepublishing.com

Produced in the United States of America

First Edition May 2025
Print Edition

Reproduction of any kind except where it pertains to short quotes in relation to advertising or promotion is strictly prohibited.

All Rights Reserved.

The characters and events portrayed in this book are fictitious. Any similarity to real persons, living or dead, is purely coincidental and not intended by the author.

ARE YOU SIGNED UP FOR DRAGONBLADE'S BLOG?

You'll get the latest news and information on exclusive giveaways, exclusive excerpts, coming releases, sales, free books, cover reveals and more.

Check out our complete list of authors, too!

No spam, no junk. That's a promise!

Sign Up Here

www.dragonbladepublishing.com

Dearest Reader;

Thank you for your support of a small press. At Dragonblade Publishing, we strive to bring you the highest quality Historical Romance from some of the best authors in the business. Without your support, there is no 'us', so we sincerely hope you adore these stories and find some new favorite authors along the way.

Happy Reading!

CEO, Dragonblade Publishing

ADDITIONAL DRAGONBLADE BOOKS BY
AUTHOR SARA ADRIEN

Wedding Fever Series (with Tanya Wilde)
Dare to Tempt an Earl This Spring (Book 1)
How to Lose a Prince This Summer (Book 2)

Miracles on Harley Street Series
A Sight to Behold (Book 1)
The Scent of Intuition (Book 2)
A Touch of Charm (Book 3)

The Lyon's Den Series
Don't Wake a Sleeping Lyon
The Lyon's First Choice
The Lyon's Golden Touch
The Lyon's Legacy

ADDITIONAL DRAGONBLADE BOOKS BY
AUTHOR TANYA WILDE

Wedding Fever Series (with Sara Adrien)
Dare to Tempt an Earl This Spring (Book 1)
How to Lose a Prince This Summer (Book 2)

Ladies Who Dare Series
Almost a Scoundrel (Book 1)
By No Means a Gentleman (Book 2)
A Knave By Any Other Name (Book 3)
A Little Bit of Hellion (Book 4)
Just About a Rake (Book 5)

The Lyon's Den Series
Beauty and the Lyon

Chapter One

Regent Street, London, 1818

"D<small>ID YOU SAY</small> Linsey?" Lady Ashley Sinclair asked her friend and closest confidant, Lady Charlene Fielding, in a whip-sharp tone. Had she heard right? "As in the *Earl* of Linsey?"

"Yes, the *Earl* of Linsey. You know, the one with fair sandy hair and eyes the color of liquid gold. Impeccable jawline. Stands a head above the average gentleman. *That* Earl of Linsey." Charlene held a purple ribbon in the air. "What about this satin one? It is pretty, yes?"

"You mean the man I loathe above all else," Ashley said, glancing at the ribbon. "The pink suits you better." Her voice softened as she added, almost to herself, "He is forever my enemy."

Ashley clutched her reticule and hoped that nobody in the haberdashery knew that she'd been jilted by a man who was running from a lost wager. In just her last season, according to her mother, she'd finally managed to do everything right—been called the catch of the season and courted by a dashing member of the Ton. But with Jordan's departure, it was all gone: her chances, her reputation, her future.

"Mr. Critton left on his own."

"My Jordan was run out of England by that earl with hair the color of liquid gold." The words tasted bitter on her tongue as if saying them out loud made them more real. As if she couldn't pretend anymore that he hadn't left.

Her most beloved suitor, the man she had planned to marry, Jordan Critton, was the third son of one of the most respected barons in the country—Baron Chiswick. He was handsome—much more handsome than Linsey. But he was also kind and generous. A combination few men in this town possessed. And now he was gone. All because of Linsey. Even now, recalling the letter where he told her not to wait for him…

Her heart clenched.

Along with her fists.

However, pain was not what she felt anymore. Any hurt had been overshadowed by fury toward that blasted earl. Who did he think he was running other people out of England? The gall of the man! But underneath the anger was a current of something deeper—fear. What if she never saw Jordan again? What if she ended up all alone? She didn't like being alone, and Jordan had filled the emptiness with warmth.

Now, the cold had once more returned.

Ashley sighed. She loved the haberdasher's shop, a well-known establishment on Regent Street, but the sheer mention of her nemesis took all the fun out of shopping. Reluctantly, Ashley traced her gloved fingers over the rows of silk and satin ribbons, each one perfectly coiled and pinned onto wooden spools.

The shop was housed in a quaint structure, nestled among the cobblestone streets of London, with its name elegantly painted in gold letters above the door. Ashley realized the letters were all brown viewed from the inside…just like the earl's devious character. The golden sheen he emanated had her friends fooled, as when you looked behind the shiny mask, he was rotten to the core.

"Be that as it may," Charlene murmured. "The earl is in London for the season. You shall have to accept the fact you might run into him."

Ashley's stomach churned as she processed the information. She couldn't stay confined in her house forever, true. But she also couldn't accept the turn of events. No, she needed to do *something*. Anything.

"Perhaps you should give the earl the benefit of the doubt," Charlene added. "I still cannot understand why the earl would run Mr. Critton off because of a wager. It seems rather like something that might only happen in a book."

Oh, my dearest Charlene. She had such a pure heart that she couldn't see the darkness in people even though it was so obvious to Ashley when she thought of Linsey. "Petty indeed."

Much more than petty, in fact.

Unacceptable.

Honestly, Ashley didn't understand it either. But she could remember the letter she received a fortnight ago word for word.

Dearest Ashley,

When you read these lines, I've long set sail. If it weren't for the wager I lost with the Earl of Linsey, I would have made good on our courtship and proposed.

Live well, my dear.

Jordan

As far as she'd gathered from this brief explanation, he lost a wager, and when he tried to negotiate the terms of that loss, he was threatened to leave England or honor the terms of the wager. Ashley didn't have any more details about the wager than that. But what wager could be worth threatening a man's livelihood over? Certainly, Jordan was at fault as well. He should have known better than to enter questionable wagers to begin with, especially ones he couldn't afford to lose. Still, could any wager warrant such madness?

A finger trailed over the blue jeweled brooch in the shape of a flower Jordan had gifted her. A token of his love. She wore it every day, as though it had become some sort of religion. A promise. They *would* reunite. She couldn't allow a whisper of doubt to creep into her conviction. It was sure to lead to her own madness.

"I heard he'll be at Almack's tonight."

Ashley started, her brows furrowing. "Almack's?" Everyone knew it was a marriage market packed into a ballroom for the Ton. No sane man with a title dared venture into the web of matchmakers and scheming mothers if they weren't prepared to be caught by the chains of matrimony. Unless…

Unless it's a man in want of a wife.

Was Linsey searching for a bride?

Hah!

The whole of England knew about his love affair with horses. A passion no woman could ever hope to match. Ashley had half expected him to marry one of his thoroughbreds. His firstborn son would probably be a centaur, with the upper body of a human and the lower body of a horse!

The thought brought a small, bitter smile to her lips. However, it quickly melted away as she imagined her mother's disappointment if she admitted that Jordan hadn't proposed. Worse, he'd vanished—and with him also Ashley's last chance to redeem herself in her mother's eyes.

She set the ribbons aside, no longer in the mood to purchase anything. However, "If he left those prized horses in the country…"

Charlene grinned. "It must be important, right? It seems to me that there might be some truth to the rumors that he has come to London to search for a wife."

Ashley nodded absentmindedly. "Do you know the source of the rumors?"

"Oh, whispers here and there," her friend answered. "However, I'm not sure how much *truth* is attached to them."

"Interesting. So, the Earl of Linsey is in search of a wife—"

"*Rumored* to be in search of a wife."

Ashley pursed her lips. Was it not the same thing? "I wonder if he has a woman in mind."

"You did hear the part where I said *rumored to be*." Her friend paused. "And why on earth would you wonder that?"

Ashley cut a look at her friend, her mind racing with all sorts of plots and twists. "Even you said there might be some truth to them. I daresay you would be correct. Are rumors not just half-truths?" She let a coiled yellow ribbon unfurl in her hand exactly the same way she wished to do with Linsey's lies and all he held dear.

"Assuredly, but we cannot forget there *are* rumors that are blatant lies."

Also, true. "But when it comes to a man and nuptials, truth and hidden agendas always stir beneath the surface."

Charlene arched her brow. "What a jaded thing to say."

Ashley waved a dismissive hand. "Where there is smoke, the sparks of a fire can be found." And there was so much smoke with this rumor Charlene had relayed that she nearly coughed from the effect of the news. Jordan's hasty departure and rushed letter still brewed in her chest. Even though they had pledged they would marry in the future, he'd left without a promise of marriage. He'd left without the promise of anything.

Not even one word of love.

That spoke volumes about what had transpired between him and Linsey. How could Linsey threaten a man away during such a sweet and endearing courtship that had the whole Ton envious? How could Ashley be left with nothing besides a broken heart and a disgruntled mother whose nagging could be felt through *her* letters? Whatever Jordan may have done, must she allow the reason for her and Jordan's calamity to get away unscathed?

No, by Jove!

The Earl of Linsey had to pay.

Even here in the haberdasher's shop, every hushed conversation, every sidelong glance, and every polite, yet pitying, smile that she encountered prickled at the rising levels of her vexation. Her whole body throbbed with the urge to meet this earl face to face and show him the repercussions of messing with a woman in love.

"Smoke or fire," Charlene murmured. "Mr. Critton could have stayed, or at least taken you with him."

Right. Ashley knew that as well, which was why the entire affair had been a tempest of confusion. If Jordan had still been here, she might not have been so vexed at the entire situation. Now, she was at the mercy of her discomforted heart and probing stares. Every fiber of her being bristled against her current state.

Jordan Critton, you just wait, too!

She would box his ears when she found him! The least he could have done was explain in person! She had done nothing to deserve such treatment from him. And perhaps some of her anger toward Jordan had transferred to the earl, but that didn't change the fact that the wager involved both of them and the outcome affected *her* as well.

The sting of being left had cut deep, leaving wounds that no amount of polite conversation or forced smiles could ever hope to alleviate with a simple explanation. Not presently. She could only channel that pain into purpose.

The Earl of Linsey's arrival must be a gift from the Heavens.

"You've got that look."

Ashley glanced at her friend. "What look?"

"That look like you're about to march into a battle with nothing but a pitchfork and a torch."

"There was a time when they were more than enough."

"Yes, to drive away beggars and witches. You need a sword if you wish to drive Vikings back from whence they came."

True. The Earl of Linsey had a reputation for standing tall and blond like a Viking. But Vikings had been a plague to this land, not heroes. He had all but handed himself over to be taught a lesson by venturing to London, away from his precious countryside. "Well, I do have a sword, if that is what you are worried about. A *hidden* weapon."

"Oh?" Charlene asked, intrigued. "What sword do you have?"

Ashley grinned at her. "Me." Her gaze caught on a bright red ribbon. How fitting. "I'll take this one."

Charlene laughed, shaking her head. "Did you just refer to yourself as a sword?"

"And why not? I can pierce, cut, and wound. Even if I must fall on my sword, I shall have my revenge." Purpose bloomed in her heart.

Revenge.

Yes.

This was what she needed.

"You do know you're saying you'd fall on yourself," Charlene said. "Why do I feel I should never have told you about Linsey? I truly fear for your future."

Too late.

"You should be fearing for him. *My* future was stolen by that man, Char. It's only fair that I snap up his, don't you think?"

Charlene bit her lip and mumbled, "Beware of losing your own life to the very cycle of retribution that you seek to perpetuate."

"I suddenly think the pursuit of retribution can be quite fruitful for the soul, Char." Ashley gave a self-indulgent smile. Why shouldn't her broken heart mend, upon Linsey's breaking? Why shouldn't he feel what she felt? What Jordan must have felt too!

Her friend lowered her voice, glancing at a group of ladies who entered the shop. "And just *how* are you going to ruin the earl's future?"

Ashley grinned. "By marrying him."

Her friend's jaw almost hit the floor of the ribbon shop. "You're going to do *what*?"

"Oh, I'm not *really* going to marry him," Ashley said. "I'm not crazy. I'm merely going to snare his attention, make him fall in love with me, and then…" The corners of her lips lifted another inch as she clenched her hand around the ribbon. "I'm going to crush his heart."

Just as he did mine.

She opened the palm of her hand and slowly balled it into a fist. "Then disappear from his life as though I was never there."

"Truly terrifying," Charlene said with a quirked brow as if she didn't believe Ashley had the courage to act on her plan.

"Watch me. I'm no longer the good girl bystander allowing other people to reign over my life."

"Utterly diabolical. Who are you and what did you do with my friend?"

"Do not tell me you have an objection?" Ashley asked. "The man may as well have ruined my life." Dramatic, she knew, but... "If he is not taught a lesson now, who knows how many other hearts he will shatter with that rotten character of his."

Charlene held up both hands. "Well, let me never stand in the way of a person dead set on revenge," she said with wide, glinting eyes. "Lest I wish to be buried as well."

"Much obliged."

"But I do have a question: How shall you break the engagement once he asks for your hand *if* he even does? Your father might let you bow out; your mother certainly will not."

"Oh, do not worry about that score. When it comes to Mama, Papa has his ways." The two might be estranged and hardly ever saw each other these days, but her father would never force Ashley to do anything she didn't want to do. According to him, Agatha Browning lost her authority over husband and daughter the moment she left them seven years ago.

Her friend regarded her with concern. "This may ruin you."

"I am aware that one digs two graves when one sets upon a path of revenge. Besides, if I can't marry Jordan, I don't want to marry at all." All her previous suitors had found her *too much*. Jordan had been the only one of them who accepted her for who she was. Which was why she was willing to pay the cost. *And if I'm ruined along the way, so be it. At least Mama will stop nagging me for the best prospects then.*

Charlene scratched her chin. "Very well. I have one last question."

Ashley arched a brow at her friend.

"How are you going to ensnare him? He is not an animal to be caught in a trap. Despite living in the country most of the year, the man is one of the most sought-after bachelors of the Ton."

Challenge rose within Ashley. "That is where you are wrong, Char. All men *are* animals to be caught in a trap." An arrogant statement, yes. But also a very simple one if one looked at the history of how women had trapped men in the past. Of course, it went both ways, but she'd wager more women had trapped men than men had trapped women. And Ashley wasn't just any *woman*. Such low tricks would never lead to love. A slow smile spread across her face, reaching all the way to her eyes. "Confidence, Char. That is how you truly trap a man."

"It's not the only thing you require."

Of course not. "As for the rest, I have just the guide on how to do exactly that." She had several guides, which she had found in the bottom of her mother's drawer one afternoon when she was bored and rummaged about.

"Well." Her friend retrieved a bright blue ribbon the color of Ashley's eyes and plucked the red one from her hand. "Then you should look your absolute best while embarking on your journey of revenge. You shall scare the man away in red."

Ashley laughed.

Ah, well.

I cannot have that.

Almack's
That Evening

THOMAS DUNBRIDGE, THE Earl of Linsey, fought an overwhelming urge to flee. Everyone around him seemed to be having a marvelous time, but he felt utterly out of place. He had been dragged into this situation by the looming deadline of a wager with a man who never forgave a lost bet. And that man, a *friend,* stood right beside him. Richard Ballard, the Duke of Paisley. He would lose his six most prized horses if he lost this bet.

And Thomas would do anything *not* to lose them.

Had it been just one, he might have considered losing the bet to Paisley. Perhaps even two. Three, depending on his mood. But *six*? By the heavens, he couldn't lose six! The horses kept him grounded, tethered to the person he truly was. Without them, he feared losing a part of himself, the one thing that reminded him of his roots, his struggles, and his victories. Memories of his father. His grandfather. He couldn't let that happen—not for anything.

Why not merely demand his life?

Though, in retrospect…

Thomas dragged a hand through his hair. "I don't bloody belong here."

"A bet is a bet," the duke said simply, not even a speck of inflection in his tone. And when Paisley's hand landed on his shoulder, a falsely congenial pat, his skin recoiled as if touched by a snake, each nerve protesting the contact.

"We made that wager years ago."

The duke shrugged. "Doesn't change a thing. Marry by the age of five-and-twenty or hand over your six most precious horses." Paisley cut him a glance. "Or do you *want* to hand over your thoroughbreds to me?"

Thomas scowled. Why did it feel like the duke's title was his only virtue, if a title could even be called such? He, at least, still had his honor even though he could hardly deny the very horses he was so proud of were in jeopardy because of his own fault. Why did he have to wager *six* horses all those years ago?

Damn Paisley for being like the loosely-drawn black shadows in paintings when devastation struck. Ruining lives was not an obstacle the duke even noticed. How many women had he bedded for sport and how many peers had he pulled over the barrel? The man wanted to win at all costs. Even if the price for his opponent was disproportionately high, he had to save face. And since he'd gotten into the duke's net of wagers years ago, he must tread with care, or he'd be further wrapped in the sticky webs and paralyzed by the duke's venom.

Thomas scowled at the man.

People usually didn't speak to him in this manner, but Paisley had been at Eton with him, then at Oxford, and they had this wager between them, so he couldn't just disregard him. This was one of the last balls before his birthday and thus, one of the last chances to find a suitable chit. His word was his bond, and since the duke refused to scrap the wager as two foolish young men up to no good, to break it would be to tarnish not only his own reputation but to besmirch the very essence of gentlemanly conduct. And with his twenty-fifth birthday coming up soon…

Thomas had to find a bride.

Yesterday.

"I'm not handing over anything," Thomas said with conviction.

"Are you certain?" Paisley murmured with a lazy smile.

His gaze hardened on the man, a dark cloud in an otherwise festive atmosphere full of crystal chandeliers and fragrant punch. He watched as Paisley winked at an innocent debutante who fluttered past him like a butterfly to a bowl of poison laced with honey, unaware of the doom that bowl represented. A bitter taste filled Thomas's mouth, his disdain for his so-called *friend* growing with each encounter.

No.

Not *friend*, friend.

Perhaps in their Eton days, but Thomas had discovered the man's rather diabolical character was not all that aligned with his. Their relationship might have started off as friendship but had soon turned to mere acquaintanceship that was more of the distant sort. Like a person one called on only once a year in order to preserve one's sanity. Once, with this man, was already too much.

"I'm certain," Thomas grumbled.

"Then look around, old fellow. Pick a bride. You don't have much time left to court her and complete the transaction."

"Marriage is not supposed to be a transaction, Paisley." Thomas couldn't keep a hint of coldness from lacing his words.

"It's nothing new at all. Marriages are forged for reasons that more often resemble business than matters of the heart. Who cares if the bride is rich and willing anyway?"

Thomas's stomach recoiled at the idea of joining his life to that of a woman for anything but love, but he couldn't say that to another peer of the realm. Especially Paisley. Romance was a weakness for a man like the duke, most gentlemen in general, and he couldn't betray his dreams in front of a man who did not hold his best interests at heart, and who would only piss on them with contempt. Thomas may have been reckless in entering the wager all those years ago, but he wasn't a fool about satisfying his debt.

He hoped against hope that the night would wash over him as nothing more than a waste of time.

You need a bride.

Fine.

For him, then, this night would be nothing more than a waste of time—with the *exception* of finding a bride.

He'd much rather be at home reading *Hopkinson's Breeding and Training of Thoroughbreds: A Comprehensive Guide to Horse Racing* than watching the debutantes in frilly dresses stare at him over their fans as if he were a piece of steak. A titled bachelor in good health was as appetizing a target at Almack's as a rabbit on a hound chase.

Should he just have approached a matchmaker?

On second thought, there was really just one girl in particular giving him the once-over and whispering something to her friend. Silly creatures, likely eager for a first kiss before the end of the season. Thomas had once enjoyed this innocence—their clumsy way of pressing their lips against his. But it had lost its appeal when he'd been tricked once.

Daisy Gotham. Baron Righton's eldest daughter. She had shown a keen interest in him. Except it had been a ruse. She had lured him into her father's study, where her sisters lay in wait. Had he been fool enough to get caught, he'd be shackled to a shrill wife and not a penny of the dowry her father had gambled away. Fortunately, his senses had been sharp, and he managed to evade the marriage trap.

Only to step into one of his own making.

Wasn't he gambling something far more precious than liberty with this wager? If only that incident had happened before he'd made the bet, then he might have thought twice before taking his bachelorhood for granted. But back then, he'd been certain he would win—convinced he'd find love long before his twenty-fifth birthday.

Thomas scowled. "One day you will eat your words, Paisley."

"Perhaps," the duke said. "But not tonight."

"Who is to say it won't be tonight?"

"I say," came his curt reply.

Damn man. Always ready to feast upon the vulnerable. He was probably a vulture in another life and managed to clean up into the dashing persona he was in this one. "Why do you even want my horses anyway?"

"It's a matter of principle."

Principle my arse. And was it his imagination, or did the man beside him just flinch? But before he could assess some more, his gaze was caught on the young woman with gold hair swept up in an elegant bun. She stood in a blue dress, her fair skin glowing in the soft light as she stared at him outright. Even from this distance, he could tell her lips were full and lush, her cheeks a pinkish hue. There was an undeniable beauty about her.

A diamond of the Ton, no doubt.

Their gazes locked from across the room, and a glint sparked in her eyes that made his stomach lurch. Something dangerous and riveting at the same time.

Thomas matched her stare, sure her cheeks would turn crimson, and she'd look away. They always did.

But not her.

No, this one, from her perch behind a marble column, she lifted her chin and met his challenge with such determination, such ferociousness, he could almost believe she was trying to call him to a duel!

His heartbeat sped up.

He forgot all about Paisley and squared his shoulders, his focus flooding with a foreboding sense of doom. Something was amiss. Something bad was going to happen. He might not lose his life in this proverbial duel, but something told him he wouldn't escape whole from this night either. One thought did enter his mind then.

Did he even want to escape a woman like her?

Chapter Two

*S*O THAT'S HIM

Ashley leaned against the pillar and gripped the ruffles of her gown as she stared at Linsey, a pillar that was placed just right to observe most of the ballroom and offered a sense of shield as well. If she chose to hide, which she was not inclined to do. She *wanted* him to feel her eyes on him. Plus, it went against her nature to hide, and quite frankly, she'd much rather be anywhere else. But now that he had arrived, she needed to act. She couldn't even admire her most favorite part of the scene before her—dancers moving beneath the sparkling chandeliers. No, her eyes were blocked by a blaze of fire, seeing only the blackness of her target's soul.

Thomas Dunbridge, the rotten Earl of Linsey.

He sported a look on his face that spoke of his reluctance and disdain.

Hah! So, he didn't want to be here either.

Good to know, Earl.

He probably wanted to muck about his famed stables with his most prized thoroughbreds. After her earlier conversation with Char, she had time to ponder his sudden appearance along with all the rumors. There are only two reasons why a countryman like him with his looks and rank would venture to London—to Almack's—in search of a wife in the twilight of spring.

One: He was impoverished and needed to refill his family coffers.

Two: He required an heir.

Both these reasons produced even more questions. Such as how the family coffers had run out. An addiction to horse races perhaps? If he required an heir, why the rush? Perhaps a provision in a will? Ashley knew enough from even her limited time in the Ton that she ought not to consider his search for a love match likely. Romance couldn't possibly factor in his devious plans, she was sure of it.

Whatever the case may be, if it were for a dire reason, it worked in Ashley's favor. For then she could rip his hope apart instead of trying to wrestle his heart away from his stable of horses. Not that she doubted she could. However, the former required a bit less effort.

She stared at the man from across the room. He was tall and towering over the man by his side by nearly a foot. He appeared rather intimidating. Not to be trifled with. *Hah!* Regardless, the earl deserved to pay for what he had done. The hearts he had ruined. He had taken everything from her this season.

Her match.

Her future.

Her *almost* fiancé.

And while everyone had declared her the ravishing beauty of the season, nobody had considered her feelings—or even her say—in what would come afterwards. She'd always been treated like a doll rather than a human being. And if she didn't want her mother to sell her off to the highest bidder next season, she had to make this one count.

Just not the way anyone expected. But if love wasn't possible for her match, then at the very least, retribution should be.

Her gaze tracked over the earl from head to toe. Despite his height, he looked normal enough. Too normal. Handsome, even. Blond hair. Golden-brown eyes. Black heart. Who knew that behind those rather attractive features a rotten core stewed and brewed? The man was even dressed in all black! No, wait. Was that a yellow waistcoat peeking from beneath his coat? Gold, perhaps? Burnt orange? She inwardly snorted. So, he had questionable taste…

Not so perfect after all, eh, Linsey?

A finger trailed over the brooch pinned to her dress at the center of her bosom, bringing her a measure of comfort.

"Why are you just staring at him? What is your plan of approach?" Charlene asked, shuffling closer to her. "And why are we hiding behind a pillar again?"

"*You* are behind the pillar, not I. And we are not hiding," Ashley said. "We are observing."

"There is another term for this sort of observing," her friend remarked.

Ashley didn't glance away from her target as she asked, "And what term is that?"

"Stalking."

Ashley gave her friend a deadpan look.

"I'm not stalking Linsey. I don't stalk."

"Oh? You aren't obsessed with him either."

Ashley gave a snort. "Only in the sense that I shall loathe him to eternity."

Charlene puffed out a breath. "Very well. If you say so. So, what *is* your plan of approach?"

Ashley pursed her lips. "I was thinking of just marching up to him and introducing myself. Cutting through all the titters, if you will."

"Why not just march up to him and propose marriage? The scandal would be about the same."

True. Without a formal introduction, she might as well lay naked on his bed and offer herself up. If she spoke to him now, the gossips of the Ton would make the same of it. "However, determined times called for determined measures," Ashley said. "But you are right. It will cause a bit of a scandal."

Charlene groaned. "Why do you sound so delighted?"

"Well for one, have you seen the girls fluttering around him?" Like moths drawn to that atrocious yellow, gold, burnt-orange fabric he wore. "It seems I shall need to stand out more than his waistcoat. And if everyone takes notice of us, *he* will notice. I need him to see me. And just me."

"Well, you should have matched his outfit then."

Ashley almost laughed. "Do not be absurd."

Charlene snickered. "Well, I'm still not convinced. What did this guidebook you found say?"

Do not let her start on that book. The information couldn't be considered bad, but neither could she claim it was good. Not for this particular mission of hers. "The usual. Act the damsel. Flutter your lashes. Stumble over your own feet."

"The last might work," Charlene said thoughtfully.

"Only if I crash through that crowd and straight into him."

Charlene grabbed her arm. "Don't look now, but the earl is looking our way."

It wasn't as if she could help it! Not that she looked, she *still* looked. Their eyes locked, and Ashley's heart somersaulted on the spot. For one short second, her mind went blank before the thrill of anticipation raced down her spine.

Yes, Linsey. I've got you in my sight.

Her chin lifted a notch. As did the corner of his mouth before his attention was once again snatched away.

Rotten beast.

Her chest constricted once more as the bold scrawl of Jordan's letter surfaced again in her mind.

Do not wait for me, my dearest Ashley.

Eight words, all bitter with no sweetness. Her fingers feathered over the brooch again, her eyes narrowing on the earl.

This is for you, Jordan.

Her heart picked up pace.

I shall make it so that you can return to London, or I shall leave to find you.

Because she couldn't accept the way he left.

And she couldn't accept how he was made to leave.

Ashley inhaled a fortifying breath. "Our eyes have already met." She winked at her friend, willing her body to calm down. "It's only natural to take the next step in our relationship. Wish me luck."

"You are crazy. What if Lord Linsey is aware of your connection to Mr. Critton?"

That would be rather interesting. "Doubtful."

"But what if he *does* know?" Charlene pressed.

"If that is the case, I suppose it shall make what I'm about to do next all the more thrilling, don't you say?"

"I don't say," Charlene countered. "In fact, I worry about your reputation. Your parents are going to kill me when they find out about this. They will never allow you to stay with me again if your plan goes awry and you cause a scandal."

"Don't fret so much, Char." Ashley patted her friend's shoulder. "I've got this under control." She did have a Plan B—leave to find Jordan if a scandal erupted and her revenge failed. "Are you coming?" After all, Ashley couldn't be ruined twice.

Charlene shook her head. "I'll observe from a distance." The emphasis was clear. Ashley was on her own, and Charlene would keep her distance, so as not to become cannon fodder for her friend's revenge.

Ashley understood.

She walked this path alone.

Besides, *she* had already become cannon fodder because of Linsey's rift with Jordan. She had lost her beloved. The earl had pulverized her hopes and dreams. Revenge was the only dish that would satisfy her appetite now, even if it meant she sacrificed her reputation and had to leave London for the time being. She would not rest until she had taken from the earl what he had stolen from her. The problem was that she also had to give it to him first, make it count, and then lead him down the path of heartbreak. She had it all mapped out in her mind.

Ashley gave a curt nod. "As you wish."

Squaring her shoulders, she made her way toward him.

This was it.

"YOU'RE RUNNING OUT of time." Thomas felt a shiver of distaste ripple through him as Paisley's groomed eyebrows arched in his direction and he leaned into him, a caricature of the perfect son-in-law plucked straight from a poorly written play. The scent of the man, a cloying blend of cologne and vanity, made Thomas's nostrils flare once more, his stomach twisting in a familiar repulsion.

He retreated a step from the man.

"I still cannot believe I'm here, in London, looking for a wife," Thomas said to himself as much as Paisley, retreating another step away from him. "I'm not interested in damn marriage, Paisley." Not this way, curse it. How could he find a bride in such a short time? How could he sift through all the eager gazes and choose the one right for him?

"Are we ever? Men are not made for monogamy. Can you imagine? One woman for the rest of your life?" Paisley made a retching noise. It sounded just as fake as the laughter that followed.

Arse.

Thomas could, as a matter of fact, imagine quite well to be with one woman for the rest of his days, for what was marriage more than the sharing of a life and a heart? It was one of those idiotic stigmas among men that love was for the frail. And yet, he had always imagined that he'd find the woman of his dreams one day—far, far away in the future—who would make his blood boil with passion. She'd make his life exciting, worth living. Not that it wasn't worth living at the moment, but he imagined his wife would bring *more*.

And he longed for more.

"And let's not forget that Almack's is the perfect place for your needs. All the women here are looking for a husband."

"My needs, Paisley, are met. Thank you for trying to look out for me."

More like rubbing salt in a bleeding wound. "But no thanks." Thomas was ready to turn away in search of a drink. He'd rather forget this stupid bet, well knowing that Paisley wouldn't let him live it down for the rest of his life.

"Come on now, old pal," Paisley drawled. "You don't want to forfeit all of your most precious beasts without even trying, do you?"

Thomas pinched his eyes shut, nearly wincing. It was as if the man wanted to see him struggle. As if the man didn't believe he'd actually find a wife to marry. But then, Thomas knew how Paisley operated. The man found perverse joy in the manipulation, twisting of fates and futures for his own amusement, oblivious to the devastation left in his wake.

The worst part, he thought bitterly, was that ruining lives was not an obstacle for the duke but merely another step in his wicked game. After all, men like him believed his title gave him a sort of supremacy over people. A fact that made his skin crawl even more.

"What if I just say no?" Thomas ventured one last attempt to get out of the foolish bet he'd entered when he was but a lad and unable to hold his liquor.

"No. I won't release you from this wager."

"What if I release myself?"

"Well, then I'll take the thoroughbreds," Paisley said.

Of course he would.

A cold dread settled in Thomas's heart at the thought of Paisley laying a hand on his precious horses, the pride of the House of Linsey. The lineage of their horses, painstakingly nurtured by generations of his family, was legendary—more than just animals, they were symbols of heritage and honor. Yet, Thomas knew the duke to be a man who reveled in tearing down legends, the sort of vile creature who'd trample upon their legacy without a second thought, solely for his own twisted amusement.

"Absolutely not, under any circumstances." Thomas furrowed his brow. How many people had he let off of their wagers? Was it so hard that one would do it for him? No matter what, he couldn't sacrifice the thoroughbred bloodline that his grandfather and great-grandfather had nurtured for selfish reasons like a love match. That was not the sort of man he was; his duty, his *convictions*, came before his desires. If it didn't, he'd be no better than Paisley. He'd fight to death to protect his family's legacy, and so, his horses.

That meant he had to find a wife.

And he had only a little over one month to do so.

His gaze tracked the ballroom filled with female titters and jitters. How the hell was he going to accomplish that? He didn't have time to court a lady. The thought brought an ache to his temples. However, he knew many of these women wouldn't be opposed to a hasty marriage if they received a title in return, but even though he was forced to marry for reasons he could no longer control, he still wanted a wife he could tolerate. One that he might come to love. At the very least, one he could become fond of over time.

A vision caught his eye.

The woman from before. The lady in the blue dress. The one who had been outright staring at him like he was a rabbit and she the wolf.

Thomas blinked.

Wait a minute. Why did it look as though she was heading his way?

Surely not.

By Jove! She was heading his way.

He couldn't mistake it. Her eyes were on him. Her feet pointed in *his* direction. She smiled when their gazes locked, and he swallowed. Just to be one hundred percent certain, he looked left and right. Even glanced over his shoulder. There still existed a small percentage that he was wrong. Perhaps she wasn't approaching him but Paisley.

Your gazes have already locked, you fool. She smiled at you.

And then, so that there was no doubt left, she stopped right before him. Them. But him. Because her eyes never once strayed to Paisley.

"Good evening, gentlemen," the vision said with a sweetness that lacked any cloyingness. "I daresay we haven't met."

Thomas couldn't help but arch a brow. "I daresay that's because we haven't been introduced."

"Lady Ashley Sinclair, and no need for an introduction. Your title precedes you. Oh, and rules are made to be broken, do you not agree?"

She was beautiful *and* brazen. And his body felt the impact. It felt dangerous. "I'm not sure I agree."

Her laughter rang through the air. "So righteous. Are you always this proper, my lord?"

Unless he was on the back of a horse… "Yes."

"I daresay I call liar."

Thomas's brows transformed into a tempest. "I call forward."

"I call *stiff*."

This little minx. "I'm not stiff," Thomas protested. Some parts of him were but he couldn't tell her that. Which bloody surprised him.

The corner of her lips lifted a sly notch. "I can hardly blame you. All men are stiff the first time they enter Almack's in search of a wife."

Thomas's eyes widened. How did she—

Her smile split open, and he knew he'd lost.

He only knew that all the retorts that sprang to his mind, moved to his tongue, rolled into silence as he parted his lips.

What he truly had lost he couldn't yet say.

Chapter Three

ASHLEY GAZED INTO the earl's eyes and kept her perfectly poised smile in place. So the rumors were true. Linsey was indeed in search of a wife. Wishing to find happiness while he'd ripped hers away?

That will not be happening, Linsey.

Not while I'm still breathing.

Annoyingly, this close to him, she couldn't help noticing that the man was more handsome than he appeared from a distance. Not that *that* made any difference. A man's appearance said nothing about his character, and this earl had proved to have a rotten one. Yet—that one little word—*Yet.*

He did not look like a man that would run a fellow peer out of the country just because that peer lost a bet and couldn't meet the conditions. Were wagers taken so seriously by gentlemen that they would ruin lives over them? Ashley couldn't fathom such a thing. *Yet,* the evidence was clear with each jab in her heart. *Yet* the man before her looked like a man that had too much honor to do such a thing.

"Do you always keep a close eye on the men who enter Almack's?"

"All ladies do," Ashley murmured with a smile. "Otherwise, how else would we meet the new arrivals?"

His eyes narrowed slightly on her. "You speak as though we are the latest fashion entering the shops."

Her lips inched upward. "Aren't you?"

Her mind raced as he arched a well-defined brow. What had the book said again? Hold eye contact with the object of your affection.

She held his gaze.

But.

Affection was not a color she'd paint this vendetta with.

Oh, the book also said she should flutter her lashes at least three times every five seconds. She couldn't manage a flutter. Grace save her, but she couldn't. There were more, weren't there. Hold gaze. Smile. Flutter lashes. Act coy. Curl a string of hair between her fingers.

Ah.

Her fan.

She could use her fan.

Ashley whipped open her fan and covered half her face with it. The man beside the earl cleared his throat. She spared him the briefest of glances. The Duke of Paisley? A wretched character, if rumors were to be believed. Of course, it made sense that Linsey would be friends with such a man. They were probably cut from the same cloth, which served as more proof that no matter how a man looked or seemed, it wasn't the whole picture.

The duke stepped forward, eyes pinned on her. "My lady, would you do me the honor of the next dance?"

What on earth? Did the man not see her interest in the earl? "Your Grace, I thank you for the offer, but I shall have to decline as I have another interest." She glanced at Linsey, holding back a bold wink. "Should we perhaps take this discussion onto the dance floor?"

Both men blinked at her, and she bit her lip to keep from laughing.

"Are you always this forward?" Linsey asked, his lips turning slightly upward. A dimple formed in his clean-shaven cheek.

"Only when I know what I want." *And I want you. In pieces.*

"What about what I want?"

She widened her gaze in mock surprise. "You don't want to dance?

I thought all men loved to dance."

"I..."

"Or is it that perhaps," she cast a glance left and right before she lowered her voice to a barely audible whisper, her eyes challenging him on every score, "you never learned the art."

His back snapped straight instantly and his eyes, for the first time, narrowed on her. "By all means, my lady. Let us take this conversation to the dance floor."

Ashley accepted his proffered arm and allowed the earl to lead her to the center of the room, waiting for the orchestra to start up a new melody.

The quadrille.

All that was left was to shine so bright he believed beyond a shadow of a doubt she was the woman for him. The only lady who could hold the position as his countess.

Her lips quirked.

"You seem awfully pleased with yourself," he said as they strode to the dance floor.

"I am."

"Oh?"

"Well, I'm the first woman you have danced with. We women come alive beneath the envious gazes of others. Didn't you know?"

"I wish I didn't."

She chuckled. He might be funny and tremendously handsome, but nothing could save him from her wrath.

Ashley caught a glimpse of her friend standing off to the side in disbelief. She winked at Charlene. Her prey was in her grasp.

Literally.

Now she just had to keep him there.

Determination intertwined with each step as he led her to where the couples twirled across the ballroom. This was her opportunity. She had to seize it with all her might. There might not come another.

"How have you found the prospects?" Ashley asked. Bold, yes. The book warned against being outspoken, but time was of the essence. The man had ventured into Almack's, which meant the man about to twirl the dance floor with her was in a hurry. And what was a book if not a guideline?

"Passable."

"Merely passable?"

"What about you?" He evaded the question. Interesting. Did that mean he also found her to be just passable? She would need to change that.

"Dismal," she answered, before her lips quirked up at him. "Until tonight."

He stared at her, and Ashley could tell he didn't know what to entirely make of her forwardness even as he indulged her in this dance. This might be a good thing. Or a bad thing. She hoped for the former. She needed to stand out in a way to make her unforgettable. But unforgettable in the way he sought her out and not someone else.

"Do I intimidate you, my lord?"

He blinked. "I beg your pardon?"

"My forwardness."

"No, of course not," he replied. "It's quite refreshing."

And you are quite the liar, Linsey.

She inwardly snorted, but the smile remained fixed on her face. "I ask because I've been told I can be a bit much. However, I am a woman who knows her own mind, and gentlemen tend to find that discomforting. I want a man who knows how to handle a woman of spirit."

"I see."

Hah! What exactly do you see, sir?

"Perhaps I made a mistake."

"A mistake?"

She bit back a smile at the lines once more deepening his brows. "I can't tell yet. You may be just such a man." She sighed dramatically.

"Or you may not be the man for me. However, I've decided you may call on me. Just to be sure."

They joined the dancers on her last note.

She couldn't have planned this better even if she'd orchestrated this herself. It seemed the universe was in favor of her method of revenge she had for this man. Her smile never faltered as she faced him, noting the small, but present lines gathering on his brow.

Envious gazes pricked her skin.

I'm doing you a favor, ladies.

SHE WAS NOT the woman for him.

Audacious, bold, and insolent.

Like a mare that hadn't been broken in yet. He was in no mood to break in an unruly lady. That should have been her mother's job. His mother would flog him for this thought. Of course, he didn't mind outspoken ladies. But there was unruly, and there was *unruly*.

He suspected this minx to be the latter.

Not that he had time to be picky, but he had hoped to snare a wife that was at least gentle and soothing. This woman had the hairs on the back of his neck standing on end.

What was happening?

Paisley had dragged him to Almack's—his intentions still suspect. He'd even tried to steal this dance. Now he'd been proverbially hauled by this woman into the one thing he hadn't wanted to do this evening—dance. People took notice with whom the fresh meat—him—danced, did they not?

Thomas swallowed a sigh.

There was nothing for it now.

However, something wasn't quite right about how this girl had claimed him. And she *had* claimed him. Of that he harbored no doubt.

Now he had to hear how he might not be the man for her?

Not the *man* for *her?*

Could there ever be a man for such a brazen wench?

The ballroom came alive with the melodies of the quadrille, but Thomas felt as though he was falling prey.

Just focus on the dance, Thomas. Would that even help?

Around them, rows of ladies in a bouquet of colored ballgowns took their positions with their partners, but Thomas scarcely noticed them, facing Lady Ashley.

He should move, right?

But he didn't. Not until she brushed her gloved fingers across his arm. A jolt sparked down his spine. Just one brush. Just one simple touch.

Bloody hell.

The blonde beauty curtsied.

His eyes narrowed on her. "You did that on purpose, didn't you?"

Her eyes widened, and he couldn't be sure whether it was in surprise or delight at his suspicion. "On purpose? Whatever do you mean?"

Whatever did he mean, indeed.

Her ever-present grin seemed to widen a touch. "Your suspicion is quite endearing."

"Suspicion means distrust. How can *that* be endearing?"

"On your face, how could it not."

He shouldn't have asked.

Best to keep his mouth clamped shut. That way, she would do the same. He didn't know how to deal with the girl's provocative flirtation. The music was light and a bit slow for his taste, but his heart raced, and his mind tried to outpace his pulse. It was an awkward moment when the couples on either side of them stepped around them. Thomas had to stay put, his mien controlled. That was the easy part; he'd learned every trick of the ballrooms at Oxford, and graduated top of his class two years ago, so shouldn't he feel ready for Almack's? He had a gentleman's education and yet his wits failed him when his gaze dipped. For a fleeting moment, he glimpsed the swell of her breast, the perfectly even skin up her neck, and the slightly pointy chin.

Very beautiful.

His turn had come.

As the quadrille continued, he took Lady Ashley's gloved hand to form the circle with the other couples; all Thomas could think of was that she held his hand. It should not be much to him. He wasn't a green boy. And yet, he failed to notice the other dancers, intent on the curly golden strand that had fallen from her coiffure and cast a tiny shadow on her collarbone, just above the lace of her dress.

"Are you doing it on purpose?"

His eyes met hers. "Am I doing what on purpose?"

"Ignoring me."

"I'm not ignoring you." He paused, and said for emphasis, "I'm dancing."

"You are ignoring me."

"I'm not."

A brow arched. "Then you are a liar."

His gaze whipped to hers once more. "Lady Ashley. You should never call a man a liar." *Even though I am.*

Well. A small lie.

"Not even when they lie?"

"A woman should not be that brazen!"

"Why not?"

Thomas couldn't answer that. For he rightly didn't know why they couldn't be brazen. Only that men prefer women who are more demure in nature. Now he sounded like his father. He certainly didn't want a wife like his mother. But then, he also didn't want a wife that agreed with everything he said. He also didn't want to answer her question, so he chose to ignore it and focus on his steps.

One, two, three, four, pivot, and repeat.

She laughed. "You are ignoring me again. You must have driven your governess up the walls."

He didn't deny it this time. "I find it best for my focus to tune things out from time to time."

"Human beings aren't things," she retorted, but chuckled, as though she enjoyed his little mishaps.

He rather felt like a fly that had gotten in a spider's web. Lady Ashley was the girl by his side, twirling elegantly to the rhythm. She seemed careless in a way that only a bird might, knowing that wherever she went, she could land softly. Her movements were graceful and elegant, her wings—ahem, arms—elongated and tipped by the silken gloves like a vulture's. Yes, if she were a bird, she wouldn't be an elegant peacock only because of the color of her dress. Neither would she be a tiny blue one like a harmless, clattering pigeon, even though her slippers lightly knocked on the parquet.

She was a bird of prey, and Thomas didn't want to be a sad little squirrel unable to escape her grasp no matter how fast he ran. But he had the lingering feeling that he would quite enjoy a swift ride through an adventure with her.

One, two, three, four, pivot, and repeat.

With a deft turn, he looked to the side of the ballroom where he expected Richard to glower and bask, but he'd gone. With every move, well-rehearsed like the ticking of a clock that merely counted time and yet remained unaffected by age and seasons, Thomas followed the steps. The rhythm was a comforting undercurrent, a lifeboat in the swirling sea that was Lady Ashley's presence, and it didn't help that he was constantly moving in the prescribed steps, losing her every time they turned. His mind was filled with the counts, the beats, the turns, and the dips, as he navigated the labyrinth of the dance floor. The numbers became his lifeline, steadying his breath and grounding his racing thoughts.

Thomas couldn't deny the warm thrill that coursed through him each time their hands brushed together in the dance.

It was over too soon. Lady Ashley gave a curtsy when they finally finished and flashed him a mischievous smile. She let her hand linger in his before she retreated two steps on a courtesy. "It's been a pleasure, my lord."

Thomas watched as her back disappeared amongst the members of the crowd.

No, she was definitely not the woman for him.

Chapter Four

The next day

"SO, HOW WAS your *tête-à-tête* with the earl?" Charlene asked as she set down her cup of tea and cast a meaningful look at the others. Sera Lyndon, the daughter of a rich merchant, and Maddie Hunt, daughter of the Viscount of Tisdale, had come for tea, as usual, ready for the post-ball debrief.

"It was fine." She hadn't stayed at Charlene's the previous night, wanting to be up before dawn if the earl decided to call. Not that he could call at *dawn*, but she hadn't wanted to take any chances.

Ashley almost pouted.

She sensed the blooms in the air, and she should have been experiencing these blooms with Jordan. Not alone. Certainly not amid a revenge plot. However, this plot to ruin the Earl of Linsey was all that kept her weathering the roses.

"*Just* fine?" Charlene asked in disbelief. "How on earth did you weasel a dance from the earl?"

Ashley smoothed her skirt. Did they honestly need to ask?

"You *danced* with the Earl of Linsey?" Maddie asked. "How on earth did you manage that? And why did I decide not to attend the ball again?"

Ashley cut her friends a look. How horrid must she be for them to be *so* stunned by the prospect? "I challenged him. How else do you get a man to do what you want?" Her aim remained crystal clear—seduce the elusive, horse-obsessed earl, make him fall deeply in love, and then shatter his heart.

He had seized what was hers, and now she'd do the same.

An eye for an eye…

A game of justice. One that she was determined to win. Victory would come when she reunited with Jordan.

"Did your mother's book teach you that?"

That book. She scowled. It didn't suit her personal style at all. One or two things she could work with, like direct eye contact, but not much else. Certainly not wagging one's brows or fluttering one's lashes!

"Did the advice not work?" Maddie pressed.

Well… "Whether it works or not is not for me to say…"

Maddie laughed. "You lost patience, didn't you?"

"It's not like I have *all* the time in the world. The earl is in search of a wife. I must be that wife."

Both women, seated in plush velvet chairs, arched their brows.

"Oh, do not look at me like that. I didn't mean *wife*, wife. I'm not going to marry the man. Just punish him for what he did to me."

"What he did to Mr. Critton, you mean." Maddie lifted her cup to take a sip of tea.

She should have offered sherry. "Is that not the same?"

Both friends remained silent.

"I know," Ashley muttered. "You think I've gone mad."

Two heads shook in all directions.

Hah! Would they swear on their souls? "I haven't," Ashley defended herself. "Justice must be served."

"What's next, then?" Charlene asked. "*After* justice has been served?"

Her foot tapped on the ground in a rhythmic, Shakespearean beat on the carpet. A bad habit. "I wait."

"Are you sure you can?" Maddie asked, her gaze darting to the devil-possessed foot. "Waiting is the definition of patience. That is not a virtue you possess."

"Darn it. I shall be waiting *impatiently*. But wait, I shall."

Charlene laughed. "Well, our conversation seems as vibrant as the floral patterns on our gowns, and the beat of that foot? Shall we change it?"

Ashley snorted. "Is that an attempt at humor, Char?"

"Lightening the mood," Charlene corrected. "Patience truly is not your forte."

Maddie nodded. "But speaking of humor, did you see the Dowager Countess's headdress at Almack's?" Maddie said, her eyes gleaming with mischief. "I swear it was taller than she!"

Ashley nodded.

A diversion of conversation was welcome.

Charlene grinned, covering her mouth with her hand. "And what about Sir James's attempts to dance the waltz? It was more like a jig!"

"If he kisses like he dances, it might be better to stay far away from him, despite his title," Maddie agreed.

Ashley joined her friends in laughter. Truth be told, she hadn't witnessed any of what they were describing. All she remembered was *him*.

The oaf—Earl of Linsey.

And his hands…expertly, and most annoyingly, surprisingly, and very vexingly, a bit breathtakingly, on her back. Not even to begin describing her hand held in his. The two things she had tried hard to ignore when they were dancing.

And failed.

"Doesn't the earl have horses that race in the Ascot?" Sera suddenly asked.

Ashley shrugged. How would she know?

Charlene nodded. "He does have a horse, if I'm not mistaken."

"Then perhaps the part of your revenge could be for him to lose," Sera suggested with a twinkle in her eye.

Lose? Did she want him to lose all he holds dear? "But how? Bribe the rider?"

"Or," Maddie said, "Feed him a tonic that renders him unable to participate."

"Like a poison?" Ashley put a hand on her mouth.

"More like a laxative. I can give you some."

Ashley pursed her lips. She knew that her friend had a medical—or perhaps chemical—solution to almost everything, but that she could influence the race was a new category of brilliance! "How does this tonic work?"

"It's concentrated senna tea. He will have to run quickly but that's all," Maddie explained. "No harm, no foul. At least, for the rider."

"But he'd miss the race?" Ashley pressed on and Maddie raised her eyebrows and shrugged.

So diabolical.

Utterly forbidden.

She loved it.

"You can truly do that?"

"Of course," Maddie said. "Anything to help a friend. Women have so little control over their lives; seeing you take charge should be an inspiration for all of us. If I can offer a little nudge in the right direction, I feel obliged."

"Then we shall go ahead and help Linsey lose the race," Ashley said without remorse. If it only took a race to ruin him, he must be already dangling, and she'd merely cut off the last branch he was holding.

A stab of remorse shot through her chest as she imagined his warm eyes widen in surprise with the realization of defeat. But Ashley thought about her future and how the earl had crushed her hopes, dreams, and chances. She'd gone from having everything to being on the brink of ruination and disrepute—who wanted a jilted earl's daughter who had no prospect except for another expensive season? It was hopeless and she saw no other way.

Just then, another thought occurred to her. "Tell me, do you think a man of experience, like the earl, could be convincingly seduced without the involvement of genuine affection?" She picked idly at the lace trim of her tea napkin, her mind whirling with unspoken worries. "I mean, would his vast experience not put me at a disadvantage?"

She didn't want to fail again.

"You mean won't he see straight through your pretense?" Charlene said knowingly.

Ashley pulled a face. "Something like that."

"He probably already has," Charlene said, chuckling.

"But that doesn't matter, does it?" Maddie pointed out. "You said he is in search of a wife. The diamonds of the season have been snatched up and there is not much time left to choose from the crop that is left. He would have to move fast if he wants enough time to woo his chosen one."

"How nice of you to refer to us as crops," Charlene muttered.

Maddie's eyes crinkled. "We must find the humor in our looming spinsterhood."

"Speak for yourself," Ashley said, but her lips quirked. "I don't intend to ever reach spinsterhood." She suddenly snorted. "But the earl wants a soft-spoken little creature that obeys him like his horses."

"Scared him off, did you?" Charlene arched a brow filled with laughter.

"I didn't scare him off," Ashley denied. "I made myself unforgettable."

"Or you gave the poor man a trauma," Maddie suggested, grinning. "I might have a remedy for that, too."

Ashley slumped back. "I need one for this conversation."

"Come now. It can't be that bad." Charlene patted her leg. "This is merely your impatience surfacing to toy with your mind."

How marvelous if that could be the case. The truth of the matter was that she didn't know. With Jordan, every moment since they met had been seamless and delightful. The exact opposite of what she experienced with *that* man.

Linsey.

Ashley bit down on her jaw.

You better not disappoint me any further by selecting a bidding lady as a future bride.

If that happened...

Then she could always burn his precious stables to the ground. Sell his horses to the post. Run away to the Americas where he could never find her or exact revenge back on her. So, tricking him to select her as his wife wasn't the only play.

She allowed that thought to give her comfort.

"Will you cover for me?" Ashley asked Charlene who set her cup down with a clop.

"What do you mean?" Charlene cast the others a look that said as much as if-one-of-us-goes-down-we-all-do.

"You know we will always support you—" Sera started.

"Even if your plans are ludicrous," Maddie added, always the more cautious one.

"Ashley," Charlene's tone was irritatingly patronizing, "I am always in your corner, and you know that." Ashley narrowed her gaze, bracing herself for whatever her friend would say. "I just won't stand by and watch you get ruined."

How nice of her to say that, even though it was a *fait accomplit*.

A moment of silence passed over them and Ashley swallowed.

"It already happened," she declared.

"What?" all three of her friends burst out, wide-eyed, and Charlene gripped the hem of her sleeve as if it could shield her from the ugly truth.

"Have you and Jordan..." Sera asked.

"No!" Ashley reassured her.

"Are you sure?" Maddie pressed for information in her not-so-subtle manner.

"I'm sure I'd know." Ashley crossed her arms.

"Oh, if I hadn't delayed my coming out—" Charlene leaned back and put a hand over her forehead.

"You didn't delay it, I did!-" Maddie said, which earned her a pitying look from Sera.

"Look, when Maddie had the chickenpox—" Ashley started but Charlene cut her off.

"It wasn't just that, rather that they kept her isolated in a room for a week. She was lonely!"

"It was your idea, however, to climb into my chambers." Maddie reached for Ashley's hand.

"But it was all of our decision to stay with you." Sera nodded. "If one of us had to have the chickenpox, we'd all have it."

"And tie our hands up in pillowcases so we wouldn't scratch," Maddie added.

"The worst was the white tincture. Do you remember the dreadful smell?" Ashley laughed.

Ashley remembered. It had been two of the worst weeks of her life, stationed in Maddie's bed with her closest friends. Yes, it had been an itchy pain, but it was shared. And that was the best part of her life, her friends.

"What if he hurts you?" Maddie asked wistfully.

"We won't let him," Charlene said.

"He already has," Ashley asserted.

And now it's payback time.

"We will be by your side wherever he takes you," Sera added.

"Not to the Ascot, I'm sure," Sera said.

A moment of silence washed over the room. Ashley met Charlene's eyes, then Sera's and Maddie's.

"So it's decided then?" Charlene asked.

"You're truly going to take this on?" Sera's question sounded more like a decision already taken.

"We will do this together," Maddie said, reaching for Ashley's hand.

Ashley gave her a little squeeze and reveled in the support her friends offered. And yet, again, thinking of the earl's warm eyes pinched her resolve once more.

"There's no turning back now," she declared.

The next morning

THE COOL DAWN air enveloped the sprawling stables, a longstanding pride of the House of Linsey, as Thomas stepped through the large wooden doors. Beside him, Sebastian Moore, the Marquess of Cambridge to most, but more of a brother to him, followed suit.

"Screechy hinges," Sebastian drawled. "How unlike you."

"I'll oil it later."

"Don't you have more important jobs?"

"There's nothing more important than the horses, the estate, and my people."

Sebastian cocked his head, but Thomas ignored him. They were both supposed to produce heirs, and Sebastian had gotten no closer to that goal than Thomas had.

Again, the blonde beauty with the feisty personality came to mind. Why was it that she resurfaced in the oddest moments? He couldn't stop thinking about her.

"I'll oil it and that's that," Thomas said gruffly. He may employ a staff of nearly forty people, but Thomas wasn't above picking up some tools for repairs himself. Few people of the peerage knew how to survive on their own, but he couldn't run an estate the size of his family's if he didn't know how to…well…*run* it. Which meant he made the decisions. Period.

Plus, it was fun to *do* something. He couldn't understand why other noblemen like Paisley just barked out orders and wasted their time at the gentlemen's club. It was the worst way to spend his time. Wasn't that what their titles were good for? To do something with one's life and to leave something behind?

That's why he couldn't squander what the Earls of Linsey before him had left behind.

His eyes took in the sight of the magnificent horses, their proud heads held high, their muscles rippling under their glossy coats. No one could fault him for how his estate was run. These were thoroughbreds that his family had cultivated for generations, their lineage as noble as his own.

His pride.

Of course, racehorses were revered animals, bred meticulously for their strength, speed, and endurance all over the realm, but the Linseys' horses were special. The breeding process was a meticulous one, paying careful attention to lineage to maintain the purity of the breed and improve upon desirable traits. He enjoyed other fast horses, too, but thoroughbreds, stemming from three key sires—the Byerley Turk, the Darley Arabian, and the Godolphin Arabian, were among the most appreciated breeds in the racing world.

"I still can't believe you'd ever enter into a wager risking your grandfather's legacy," Sebastian said. "You may have just wagered his trophies, too."

"He was an icon, Sebastian. I'll never live up to him," Thomas mumbled.

"Well, you might. He shone at the Epsom Derby and the 2000 Guineas Stakes," Sebastian said appreciatively. "And your thoroughbreds will be the strongest at the Royal Ascot this year."

Thomas sighed. He could only hope so. The race held immense

popularity, drawing crowds from all strata of society, affirming the significance of horse racing in British culture.

"I just don't know if I can live up to what my father and grandfather have created."

"They didn't create any of it. They managed it extremely well."

"Not sure I can," Thomas admitted. Of course, he'd never have told another soul, but this was Sebastian. He'd always been there, and he was the only one who knew Father and Grandfather. He understood.

"Look, nobody realizes just how much you've put in. You need to win the Ascot and shine."

So Paisley takes it all. Thomas tasted acid.

"You're doing what nobody has ever done, Thomas!"

"Losing my family's legacy? I'm pretty certain I wouldn't be the first."

"No. You're ensuring that the horses were not just bred but compatible."

"It's almost romantic, isn't it? A fairy tale," he growled, taking stock of all the work he'd lose if Paisley got his horses.

"You and I both know that they are feeling creatures."

"Paisley?"

"No, not him. The horses."

As a result of his careful breeding, the foals were stronger, faster, and their coats even shinier than any his grandfather had bred. Thomas couldn't get himself to let the horses mate for the sake of procreating. It would be no different than if he merely impregnated a woman for the sake of producing an heir. There had to be the matter of the heart, something he couldn't discuss with anyone except for his best friend Sebastian.

"You do have a way with them," Sebastian commented, his tone light, yet carrying an undertone of reverence.

"Horses?" Thomas nodded.

"No, women."

"That's not true."

"It is." Sebastian combed both hands through his hair. "You go to one ball, make a rash decision to marry so Paisley won't get the thoroughbreds, and the prettiest woman comes to you."

Thomas's heart dropped. She was very pretty and spirited. There'd been a wealth of intelligence in her eyes and wit in her manner of speaking. And when they'd danced, his hand trailed down her back and for a fleeting moment—just a fraction of a second—where he thought about something more. Not love, of course not. Compatibility perhaps?

She was the daughter of an earl after all.

A very pretty and forward one, to be exact.

The soft neighing coming from below interrupted his daydreaming.

Thomas chuckled, his eyes softening as he approached a frail foal tucked away in a corner. If he had *a way*, this weak little one wouldn't have been born so fragile, but he would do anything in his power to save this little one.

"They are my responsibility, Sebastian. They depend on me, just as my people do," he said, his voice barely above a whisper as he stretched out a hand, allowing the foal to recognize his scent.

Thomas crouched down beside the weak little horse whose legs seemed no thicker than matchsticks. His heart melted.

"This little one almost died last week," Thomas said as his expert hand rested on the foal's heart. "He was even too weak to drink milk."

"So you fed him?" Sebastian asked.

"A bottle, yes. I made him oats and milk with egg yolks. He looks better now, doesn't he?"

Sebastian gave an appreciative smile, leaning against the stable's doors. "You know, if you were as kind to yourself as you are to these horses, you might find a way to fulfill the desires of your own heart."

Thomas glanced up at him, surprised. He opened his mouth to retort, but words failed him. Instead, he looked away, his gaze falling back onto the frail creature before him. "I am an earl, Sebastian," he finally said, his voice steady despite the uneasiness he felt within. "My desires are secondary to my duty. I wasn't trained to listen to my heart."

Sebastian sighed, pushing off from the door, and patted a hand on Thomas's shoulder, giving it a firm squeeze. "And yet," he murmured, his tone gentle yet firm, "even earls are allowed to have the attention of a woman they love. And hearts, my friend, are not designed to be ignored."

If only...

The silence that followed was punctuated only by the soft whinny of the foal and the distant crowing of a rooster. Thomas didn't want to marry, especially not any of the debutantes he'd met at the ball. They were either too young, too done up, or just altogether wrong. The one that had irked him the most was this Lady Ashley. She'd been forward and rather bold, if not outright rude.

Thomas chuckled.

She *was* amusing.

"What are you laughing about?" Sebastian asked.

"Oh nothing..." *Just the hotblooded female I can't get out of my mind.* Come to think of it, she was right about what she'd said, and her observations were, whether he wanted to admit it or not, true. And what was also true was how outright beautiful she was in her azure dress, shimmering with every movement.

Ah.

The way the fabric had clung to her...the dress had seemed an extension of herself, accentuating her perfect proportions and complementing her striking blue eyes. Those eyes... So mysterious and clear at the same time. The play of the soft lighting of the chandeliers in the ballroom and the warm sheen of the parquet had complemented the cool tones of her eyes. Yet, there'd been a flicker of a heat in her gaze that made Thomas's stomach lurch now that he considered it again. It wasn't desire exactly—he knew what that looked like in a woman. Certainly not like that with her lips pinched and her lids drawn low as if she were calculating how best to dissect him.

She seemed to be plotting something. There was certainly more to her than she'd let on.

And Thomas couldn't help but wish to fit into those plans.

Surely nothing evil could go on in that pretty head of hers, just as nothing vile could emerge from the kissable mouth... *Stop!*

Even though she was a beauty without a match as far as Thomas could remember, the blue fabric made her seem like she had stepped out of a Renaissance painting. Every detail of her was exquisite, making her appear less like a woman and more like a master's sketch of the perfect woman. It was an unsettling, yet intriguing, realization for him.

Because she attracted him.

"You are thinking about a woman, aren't you?" Sebastian said, crossing his arms.

"What makes you say that?"

"Your cheeks are red."

Thomas's hands shot out to cover his cheeks, glaring at his friend when he laughed.

"So," Sebastian asked, clearing his throat. "Who is she?"

Thomas thought about the little beauty. "Someone suspicious." She was boldness personified in a manner he had never quite encountered before. However, she seemed too good to be true. Had she planned to meet him and merely lost patience to wait for a proper introduction or was there more to it? Could Paisley have had a hand in their meeting?

Thomas broke out in goosebumps.

She rather seemed like an order placed but yet to be picked up.

Was there a trick? Had she so little regard for her reputation, she'd forgo a proper introduction? She was practically ruining herself—or was she already ruined?

So many question marks surrounded her.

A low rumbling tugged at Thomas's heart, stirring a sense of suspicion that was tough to quell—and he hated it. Could Lady Ashley's seemingly haphazard acquaintance with him have been an orchestrated ruse?

No, Paisley wouldn't go that far, would he?

He wanted to *win* the bet, right?

An unsettling chill ran down his spine. As much as he was drawn to Lady Ashley, this suspicion cast a dark shadow over his initial impressions. If she didn't come to him on her own accord but she'd been sent, Thomas wondered if he'd still want her. Yet, nothing could distract him entirely from her mesmerizing charm. He was caught in a bewitching paradox, torn between charm and caution.

"Ah," Sebastian said. "You met her at the ball you didn't tell me you were attending."

"Don't look at me that way. You and Paisley don't get along."

"That doesn't mean I don't know how to behave," Sebastian muttered. "So, who is she?"

"*She* is called Lady Ashley."

A little spitfire.

She would make for a rather interesting match.

Sebastian quirked a brow and gave Thomas a suspicious once-over. "You mean—"

He stilled. By Jove, was he already thinking about her as a match? Well, she *was* smart and not shy, which could be beneficial for him.

And...

A certain other spot. Like, say, the bedchamber. He was used to breaking in wild beasty horses and expected no less of this blonde beauty.

What are you thinking?

He rubbed the back of his neck.

Why had she chosen him? Had a certain sense of wicked curiosity fueled her to approach him or was it just plain sauciness? He thought of some of the beauties he'd met over the years. Most of them had acted either spoiled or entitled, as though their attractiveness was a currency, and they'd use it to get what they wanted. But not Lady Ashley. So, it must be something else.

Call me intrigued, Lady Ashley.

"Is this Lady Ashley the one you're going to marry because of your wager with Paisley?"

"I don't know. Maybe. She might say no."

"So you are seriously going forward with this?"

Thomas rubbed the foal's head. "I don't have much of a choice." And she was the only woman who stood out to him.

Then why did he feel so uneasy about this infatuation with her?

Damnation.

Whatever her motivation, or situation, whether she was innocent or not, he could marry her and get Paisley off his back, deposit her somewhere in a country estate, and then go home to look after his prized horses.

It was that simple, right?

Yes, he could do that.

So why did the idea pull at his heartstrings as if he were making a questionable choice?

Chapter Five

ASHLEY SLID BACK onto the sofa like a starfish, her limbs sprawling over the plush pink cushions, surrounded by the delicate green-and-pink bird-themed décor of the drawing room. The sun filtered through the curtains, casting a warm glow over the room, but it did little to lift the dark cloud hovering above her head. Luckily, her dearest friends were with her: Sera, Maddie, and Charlene.

"Why is life so hard?" Ashley groaned.

Maddie lifted a brow, the corners of her lips twitching in amusement. "Life is not *that* hard."

Not. That. Hard.

Pah!

"Are you jesting?" Ashley leaned back and felt as though the air had been siphoned from her lungs.

Two days.

It had been a mere two days since the ball, and yet it felt like an eternity, a never-ending cycle of introspection that twisted her insides into knots. Two days since she last saw Linsey, that incorrigible rapscallion who had disrupted the calm waters of her existence. Two days of sitting around, draped in her own discontent, questioning every choice that had led her to this very moment.

Why hadn't he called on her?

She turned her gaze to the ornate clock on the mantel, its ticking seeming to mock her. Dratted man. Hadn't she been obvious enough? She thought she had. And his silence was driving her mad. Hadn't she made herself clear? How could her blatant hints not have landed on his square, handsome head.

Charlene chuckled. "Certainly not life for the privileged."

Ashley eyed her friends miserably but couldn't help a laugh that escaped. Was her plan of revenge dead even before it had a chance to live? "I have no *privilege* when it comes to that man. He is doing this on purpose. Making me wait. Setting me on edge."

"Perhaps I wasn't obvious enough?" Ashley whispered more to herself than her friends. But when Sera spluttered a laugh and instantly covered her mouth with both hands, Ashley slumped.

"You should have kissed him," Sera said. "That would have made it so clear that he couldn't miss it even if a pile of horse manure hit his face." She laughed.

Not funny.

"What a vivid image," Charlene complained, pulling the corner of her lips upward.

Sera shrugged. "Isn't he obsessed with horses?"

"Perhaps you should talk in horse references when you speak to him in the future," Maddie suggested. "You know, *mounting* hints that *stirrup* his interest."

Ashley groaned. "Slice my wrist now."

"Well, you have chosen to *saddle* yourself on this path of vengeance," Charlene said with a smile. "You can't stop your *canter* now."

"You are the worst," Ashley muttered.

"Yes, perhaps the earl needs more grooming before he *gallops* over for a marriage proposal," Maddie said.

"Agreed." A twinkle sparked in Sera's eyes. "You should start with a horse bit. Stuff him with the mouthpiece of the bridle used to control the horse, *him.*"

"Then strap him with the reins," Charlene said. "Whichever comes first?"

"Dear me, have all of you gone mad?" Ashley asked. "All I need is a riding crop and then I'm ready to trot into the sunset, it seems." And who had time for all of this? *Time.* It was both a blessing and a curse, and right now, it felt like an enemy.

Sera laughed. "A riding crop! Why didn't I think of that? But yes, you are beginning to grasp the picture."

Maddie chuckled. "Send him to the hayloft when he is not cooperating."

"Well, I'm not going that far since I had no intention of wedding the man from the start. That would give him what he wants, wouldn't it, and I have determined to take away all that he wants and desires."

"Then you shall have to take away his horses," Charlene said.

Ashley nodded. She hadn't gotten all that far in her plan. She was taking it one step at a time, since there were many things for which she still didn't have answers—answers she would get from the man no matter what. And if he didn't come to her, she would just have to go to him. But hopefully, it wouldn't come to that.

"You do know you haven't spoken one word about your Jordan today," Maddie pointed out.

"True," Charlene said, tilting her head to the side in thought. "All she goes on about is Linsey this, Linsey that."

Ashley tossed a pillow at Charlene. "What are you talking about? Everything about Linsey is about my Jordan."

"If you say so," Sera murmured, pouring herself another cup of tea.

"I *do* say so."

"Just don't fall in love with your enemy," Sera cautioned. "A woman can rarely compete against a man's obsessions, and his obsession seems to be his horses."

Maddie nodded. "We'd hate for you to be leg-shackled to a man you loathe. The path of revenge is never easy."

Ashley nodded. "I know, when this is all over, I plan to find Jordan, so do not fret too much about me."

"Oh!" Charlene said, a sparkle suddenly entering her gaze. "Does the book not have any advice on this particular predicament?"

"What is that?" Sera asked with curiosity.

Ashley scowled. "Oh, just a guide to win a gentleman's heart. It has all sorts of chapters from winning a man's heart to seducing your husband away from his mistress and what not. Even how to teach them a lesson. The book is rather tame for my taste. I've been updating it with notes."

"Goodness, and they print these kinds of books?" Maddie said. "I'm surprised they are not banned."

"Well, if it's too tame for you," Sera murmured, "you should lend it to me. I've been looking for interesting reading material."

Ashley nodded. "After I'm done with adding my thoughts, I'll be more than happy to pass it along."

"Ashley." Maddie suddenly grabbed her elbow. "A carriage just pulled up in front of your house."

Ashley's head whipped to the window, her pulse leaping. She craned her neck to stealthily peer through the glass. She sat up straighter on the sofa, every muscle tensing as her gaze fixed on the view outside. Without standing, she twisted in her seat, craning her neck to get a better angle. The drapes were parted just enough to offer a glimpse of the street below. Was it Linsey? She rose from her seat.

"Don't look!" Sera admonished. "What if he sees you? You are aware there is a difference between obvious and desperate?"

"I'm not so sure about that," Maddie said, biting her lip to keep from laughing.

"Feign nonchalance and don't look," Sera suggested. "Charlene is the closest. She can sneak a peek."

Yes, remain calm.

She could do that.

I can be calm. I can not look.

"What's he doing?" Charlene asked, squinting.

Ashley stiffened. "What do you mean what is he doing? Is it Linsey?"

"Yes, it's him all right, but he is just staring at the house," Charlene said, her brows furrowing. "As if he's deciding to come in or not."

Don't turn away, you coward.

I have plans for you.

Ashley swallowed hard when her heart fluttered. It had never quite leapt so with Jordan, so why did she react so to the golden-haired earl?

Was he still just staring at the house? Was he having second thoughts…right there on her doorstep? If he dared to turn around now, she would hunt him down and be done with him once and for all. Revenge completed. In fact, she didn't have to go that far, but she wanted him to feel what it feels like when you lose what you adore most.

"He might be of two minds," Maddie echoed her fear.

Ashley's head whipped to the window again. To the devil with being calm and not looking. She wanted to witness his decision firsthand. And sure enough, the unwelcomely handsome man stood there, just staring at the house. "Two minds my *derrière*. He came all this way, didn't he?"

This is no catch and release, Linsey. I'm reining you in no matter what.

"All the way? He doesn't live that far from here," Charlene pointed out.

"He still made the choice to come here today."

"I suppose you are right," Charlene said. "He did at that."

Ashley shot a hot look at her friend.

"Oh!" Maddie exclaimed. "He's coming up the steps now."

Sera laughed and clapped. "The anticipation!"

Yes, the anticipation…

However, he was here. That head of his hadn't been so square and dense as she first believed it to be. He had absorbed her hints, and he had made a choice.

Ashley grinned.

I did it.

The rest would be easy.

>>><<<

One minute earlier

THOMAS PAUSED, STARING up at Lady Ashley's townhouse, wondering what he was doing. This was harder than he'd imagined.

So much harder.

Should he have brought flowers?

Perhaps he ought to go to Regent Street and purchase red roses... No! That would be a lie. A declaration of love and promises of passion called for red roses.

Pink perhaps? For chaste affection.

Or white? A virginal bride.

He didn't know what Lady Ashley's preferred flowers were. His mares liked dandelions and daisies, but Lady Ashley wasn't going to eat them.

No, better no flowers at all, lest he wish to go for white lilies and that could be misinterpreted. His intentions would be clear; words must suffice.

His heart and his mind fought a brutal war, as they had since the moment he set eyes on Lady Ashley. But there he stood, and he had no intention of turning back. He just needed to collect his breath. This was, after all, marriage, and no matter what reason for the proposal, it was no small thing. Even if it started as a dandelion, a seed of affection could grow into moments worthy of red roses. Perhaps he'd give Lady Ashley some in the future.

And that possibility strengthened his resolve. A secret hope that the brazen beauty could feel as strong as her word choice encouraged

Thomas. It was a seed after all.

Time to go in.

Thomas straightened his back, tugged at his cravat, buttoned his coat, and faced Lady Ashley's home. Inhaling deeply, he ascended the steps to the elegant Georgian masterpiece in the heart of London's prestigious district. His heart pounded with a combination of apprehension and excitement. Hailed as one of the city's architectural gems, the townhouse boasted four floors, each window reflecting the soft sunlight, imbuing the white stone with a warm glow. The iron railings and the stately front door painted in a deep, rich blue instantly announced the status and wealth of its inhabitants.

Get your head together, Thomas!

Architecture was not important right now. But then, he needed to recenter his mind away from Lady Ashley. Just for a moment. But it wasn't enough for him to race over the perks of his decision again. She was pretty, young, intelligent enough to maintain a witty conversation, and wealthy. Suspicions aside, what more could he ask for in a bride?

Love?

Pah!

Passion?

He sucked in his cheeks. A future for his estate, an heir, and the dignity his station commanded. No flowers and kisses for a long time. Seeds needed time to grow—if they ever sprouted. And if he stayed on the doorstep much longer, he'd be noticed and ruin his chances for the most compatible match with the lovely daughter of a fellow earl.

Right.

That would do.

Compatibility as with the horses…to make for healthy offspring…

Then why didn't he have a spring to his step on the path toward a proposal? He felt as though he'd walk toward a cliff and hand her the ring to push him over the edge.

Perks.

Just think about the perks.

Besides being an ideal wife under his current predicament, he did want to discover other qualities in her. Other reasons to marry her besides sufficiency and good timing. She was a stranger, and he was going to invite her into his family.

She would become his family.

Would she mind living in the country for the better part of each year? The thought nibbled at him as he imagined her in the quiet solitude of his estate, so far removed from the bustling life of London she likely preferred. If she accepted his offer, they'd have a lifetime to sort out the intricacies of married life. But it was a hollow consolation for losing the opportunity to wed for love.

Four-and-twenty was still young.

But then, given he was wedding to save his horses, he supposed he was marrying for love. Just love of a different sort. Perhaps they could become friends over the course of their engagement. That was also a form of love, was it not?

He lifted his hand to rap on the door, his heart pounding in his chest like a kettledrum, each beat echoing his mounting nervousness. He heard his own breathing, and his whole head felt as though it was galloping with his heart as if it tried to get away from what he was about to do.

Here we go.

With firm resolve, he rapped at the door.

The door swung open to reveal a tall, wiry butler, his face impassive and professional. With a quick, rehearsed nod, Thomas handed over his calling card, his name inscribed on the thick paper. He couldn't help but feel a strange sense of finality, as if he was about to embark on an irrevocable path. "I'm here for Chaswick."

The butler glanced at the card, and then back at him. He gave a curt nod. "Please, follow me."

Did they expect him?

He suddenly wanted to laugh. Given that brazen minx, they probably were.

The servant led Thomas to a richly decorated study where Ashley's father, the Earl of Chaswick, a portly, stern-faced man, sat behind a mahogany desk stacked with documents and maps of his numerous estates.

"Linsey," the earl said as he rose and motioned for Thomas to take a seat. "I've been expecting you. Tell me, are you the Thomas who studied moral philosophy under Professor Copperman at Oxford in 1814?"

Thomas couldn't help but narrow his gaze. "How did you know?"

He'd been more than expected, they'd researched everything about him, hadn't they?

"It's not important." Chaswick waved him off.

"Then why did you ask?"

"Just a shared connection, that's all. Now to Ashley."

As I thought. "I take it your daughter informed you that I would call on you."

"Her exact words were: If the Earl of Linsey calls to offer for my hand in marriage, don't stand in my way."

Thomas blinked. Well…he couldn't claim he was all *that* surprised. But then, how could she possibly have known? "Your daughter has a refreshing boldness about her."

Chaswick scoffed, but his eyes had softened. "I was too lenient in raising her. I still dote on her too much." The man lifted his chin to stare at Thomas with a hard look. "If you are here for my daughter's hand in marriage—"

"I am."

"—then you may have it. That being said, when I asked her if you were the man for her, she shrugged with a rather unsettling smile. But if you treat her wrong, you will be staring down at the barrel of my pist—"

"It won't come to that," Thomas assured him. He'd surely treat her right and never force her to do anything she didn't want. A chill slithered down his spine. She might force him though, wouldn't she? Call him to London for the season? That would be Lady Ashley, too. But first and foremost, he wanted to reassure the earl, "I have no ulterior intentions."

Unless a marriage of convenience for the sake of keeping my family's fortune and the pride of the House of Linsey is an ulterior motive, nah!

"Good."

Thomas nodded his head absently. He had expected the subsequent discussion to be as transactional as a horse sale at the market. Yet, no talk of a transaction had taken place. The process had been too easy, lacking the emotional depth he had thought would accompany such a monumental decision—a father releasing his daughter to another man, and said man taking a wife. Well, such was the nature when marrying for a wager, he supposed. No use in being disappointed about it. It was how the world worked, the daughter of an earl for an earl. Love, romance, and passion were not required for people like them. They were cut from the same cloth, and that was all her father needed apparently.

"Ashley," the Earl of Chaswick suddenly said, and Thomas started. His head whipped around to glimpse the door creaking open and Ashley stepping into view. "It would be prudent to practice some patience."

She grinned. "I'm not so sure. Impatience has worked quite well for me up to this moment."

Snickers sounded behind her, and Thomas leapt to his feet.

Chaswick scoffed, rising to his feet. "Since you are here, I'll give you a moment to discuss your partnership." He strode to the door, leaving him alone with Lady Ashley. "Ladies," he murmured as he passed her friends.

One of them mumbled something to Ashley and Ashley gave her a mock pinch on the arm. Each of the ladies gave Thomas a once-over before they, too, gave them some privacy.

"I'd offer you tea," Lady Ashley said, sauntering over to a nearby shelf. "But since it's a study, cognac is all I have available."

"No, thank you." He would like a clear mind in dealing with this spitfire of a woman. "Do you usually drink cognac at this time of the day? Isn't it more cordial…ahem…feminine for after-dinner?"

"You think I'm not feminine?"

Thomas shut his eyes for an instant.

You can do better!

She cocked her head at him. "So to what do I owe the pleasure of your call today?"

As if the minx hadn't expected him. He studied her closely. "I wish to ask for your hand in marriage."

"Oh? After only one dance?" She sounded almost intrigued. What she didn't sound was surprised.

"This should be called a brief courtship," Thomas announced as though he had every idea what he was talking about. "Spanning over a dance and a conversation."

"*This* one? Has it started yet?"

Thomas nodded, trying to decipher her smile. Was this the one her father had talked about? If so, he could understand Chaswick's sentiment. Gooseflesh spread over his scalp.

"What about the length of our engagement?" she asked. "Shall that be fleeting as well?"

Very fleeting. "Yes, I'd like to marry by way of a special license."

Her grin spread. "When?"

"As soon as possible."

"You shall have to be more specific than that."

"Then at the end of the week." Thomas expected more of a shock but all he got from Lady Ashley was an amused expression that made his blood curdle. Was the chit enjoying this? He suddenly thought of that spider that ate their mates. What was it called again?

"Why so fast?"

Thomas cleared his throat. "I have my reasons."

"As your wife, would I not be privy to those reasons?"

"As my *wife*, you would." He cleared his throat. "But you're not my wife yet."

She suddenly laughed. "Well, I have my reasons for a longer engagement. We shall have to compromise. Is that possible?"

His brows furrowed. "That would depend on your definition of long."

"A few weeks, not just one."

Thomas nodded. He could do a few weeks. Just not a few months. "Very well, but I have one condition, then."

"Oh?" She leaned against one of the shelves. "Do tell."

"You shall accompany me to my country estate for the duration of our engagement." He couldn't afford to let her out of his sight. It would be a disaster if she changed her mind while he wasn't paying attention.

"Why, I would love to join you," Lady Ashley said, pushing away from the shelf and sauntering up to him, her eyes bright. "So, then, my lord, will you marry me? I would be honored if you became my husband."

Thomas blinked. What…on… "Did you just ask me to marry you?"

Her smile remained in place, and the hairs on his skin prickled as the sweet scent of jasmine filled his lungs. *So close.* "I did."

"Am I not the one who should ask?" Thomas asked gruffly.

Her smile turned mischievous. "Says who?"

Vexing minx.

"Before you give your answer, I do have a condition though."

"Name it."

"My dowry stays my own."

That's all?

"Of course," she went on, "I am aware it doesn't matter if you sign my dowry over to me or not, it's still all yours by right, but I'd appreciate the gesture."

"I see no reason why not." Thomas didn't understand why she'd ask this, but he supposed, like him wedding her, she had her reasons for wanting access to her dowry. And it was a small request. "It's not as if I'm wedding you for your dowry."

"Good, then what do you say, Linsey? Shall we marry or not?"

Thomas inhaled deeply. "Yes, I will marry you."

Chapter Six

THE MAN WAS a conundrum.
And not just any conundrum. A *conundrum*-conundrum.
He didn't want to marry her for her dowry.
He passed *that* test.
But marry within a week? Hah! The only reason she could think of, well two reasons, was he either required an urgent heir, or it had something to do with his infamous prized horses. Since he didn't look like a dying man—everyone but Adonis and Hercules would envy him for his physique—her bet was on the latter. But just what had prompted him to hastily wed the first lady who showed interest in him?

It could spell trouble for her plans if she remained in the dark about his true motivations... Ashley felt a little like a fox considering whether to go into a trap or not. But this wasn't one she couldn't get out of. All she had to do was dissolve the engagement, break his heart, if he had one, and... Well, she did not believe that to be the case.

She had to keep her wits. *I have it in spades.* That was all she required. She had a plan and would fall on her sword if needed—after slicing his most precious treasure like a ham.

They were, however, leaving in the morning for his country estate.

Thus, the next morning, after her servants packed her essentials and she arranged for the rest to be delivered later, Ashley felt ready for battle. She'd donned her favorite travel dress and slept with her hair wrapped around red ribbons for the extra spring in her locks and the added encouragement. If she looked invincible, the rest would come on its own, surely.

"Are you certain this is what you want?" her father asked, nodding at a servant who cleared his breakfast plate. "It hasn't been that long since you were sulking in a dark chamber because of that other fellow. What's his name? John Crisson or something."

"Jordan Critton."

"Not a memorable name." Her father gestured and winked at her.

"Papa."

"Fine, I won't nag, but I like Linsey better than the previous one. He appears to be an upstanding man."

Upstanding? What poppycock. But then, she supposed men had other criteria for liking or disliking their own kind. It wasn't the same for her and didn't factor into her vendetta. "The earl is quite something."

"However, a sudden engagement is one thing, but leaving for his country estate is another."

"You can always join us, if you wish."

"No, I still have business in London," her father said, scratching his chin. "But if Linsey has any ill-intentions, say the word, and I'll break his arms and legs."

What I will break is far worse than a leg. "Rest assured, Papa, I can handle Linsey."

"I've never doubted your ability," her father said, "but neither do I doubt his." Ashley smiled but her father's subliminal warning didn't go unheard. Her father was ever indulgent, and they told each other, for the most part, everything. But she couldn't share the truth about Linsey and Jordan with him. Not yet. She couldn't give him a reason to stop the engagement lest she fail to achieve her goal. And if she didn't avenge that she'd been used like a doll in the lives of these men without consideration to her feelings and future, then why should they fare any better?

And there was more now, Ashley realized. She wanted to succeed for her friends.

"Your mother will be over the moon when she learns of your engagement."

Ashley's eyes widened. "No! She cannot find out yet!" Her father joining them at Linsey's estate was acceptable, but her mother? She would nag her and Linsey endlessly about every little detail of this engagement. Usually, her mother loved to travel with her friends and spent more time away from home than at their home. The woman didn't have a maternal bone in her body. But planning a wedding could draw her out. Not because it was about Ashley but because Mother had a chance to use her as a pawn in society, of course.

Her father arched a brow. "She is bound to learn of your engagement sooner or later."

"Yes," Ashley said, suddenly parched. She poured herself another cup of tea and took a big gulp. "But don't tell anyone, yet. I would like to enjoy my engagement for a bit. Let this be mine for a while, please."

Let revenge be mine.

Her father chuckled. "That is true. Your mother loves to fuss and would distract your attention from Linsey."

Exactly. Which was why she wanted to start and end her plan of revenge before her mother learned of Linsey. Ashley would like to avoid unnecessary complications if she could! "Her need to make a statement is the worst."

"Do not worry. She will not hear about your engagement from me."

Ashley grinned at her father. "Thank you, Papa."

"The things I do for my daughter," he muttered, but there was amusement laced in his voice. "So, will you not tell me why you chose Linsey?"

Ashley shrugged. "He is handsome."

Her father arched a brow. "That is all you have to say about the man?"

"He loves horses, too."

"And you don't," her father pointed out. "You love balls."

True. "He owns a castle in the country."

"You loathe anything beyond Piccadilly."

Ashley nodded thoughtfully. Her father knew her too well. "I can see why you might be concerned. So why did you agree? Surely not only because I asked you?"

"Is that so?" He gave her a kiss on the top of her head like he used to when she was little.

"I'm not concerned, though I am a touch suspicious. What father would do it so quickly?"

"Love is quick sometimes. I hope you'll know soon enough."

"Of course, Papa," Ashley said dryly. Thankfully, her father was not so heartless. "Enough about me, Papa. I'm more concerned with what you shall do without me."

"Worry less, I imagine. I'm not entirely dependent on my daughter."

Ashley grinned. "That is good to know, Papa." But she didn't like to leave him alone.

A question suddenly popped into her head. "Why are some men so obsessed with horses?"

"Why are some women so obsessed with shopping, dancing, knitting, reading, or like you, driving your father's heart rate up?"

Ashley cast her father a deadpan look.

He chuckled, then shrugged. "We all have hobbies."

True, still... "How can a hobby turn into such an obsession?"

"That I cannot say," he murmured. "I suppose that it is different for each person. You are talking about Linsey, right? Perhaps he has nothing else to keep him occupied, or perhaps he's using it to escape something else."

Escape something else…

Intriguing.

Was Linsey using horses to escape something else, something deeper, or did he simply have only horses in his life to entertain him? Considering the man's character, it might be a bit of both. The more she thought about it, the more she wanted to understand what drove him. In fact, it wouldn't be wrong to say that everyone had something, no matter how small, they wanted to escape from and into something else.

She could relate to her father's assessment.

After all, she had felt the loss of her mother's affection when she was little. Once Ashley had accepted that she would never be enough for the countess, and a constant disappointment, she'd found a way out. An escape, as her father would use the word. Back then, she had escaped into her father's love and embrace. Now, she had the loss of Jordan, and she was escaping into vengeance.

But she wouldn't exactly call it an obsession.

Which was why she couldn't tell her father, even though she had never hidden anything from him before, what she had in store for Linsey. He was the only person in the world who could stop her from exacting retribution.

And she would listen to him.

But she didn't want to.

Not with this.

Her vengeance would be sweet. It would also be bitter. And it all started tomorrow when she left London with the very man responsible for tearing her beloved from her proverbial embrace.

She almost felt sorry for him.

Almost.

To Thomas's surprise, Lady Ashley had been ready when he came to pick her up. He'd chosen the landau for the occasion. It wasn't his finest carriage but certainly the sensible choice for an extended journey with a near stranger. He wanted to assure this stranger's comfort, since she'd be his wife after all.

Thomas stared at Lady Ashley, seated across from him.

His soon-to-be countess.

His wife.

The hairs on the back of his neck rose. He'd been mentally chastising himself for the fool he'd been to enter a wager with Paisley, fighting the lingering sensation that he'd come to realize how much he'd gambled away even if he won the wager. But now...other thoughts pierced his initial unease.

This was no longer between him and Paisley, but between him and Ashley now—if she went through with it. And that, he had to ensure, she would.

She was riveting.

She kept her gaze out of the window, and he couldn't quite see her face fully under the ruched bonnet, but the shadows danced across her features, almost like a spell, and he feared the enchantment might spread to his very bones. He hated to admit it to himself, but he knew when he was in trouble. Lady Ashley *was* trouble.

She wore a dark-green dress that complemented her eyes. Two blonde locks escaped the coiffure under her bonnet, adding a hint of sweetness to her. He inwardly scoffed. Dainty she may be, but she was a woman of surprising strength. Her beauty was not the typical overt kind—it was a quieter, more bewitching allure, as if she carried a timeless grace that lingered in the air around her, capable of drawing him in without a single touch.

His gaze dropped to where she peeled off her gloves, picking at her nails. An unguarded gesture. One that belied her usual tart remarks.

She was nervous.

It pulled him in further, despite his better judgment.

And then there were her lips. He found his gaze locked there, momentarily captivated. She had the most enchanting mouth, lips full and pink, glistening from a tongue that darted out to moisten them.

"You are staring."

Their eyes locked.

Thomas started, staring into twin pools of blue, clear as a summer sky after rain. He coughed behind his hand. "Would it be inappropriate to say I cannot help myself?" Because, truly, he couldn't.

"Yes."

He chuckled. She had a way to make him laugh with nothing but a one-syllable word. Yes, he thought to himself, she was more than her beauty.

He shifted in his seat. "Are you nervous?" He sure was.

A snort answered him.

So, not nervous, then.

"Are you afraid? Not even a little?"

Her brow arched. "Of what? You?"

Well... Yes, and no. "Our future, I suppose."

She cocked her head to the side, her gaze probing his. "I'm not. Are *you* scared, perhaps?"

"Don't be absurd," Thomas said gruffly. "An earl and the daughter of an earl. Soon there'll be heirs and spares, and what's not to be thankful for?" Suddenly, he felt sick to his stomach, worried and nervous all at once. The abstract ideas of matrimony and a family were suddenly so much less abstract with her looking at him, his fiancée. "I'm as happy as a peach."

She laughed, the sound light and teasing. "I imagine peaches aren't very happy, seeing as they get eaten."

Thomas swallowed hard, doing his best to keep his mind from exploding at the spectacular imagery that saucy comment provoked. But no, he wouldn't give her the satisfaction. "Peaches," he said smoothly, "are happy to serve as the succulent fruits they are."

"Succulent, you say? I wouldn't know," she said tartly. "I've never particularly enjoyed peaches." She leaned in, her voice softening as if sharing a secret. "Tell me, Thomas, are you an expert on such delights?"

His pulse stuttered for a moment, but he managed to keep his composure, his gaze holding hers. "Naturally. A gentleman ought to be well-versed in his fruit."

"Fruits are important, yes."

Hers were like large oranges, perfect fistfuls.

Control yourself, Thomas!

His cravat suddenly felt tight, and he tugged at it. "Just as vegetables. Very healthy." Just like her breasts, he imagined.

Wait, what did he just say? He gave another tug. Vegetables were on the safer side of temptation—they weren't tempting at all—and with her, nothing ever seemed quite safe.

But then, she was saucy, just like a peach.

A peach with a big question mark. "Lady Ashley, if I may be so bold, is there a particular reason you agreed to a hasty marriage?"

Her eyes widened slightly. "What reasons do you mean?"

He coughed, his throat suddenly dry. "For instance, whether you, um, still possess your virtue."

Her eyes flew wide, revealing the whites around her striking aquamarine-colored irises. For a moment, silence stretched between them, the rattle of the carriage wheels the only sound accompanying them. Then she blurted, "*Excuse* me? Why would you ask me such a thing?"

"I—" Hell and damnation. He himself didn't know why he'd asked such a deuced thing. He just couldn't understand why she'd chosen him, and why she agreed so quickly to a hasty marriage. Or perhaps, just perhaps, he wanted to find flaws in her reasoning because of his own reasons for doing the same thing. "My apologies."

"Yes," she muttered. "You should be sorry." Her eyes narrowed on him. "I certainly never inquired about your virtue."

Thomas froze, and it was his turn to open his eyes wide. Better not to touch that remark. Though, he couldn't quite blame her. He didn't press the matter, lest *he* wanted to be pressed. And he didn't. Plus, he was an earl. He was expected to have a certain degree of experience. And he rather wished not to imply that he didn't.

"I don't care about such things," Thomas clarified. "I am just curious about you."

"That makes two of us, my lord."

That made his pulse quicken.

She bit her lip. Bloody adorable.

There was something utterly disarming about the way Lady Ashley spoke—direct, with a hint of teasing that left him unsteady. She entirely unmoored him with one look. His gaze dropped to where she bit her lip, and he cursed himself for wondering just how often she bit it like that. Was it intentional, or did she truly not know the effect of that tiny action?

"Do you often leave men speechless?" he asked, quirking a brow. "Or is that reserved for the lucky few who find themselves trapped in a carriage with you?"

"Trapped?" She raised her chin, eyes gleaming with mischief. "Only those who believe themselves to be trapped, I suppose. And you are the only one."

A grin tugged at the corner of his mouth. "I see. Then I must count myself fortunate. Though I fear my wits may not be on par with yours," he finished dryly.

"Your modesty is refreshing, my lord," she quipped. "Quite different from the grand tales I've heard."

"Grand tales?" How could that be? His brow lifted in amusement. There was nothing grand about his daily life. "What exactly have you heard, Lady Ashley? Should I be concerned?"

Her lips twitched. "Oh, nothing that would alarm a man of *such* noble character. Just the usual gossip—something about a wild stallion and a wager."

He coughed instantly to feign innocence. Had she heard something? He didn't want her to know this. Not yet. Not while their relationship could still be considered fragile. "That hardly narrows it down. I've made many wagers, most of them unwise." This was no different than other peers of the realm, was it?

"Most wagers are."

He studied her. "Have you never made a wager before?"

"Oh, I'm not the wagering type, my lord. But if I were, and if I were to make a wager right now," her eyes sparkled at him, "I'd wager you've never met a woman like me."

Thomas chuckled, leaning back in his seat as the carriage jostled over a bump. "And I'd wager you might be right."

A faint scent of jasmine from her gloves wafted through the air, mingling with the musty aroma of the carriage, a comforting layer that Thomas inhaled deeply. His body couldn't help but react.

The wedding night suddenly blasted through his mind.

Ah, hell.

Obviously, his loins had sent a clear message that his head tried to ignore.

But it wasn't just that.

Something in him recoiled at the thought of a cold, dutiful marriage, the kind so many of his forebears had endured. He wanted more—needed more. Passion, perhaps. Even love.

Don't be foolish, Thomas.

At the very least affection.

Mutual affection.

Having his future bride with him alone in the carriage was wreaking havoc with both body and head. He shifted uncomfortably.

Horses. Just think about horses.

Horses were easier than women.

They required little more than an understanding of their language—a skill Thomas had mastered with both ease and passion. Lady Ashley was a puzzle yet unraveled, each uncertain smile, the gentle play of her fingers in her lap, a riddle so unlike the scorecards of courtship games.

Thomas had ridden more horses than women but rather feared that Lady Ashley would tame *him* like he did a wild French stallion.

Wait, no.

Thoughts of horses were *not* helping.

The carriage hit a sudden rut, jolting them both from their seats. Before he could react, Lady Ashley was thrown forward, tumbling against him. His arms wrapped around her instinctively, and for a moment, time seemed to still. Her breath, quickened and warm, teased his neck.

Her eyes met his, wide with surprise, and then…something else. A glint of mischievousness, and maybe even a trace of amusement. Instead of pulling away, she stayed where she'd landed—pressed against him in a way that felt both improper and entirely scandalous.

Perfect.

She grinned at him, stunning him into a gaze.

Everything else vanished, and he tightened his hold, his body reacting in ways his mind scolded him for, but he drowned out all reason. There was nothing happening he couldn't answer for. They were already engaged to be married.

The sweet scent of jasmine cloaked him.

This might have started as a bet, but…

I'll take care of you, Ashley. When you fall, I'll catch you.

As if reading his thoughts, she exhaled softly, her lips curving even more, pushing the smile into her eyes. It was the kind of look that could undo a man entirely.

It undid him.

Chapter Seven

SHE HAD THOUGHT Linsey the puzzle, but no, she was the biggest one.

Why was she sitting on Linsey's lap? She should get off. Put distance between them. Instead, she remained there, her body curiously unwilling to budge. His eyes, an intense shade of golden-brown, seemed to flicker with some unreadable emotion—desire? Confusion? His chest rose and fell beneath her with a steady rhythm that felt impossibly calming and yet stirred something wild inside her.

His scent was impossible to ignore.

The earthiness clung to him, mingling with the crisp outdoor air that crept into the carriage. His warmth surrounded her, and she couldn't help but notice how solid he felt beneath her, all lean muscle and strength. His jaw—sharply defined and slightly shadowed with the hint of stubble—drew her attention.

A sudden urge to run a finger along the line of his face filled her, but more than that, a reckless urge to kiss him. She could hardly believe herself, yet there it was, a wild temptation that made her fingers twitch. But then, once she set her mind on a task, she gave it her all. And, well, Ashley refused to miss the perfect opportunity to grab the man by the lapels and boldly rob him of his breath!

So, she did just that.

She yanked him to her, planting her lips firmly on his. The man had the gall to speak of virtue. Well, then, she would have the gall to kiss this vexing mouth into submission! His heart would, hopefully, follow soon enough.

His body tensed beneath her, his hands coming to rest on her waist, probably unsure of whether to pull her closer or push her away. But he didn't push her away. She wanted to take charge, to sculpt this impulsive moment into something she controlled. But no. Linsey met her passion with an intensity that startled her, a force that left her breathless. His hand cradled the back of her head, a tender gesture that contrasted with the hunger in the kiss.

So good.

Ashley's senses reeled, torn between the desire to lead and the unexpected thrill of being met with equal force. The air around them pulsed with the heat of their intertwined spirits; even as she fought for control, she couldn't deny the electricity sparking from his touch, setting her every nerve alight.

Ashley's senses spiraled, caught between her desire to command and the thrilling shock of his equal thirst. The air between them crackled, pulsing with heat and tension, every touch sparking a fire along her skin. She could feel the strength in him, the restrained power beneath the gentlemanly bearing, and she hated how much she liked it.

She was in his lap!

Her weight pressed him back into the corner of the bench.

Then why, oh why, did it feel as though he had taken complete control of their kiss? Over her senses?

No! Ashley wouldn't allow it.

Her free hand cupped the back of his head, pulling him closer, deepening the kiss, intent on reclaiming the reins. She was not one to yield easily!

But then... *Oh.* His teeth grazed her lower lip before his tongue pushed in. Her heart stumbled, skipping a few beats.

And then it stopped altogether.

The man could kiss.

And how he could kiss!

Every breath, every movement of his lips against hers sent a dizzying thrill through her, unraveling her willpower in a way she hadn't foreseen. This wasn't a mere kiss. It was a claiming. And it was far too spellbinding.

Ashley had never been so bewildered before.

How was it possible that his mouth could simply touch hers, and her insides leapt with a giddy thrill?

No, it wasn't merely that.

It was a heady blend of sparkling contact, a fiery dance of tongues, and his intoxicating scent overpowering her senses. Her heart had ceased its rhythmic beats, and her lungs forgot how to draw in air. Breathless and dazed, Ashley's bones turned to cotton. Kissing like this, the man certainly didn't seem like the villain who would send another man fleeing from London.

He seemed like just the right man to hold her in his strong arms and kiss her for as long as she existed. Anyone who claimed a woman like that—claimed her like Thomas did—would surely be—

And then it was over.

He pulled away and stared down at her. Ashley stared back, no words ready to fire from her tongue. Was this what they called speechlessness?

Oh dear, it was horrible!

The tips of his fingers brushed over his mouth. "What did you just do?"

"I, I kissed you." *And you devoured me back.* She suddenly laughed. "Why? Are you afraid?"

"Yes, I'm terrified." He turned his gaze away for an instant.

The Earl of Linsey terrified. Ashley would take it. At least she wasn't the only one with a momentary lapse of wit.

"Not that I mind, Lady Ashley," he went on while she still gathered her internal dictionary. "But you are still sitting on my lap."

Ashley launched herself back to her seat. How could she have been sitting on his lap all this time without a worry or care!

Compose yourself, Ashley.

But she could still taste him.

Smell him.

It was intoxicating—and infuriating. She didn't want to feel that way. After all, he had upended her life, hadn't he?

The implication: How could she compose herself?

She felt a pinch of pity for her plan of revenge.

But that didn't stop her from forging onward using the best of her ability. She planned to find Jordan when all of this was over. But even she wasn't so jaded to believe that when she did find him, all would go as she dreamed.

For one, Jordan had left with nothing but a note. He hadn't even had the courage to say goodbye in person. She had tried not to think about that, but it still brewed in the back of her mind. Also, why hadn't he taken her with him? She'd have run away with him if he had asked. But he hadn't even bothered to do that.

Plus, Jordan had never kissed her like that—he hadn't kissed her at all except for her wrist. Which meant…

Linsey was her first true kiss!

Her eyes fixed on Linsey, and he stared back steadily. "I came to London to search for a wife," he suddenly admitted.

Her lips parted and closed, brows furrowing. "I've deduced as much. And you found one." *But do not count your foals before they are colts, Linsey.* "I also heard there is a reason you are searching for a wife. A reason for you to find one sooner rather than later."

He sighed, dragging a hand through his hair. "There is."

She arched her brow. "But you don't want to tell me, is that right?"

"I don't," he admitted, then said softly. "But…" His chest rose and fell with a deep breath. "If I don't marry, I'll lose a bet."

Ah, so she had been right. "Something to do with horses, I suspect."

He nodded. "If I don't marry by my birthday, then I'll lose six of my prized steeds."

Well, at least it wasn't one.

Still. "You would marry just so that you don't lose your horses?" Unbelievable. No, considering this was Linsey, very believable.

"You sound incredulous; however, my horses are everything to me."

"Oh my word! Why?" There must be something more here. A reason behind his obsession. A man who kissed like that must have more depth than the mere pleasure of horsemanship, right?

"Are you obsessed with anything, Lady Ashley?"

Does revenge count? "Perhaps." Perhaps not becoming as frivolous and detached as her mother? That certainly had been an obsession of hers. She had no true hobbies. Well, except if she counted spending time with her friends.

Goodness!

Could she be becoming her mother by obsessing how *not* to become like her mother? Was there something wrong with her because she had nothing she was that attached to, except for him? She almost wanted to ask if he'd marry *them* rather than give them up?

"I can't say that I am," she finally murmured. Nothing she would openly admit to, anyway.

He nodded thoughtfully. "Perhaps you just haven't found something you are passionate about."

If only you knew, Earl. "I have you now, do I not?"

He chuckled. "You should never place your passion onto people, Lady Ashley. They inevitably disappoint."

She cocked her head. "That is quite jaded." And this from the lips she just kissed!

"But the truth."

"Well, horses disappoint, too, you know."

That earned her a raised brow that practically shouted, "How so?"

She shrugged, settling into her seat. "They may run away, too."

"Who's the jaded one now?"

Ashley smiled, pointing out, "They also lose races."

Linsey laughed. "That has to do with the rider as well. The blame cannot be entirely put on the horse's head."

The carriage jolted once more, and Ashley pressed herself more firmly into the seat. She couldn't have a repeat of earlier! "I believe human or beast, we are all at the mercy of transience."

"I doubt that horses give such grand philosophical ideas much thought. They are simple creatures, loyal and unchanging."

"Well, if that's your reason for being so enamored with them, I fear for my poor future husband."

Amusement flickered in his eyes, a genuine curiosity beneath it. "And why is that?"

You'll know soon enough, Linsey.

"They may never betray you, my lord, but what about you? What—or who—are you betraying by keeping them so close to your heart? So much so that you'd marry me without truly knowing me?"

"Oh? Then what about you, Lady Ashley? Were you not the one who asked me to wed you first?"

Ashley waved a hand. "Only after you asked my father."

"Yes, but you now know my reason for a hasty marriage. What is your true reason? I'm thoroughly curious."

He surely was. But any answer she gave him now would be a lie. This entire betrothal was built on deceit, and he had yet to realize it. If he suspected too soon, she wouldn't accomplish what she'd set out to do. And, with any luck, by the time he discovered the truth, it would be far too late.

She suddenly sensed his underlying suspicion.

His eyes were sharp, not only capable of piercing right through her ploy but straight through her soul.

Don't falter now, Ashley. Don't forget what he took from you.

"If you are looking for reasons, my lord, you need look no further than my age. I'm not a woman meant to even touch the outskirts of spinsterhood."

He stared at her, then suddenly laughed, shaking his head. "Very well, Lady Ashley."

She inwardly stuck out her tongue at him. "You should get some rest," she muttered, averting her gaze. She could do with rest too. Space. Even if it was only mental. Why did he assume she wanted to marry in such haste? As a man, he was probably imagining the worst. His earlier comment about her chastity came to mind.

Wretched thing.

Hah! Horses do not betray? What, then, was he betraying by marrying the first girl—chaste or not—just to keep his beloved horses?

<hr>

THOMAS HAD NEVER been so relieved to escape a carriage. What had just happened? The crunch of gravel under his boots was a welcome distraction as he took a few brisk steps away from the carriage, breathing in the cool air of twilight.

They kissed.

No, *she* had kissed *him*.

But he'd kissed her back.

Then she kissed him back *more*.

And he kissed *her* back more.

So she'd started it. More importantly, she made him feel things. Things he hadn't expected, things he wasn't even sure how to name. What unsettled him even further was what she had said. Her words echoed in his mind, a challenge he couldn't shake. *They may never betray you, Linsey, but what about you? What—or who—are you betraying by keeping them so close to your heart?*

The question rattled him.

Because he didn't know how to answer it.

Thomas scrubbed a hand over his face, trying to focus on his breath. The sensation of the kiss still lingered on his lips—a heady mix of sweetness and something deeper, something that set his pulse racing.

Breathe in. Breathe out.

This was the type of experience that authors and poets strove to depict with elaborate prose, yet here he was, living it. Vivid. Uncontrollable.

He hadn't expected this.

It was going to haunt him.

The kiss had started soft, a tentative immersion, but then there had been a shift. Her lips became more insistent, daring him to follow her lead. And he did—though perhaps not fully understanding what it would awaken in him. He inhaled sharply, remembering the tenderness of her touch, a delicate suckling that had pulled him deeper into the moment. It was a dance of breath and longing, each movement synchronized silently, a promise of more to come.

Bloody hell.

He was reliving it as though it were happening again. She'd stirred a longing deep within him that he knew he wouldn't be able to satisfy. Perhaps ever!

Only she could.

A mix of awe and bewilderment seized him. He ran a hand through his hair, disheveling it. What was this? A simple kiss, and yet his whole body had responded, sparking a fire that refused to be extinguished. His heart hammered as he recalled how she had made him feel.

No, not just feel—desire.

He glanced down at the strain in his trousers.

He shifted, turning slightly as she exited the carriage behind him. Thomas snatched his hat from his head, using it to hide the evidence of his desire. But this wasn't the worst of it. He wanted her near again. Wanted to taste her again. To feel her breath against his skin.

Clearing his throat, Thomas gripped the brim of his hat tightly, as though that could steady his thoughts.

Think about something else, Thomas.

But it was impossible. He was no novice when it came to kissing and had stolen many a kiss before. Yet this—this had been something entirely different. It wasn't just a kiss; it was a revelation. She had kissed him like she *knew* something, as though she carried a secret knowledge of how to stir a storm within the human soul. As if she held the secrets of how to unravel him completely. He shivered despite himself.

It was disconcerting.

Exhilarating. Terrifying.

How could he get more?

Yet, how had one kiss left him so undone?

He stood there, erect and perplexed, wondering how such an encounter could leave him so unmoored. And there lay his dread, raw and unbidden, that this unexpected maestro of emotion could lead his life into a tempest of disarray just as easily.

Damn it. A thrum of nerves competed for the ranks of his racing heart. He was taking her home. *Bringing her home.* And that act suddenly seemed to carry a weight far greater than he'd first imagined.

"What are you doing?"

Thomas jerked at the voice that crept up from behind. "Oh, merely observing our surroundings," he said quickly, cursing his dull answer. His gaze met hers before sweeping the area, the area as if searching for something to point out. It landed on the inn they had stopped at. The roof sagged, puddles had formed where the rain had broken through, and the whole building looked as though it might crumble with the slightest nudge. He'd been there a few days ago. What happened?

"Are we staying *here*?" Ashley asked, stepping up beside him, her tone laced with disbelief.

Thomas cast a glance at her, noting her elegant figure against the shabby backdrop. This wasn't the grand ballroom or elegant estate she was used to. This was Sleepy Oak—a far cry from her usual surroundings. But there was no other choice. The horses needed rest, and so did he. "It has its charm."

"Charm?" She arched an eyebrow. "I don't see it. Unless by 'charm' you mean the imminent collapse of the roof."

"Precisely," Thomas quipped. "It's part of the rustic experience. Builds character."

"Rustic experience? You should write travel pamphlets," she said dryly. "You'd sell none."

"'Tis as far as the mares will take us," the driver announced, echoing Thomas's thoughts.

"Well," Lady Ashley said, her voice dripping with resignation, "at least the horses get to enjoy it. They do deserve better lodgings than we, after all."

Thomas gave her a wry look as they approached the weathered oak door of the inn. "Oh, without question. In fact, they usually have fresh straw. We'll be lucky to have that much." An exaggeration, of course.

"Fresh straw? You really know how to spoil a lady."

He grinned, opening the door. "I live to serve, my lady."

Lady Ashley rolled her eyes but couldn't suppress a small smile as she eyed the crumbling inn again. "I hope you have better plans for our future accommodations."

Inside, the inn was a scene of hasty repairs—men sawing wood, women collecting buckets filled with rainwater. The innkeeper, a rotund man with a bristling mustache, greeted them with an apologetic smile.

"Good evening, milord. I'm afraid we have a situation at hand."

Thomas's eyes darted toward the ceiling, where water dripped steadily from above. "What happened?"

"Rain, milord. The roof couldn't hold. I'm afraid the rooms are all out of commission."

Thomas sighed, rubbing his temples. They were miles from the next village, and he couldn't push the horses any further. "Do you require any help?"

"Just time, milord. My daughters help, and each of my sons-in-law are here, and my brother's come, too."

"And there isn't a dry place left?" Thomas had to confirm.

"Only the stables, milord. We will sleep at my daughter's cottage and the stove's unlit."

"Have you anything for the mares?"

"There're carrots and apples in the stables," the man said. "No charge, if you promise to stop here after we repair the inn."

"Of course." Thomas pulled a bank note from his coat and placed it on the counter. "To help."

"Milord—"

"Keep it," Thomas insisted before the man could protest. "You will need it, and I shall need future accommodation again. We shall make do with the stables tonight." At least his body had calmed.

The man nodded. "Very well, milord. I shall show you there in a moment."

Thomas nodded and strode over to Lady Ashley. "There's no room at the inn," he said, his voice soft but firm. "They'll let us stay in the stables," he said, then added, "There are apples and carrots."

She raised an eyebrow, smoothing out invisible wrinkles on her gown. "Ah, so we do get to sleep like royalty tonight. I almost feel honored."

He chuckled. "It could have been worse, trust me."

"Very well, then. Who am I to argue."

Thomas marveled at her composure. He thought she might fuss, but surprisingly, she took the news very good-naturedly. This was what he liked about her.

Nothing seemed to faze her.

Not kissing.

Not spending a night in a stable.

Not him.

It was going to be a long night!

Chapter Eight

ASHLEY'S GAZE SWEPT over the interior of the stables, starting at the hayloft where their bed had been prepared, her eyes taking in the rough wooden beams, the flickering shadows cast by the lantern, and the shuffle of horses in their stalls. There truly seemed to be a first for everything. For all her daring and boldness, she had never imagined herself here—facing a night surrounded by hay, horses, and the man she intended to ruin. The thought was utterly absurd. Laughable even.

The very idea of spending the night under these circumstances, with *him*, made her stomach knot in ways she couldn't explain.

She had expected the stench of manure, the damp rot of straw, but to her surprise, the air was rather...pleasant. Earthy, rich with the scent of hay, leather, and something else she couldn't quite place. It most certainly wasn't unpleasant. If anything, it was grounding. A far cry from the cloying perfumes and the stiff, polished airs of London's drawing rooms. It felt real—like the world stripped of pretense and nonsense.

Like him.

Which was even more absurd!

Perhaps this was why the arrangement made her so uncomfortable.

Her gaze flicked to Linsey, who was speaking in low tones to his driver, helping the man settle the horses in their stalls. She watched him quietly, trying to make sense of the man before her. He moved with a kind of ease, a familiarity that spoke of someone at home in the countryside, at home among the dirt and the animals. It was so at odds with the image of him that she had constructed in her mind—the beast-like earl, who had ruined a man's life over a simple wager.

But watching him now, as he took the reins from his driver's hands and murmured something softly to his horse, she found herself questioning that image. Could a man who cared for his horses with such tenderness, who made jokes at her expense with such warmth, truly be the heartless rogue she believed him to be?

It doesn't make sense, she thought, her brow furrowing. *If he is so heartless, why does he seem so human?*

But then, it was easier to love animals than it was to love people. This much, she had seen with her own eyes. Her mother's annoying pug came to mind—an obnoxious creature with a bark far worse than its bite. The countess would forever choose that beady-eyed animal over anyone else.

She inwardly scoffed.

Linsey suddenly looked up and grinned when he caught her staring. Ashley's ears heated, and she suddenly recalled their kiss. An infuriating, heart-pounding, earth-shifting moment that she had not planned for. The way his lips had lingered, teasing, tempting—she had been caught entirely off guard.

"What are you grinning at?" she muttered at the man.

His grin turned roguish, and an unrepentant glint entered his gaze. Hah! She ought not forget that there were many sides to a man. "I'm grinning at the woman who is staring at me."

"I'm observing. There is a difference."

That grin widened a notch. "A stare is a stare no matter how you *look* at it."

She snorted. Incorrigible.

Before she could respond, the innkeeper's wife bustled into the stable, carrying a tray with bread, cheese, and a jug of wine. "I thought you might need something to line your stomachs," she said with a warm smile. "It's not much, but it'll keep you warm through the night."

Ashley blinked, momentarily startled by the woman's kindness. "Thank you," she said as Linsey hurried to accept the tray. She'd never been so grateful to see wine!

"This is most generous of you," Linsey said. "We shall enjoy it."

The woman waved her hand dismissively. "It's no trouble. You'll find the loft cozy enough once you settle in." With a nod to the earl, she disappeared again. The driver followed, having offered to help with the repairs that would last through the night.

Linsey carefully brought the tray up to the loft. "Is this not heaven?"

Ashley scoffed. "Are you sure you live in a house and not a stable?"

He chuckled. "This is familiar to me. Comfort."

"I can see that. You must have been born a horse in your last life. Why are you so delighted to sleep in the stables?"

He inhaled deeply. "Don't you just love the smell of livestock and fresh straw?"

"It's not my most favorite scent in the world."

He chuckled. "This is the simple life."

"You truly are a country bumpkin, aren't you?"

He shot her a grin. "You sound rather disgruntled at the thought."

Disgruntled? Her, a lady? Absolutely not. It had nothing to do with her whether he was a country bumpkin or not. What did concern her, however, was how she found him mucking about the stable rather attractive. In a pure, raw sort of way. He'd stripped to just his shirt, sleeves rolled up to his elbows—exposing his muscular arms and the hint of a vein popping up on the underside.

Urgh! It's the stables, Ashley! There is nothing pure or attractive about it. Raw, yes. The rest, no.

She turned to the makeshift bed of hay and blankets in the loft. "Cozy, she says," she murmured. "What a quaint way to describe sleeping in a barn." But it wasn't all that bad. It did *look* cozy. The bed might not sleep all that comfortable, though.

"Just where do you expect me to sleep?" It was best to focus on the immediate matter at hand rather than the man's muscles.

"With me."

That wine would be good right about now. Perhaps even cognac, not that she had any. Nor did she have any clever retort.

"What? You can kiss me but not sleep next to me?" He raised an eyebrow.

She had honestly tried not to think about it at all.

"Nothing some wine can't fix," he replied, setting down the tray and pouring her a cup. A cup! Not a glass at a nicely set table. Their first meal was going to be wine at the stables.

Well, at least this betrothal wasn't going to mature into more than she'd planned.

"Agreed." She accepted the wine, taking a sip and secretly savoring the warmth that spread through her.

"Good?" he murmured, pouring a cup for himself.

"Exceedingly so."

"Very well, then. We have ourselves a feast." He gestured toward the bread and cheese. "A night in a stable with fine cuisine. Who could ask for more?"

Ashley tried but couldn't suppress a smile. "Only you would find excitement in muck and hay, Linsey. I suppose it beats the latest ball, where one is required to nibble delicately on pastries while dodging unwanted suitors."

"Only because it comes with such delightful company," he countered smoothly, raising his cup in a toast.

Ashley felt her heart flutter at his words, and she raised her cup in return, her gaze locking with his. "To scandal and stables," she said, laughter dancing in her voice. "May we survive the night."

She would survive, but she'd hoped for more triumph than that.

And it was only their first night together.

THOMAS LEANED AGAINST a wooden beam in the hayloft, staring at Lady Ashley with a smile before his gaze shifted over at the bed of hay in the corner.

Swallowing another sip of wine.

He could do with something stronger.

"Not so inviting after all?" Her teasing voice came.

"Not at all." Quite the contrary. The thought of sinking into that prickly mound made his heart race with nerves. He glanced back at Lady Ashley, suddenly laughing at her suspicious look.

"So long as we are warm, nothing else matters," he remarked, a wry smile tugging at the corner of his mouth, keen to lighten the air that seemed to thicken with unsaid thoughts. Now that he knew with how much boldness she kissed, that lumpy bed looked like a dangerous weapon. He gave another curse as his mind conjured all sorts of hot images of sharing a bed in the stables.

"What if there's a mouse?" Her eyes trailed over the drafty planks that made up the stable walls. "I can tolerate many things, but I'm not sure about a mouse crawling over me."

"Why would there only be one? The cats would starve." She was too adorable not to tease a little.

He noticed the rise of goosebumps tracing her neck. "But do not despair. There is no animal that will get past me while I watch over you sleeping." And he meant it. Her gaze lifted to him and there was a fleeting crack of her usual composure. An allure that made him feel more man than his title, estate, and any riches ever had. "I promise. No mouse will touch you." He'd gladly slay not only a rodent but even dragons on her behalf.

Ashley laughed. "Oh, I can take care of myself, rodents or not. And while I am taking care, I shall take care of you, too."

Thomas's chuckle rumbled from deep within his chest, but he'd leave her that. Her wit still sparkled with the sharpness of cut glass, and he found himself unwilling to look away, captivated once more. Or captivated still; he couldn't tell. This was all too new for him. It was a curious thing, this magnetic pull she had over him—a mystery he hadn't given much thought to solve but now found himself entangled in.

"This bedding shall do," she finished with a nod, taking another sip of wine.

"Very well," she said, settling onto the bedding with a resolute nod, picking up a piece of bread from the tray. "This bedding, this *straw*, shall not defeat me."

Hmm...bedding.

Bloody hell, Thomas.

He eyed her as she nestled into the straw, her deceptively delicate air completely at ease. It was not the marriage of convenience he had envisioned—no, here beneath the wooden beams he sensed the stirrings of something far more powerful than convenience.

Perhaps all was not lost.

Thomas made a silent vow. She might be his fiancée by circumstance, but he was responsible for her and would ensure her wellbeing, and he was going to steal her heart right from under her bold toes.

He plopped down himself, tearing off a hunk of bread for himself. They ate in companionable silence, the quiet punctuated by the occasional snort of a horse or rustle of hay.

"You are welcome to invite your friends to visit," Thomas suddenly said. "It must be hard leaving them behind."

Her eyes lit up. "Really? Then I shall send them a note before we leave tomorrow." She cocked her head. "Why did you suddenly think of them?"

He shrugged. "This might be a marriage of convenience, but I still want you to be happy." And it seemed her friends made her happy. To win her heart, happiness was key, was it not?

She sent him a riveting smile. "Thank you."

"Think nothing of it. My home is your home after all. Speaking of which, I'm surprised your father agreed so readily that you travel with me."

She waved a hand. "Ah, well, Papa has always wanted me to live a life I chose. He wanted me to have no fewer privileges than a son would have."

"And yet, you're obviously not one. A son, I mean."

"No. But I received as many privileges as a daughter could. Tutors, books, and any luxury I ever desired."

"He must love you very much." Thomas tasted the words. It would probably be easy to love her, spoil her, and give her everything she wanted. Except that he didn't quite know yet what exactly she wanted from him, really wanted…besides the obvious marriage to become his countess.

"Well, he said it was an investment in my future." She tugged at her dress as if the conversation of her future almost unsettled her.

"Very forward thinking of him," Thomas remarked. "I understand now why you dare to be so bold. What of your mother?"

She pulled a face and took another sip of wine. "That surprise I shall not spoil."

"Now, I am terrified."

A small laugh. "You should be," she murmured. "What about you? What about your family?"

His family.

"Nothing too overly complicated or terrifying. I'm the heir and the spare. You know how these things go. My mother is touring the continent with her new husband. So, it's just me."

"That sounds lonely."

"Well—"

"Well," she interrupted. "You also have a *stable* family, don't you?"

Thomas gave her a deadpan look, then laughed, shaking his head. He couldn't believe she made such a joke! "I do have a stable horse family; you are not wrong."

"You know," she murmured, her lips pursing in thought. "I don't believe we have one thing in common."

They didn't? "I don't believe that is true."

"Oh? And what do we have in common?"

"Mettle."

"*Mettle?*" A bubble of laughter escaped her lips. "I suppose that is true."

"We also value our friends." He thought of Sebastian. He might only have one true friend, but that was enough for him.

"And gumption." Thomas's leg brushed against hers.

Her body tensed slightly at the contact, but she didn't pull away. Instead, she turned to him, her eyes glinting. There was no mistaking the challenge in her eyes—a dare almost, wrapped in that silky, teasing tone she wielded so well. She was daring him now, in ways she perhaps didn't even realize.

"These are not things that keep conversations flowing."

True. *But.* He shifted closer, feeling the heat of her body against his side, her scent—something faintly floral—wrapping around him, teasing his senses. His pulse quickened. The hay bed beneath them felt increasingly irrelevant. "But then we also have…"

Her eyes twinkled. "What? What do we both have?"

He swallowed, his gaze dropping briefly to her lips before returning to her eyes. The desire to close the small gap between them was becoming harder to ignore, but he didn't move. Not yet. Instead, he leaned in just slightly, enough to feel her breath hitch in response.

"Determination," he said quietly. "Neither of us backs down easily. And I'm certain we shall find things we very much have in common."

Though the thought of discovering what those are may just undo me.

Chapter Nine

THOMAS HAD FACED many crises in his life. Some of the most difficult had been navigating the aftermath of his father's sudden death, rescuing his horses from his barn that caught fire, and even wrestling a panicked mare out of a flooding river.

But the crisis he felt at the moment, staring into Lady Ashley's eyes, was unlike any of those. It was the quiet, burning kind—the kind that settled deep in his chest and threatened to unravel his carefully constructed world. Because in her gaze he saw not just a woman but a future, a temptation, and the terrifying realization that if he wasn't careful, he could lose far more than his composure.

Yet the unbidden thought still came. *What do you do with this future countess in a hayloft? Especially one that set his heart into a gallop?*

"Of course, anyone who digs deeper can find something in common with another person," she murmured, holding out her empty glass for him to pour more wine.

He obliged, holding the hand with the cup steady in his. The skin of his whole body burst out in ripples. "I don't mind digging deeper."

Oh no...that came out wrong.

They were now almost too close for comfort. He could easily reach around her waist, pull her in, and press her body against the length of him. She slowly retracted her hand, her gaze never leaving his. What had he gotten himself into with this woman? He had the breathtaking thought that he would never be able to win against her.

Control yourself, Thomas.

She's a lady, and you're the earl now, not a randy stableboy.

Her smile turned impish. This woman knew how to use her charm like a lethal weapon.

She leaned in and licked a drop of wine from her lips. Thomas's heart skipped a beat, knowing exactly how dangerous those lips could be. Then, as if oblivious to the chaos she was creating in him, she took a slow bite of the cheese, her teeth sinking into the soft wedge. He watched, captivated by the movement of her mouth, and swallowed hard. Heat knotted low in his belly. But all he did was sit there, transfixed, gripping the cup of wine as if it were the only thing tethering him to reality. How was it that a simple piece of cheese could look so enticing? He hardened in ways that made him want to snatch his hat again, but his hand came up empty.

Devil take it. His hat was tossed aside on the ground floor.

She held his gaze as she chewed, her lips curving upward in the slightest smile—a wicked little thing that told him she knew exactly what she was doing. And when she swallowed, he had to look away, but he couldn't look away for long.

"Something wrong, my lord?" Her voice was a purr, dripping with mischief. "You seem distracted."

Distracted? He was utterly undone. He forced a laugh, though it came out strangled. "I'm only wondering how cheese could look so delicious."

Her brow arched, a spark of amusement dancing in her eyes. "It's just cheese, Linsey," she said, then took another bite, her teeth grazing the edge with infuriating precision.

His pulse kicked hard, and he couldn't stop the grin that tugged at his lips. "Perhaps," he conceded, watching as her tongue darted out to catch a morsel from her lip. His gaze followed the movement, his body stiffening in response. Goodness, what had he gotten himself into with this woman? She was toying with him, and he was more than willing to play her game.

He reached for the cheese, but before he could take a piece for himself, she leaned forward, offering him a bite from her hand.

You are going to marry me, so why hold back?

The thought came unbidden, and taunting.

And yet, who started this? He leaned over to take the cheese with his mouth, and let his lips linger, just for a second, on the edge of her fingers, before he pulled away. The taste of the cheese was sharp, earthy, but all Thomas could think of was the taste of her.

Her breath hitched, and she pulled her hand back slowly, her eyes locked on his. The teasing glint had dulled, replaced by something deeper, more dangerous. The space between them seemed to narrow, though neither of them shifted an inch. The air was not heavy with tension, but rather with the subtle promise of something unspoken—a spark waiting to ignite, should one of them dare. And it was well-known that a spark in a hayloft could set the whole stable ablaze.

Thomas wanted nothing more than to shed the shackles of restraint and embrace the raw, untamed nature of the place—pure and honest, so unlike the perfumed parlors of the city. And he'd let her flames light him up, as any spark from Ashley would. He'd burn the whole place down tonight, if she let him.

But tonight was not *that* night.

If he was going to set any stables ablaze with passion it would be his own.

However, he could still tease, so with deliberate slowness, he brought his thumb to his lips, tasting the faint remnants of the cheese—and of her. "Sweet."

She blinked, a light blush sweeping over her cheeks. "The cheese?"

Thomas leaned in, his hand moving to rest on the hay beside her, bringing him closer—so close he could smell the soft scent of her. "You."

She let out a breathy laugh, her eyes flicking to his lips before meeting his gaze again. "Incorrigible."

He grinned, his gaze dropping to her lips, and without thinking, his thumb grazed the corner of her mouth where a tiny bit of imaginary cheese lingered. "I am merely matching you. I think you want that."

Her eyes narrowed on him, and he loved that look. "That's not fair." She copied his actions, trailing her thumb over his lower lip. She placed her thumb in her mouth.

"You make it difficult to behave, Ashley."

Her grin was slow in coming. "Behaving is for children."

How the devil was he supposed to resist in the wake of that bold statement? He couldn't. His lips found hers in a swift, searing—just as bold—kiss, the taste of wine and cheese mingling with the heat of her mouth. It was both a surrender and a victory, the culmination of all the teasing and tension, and yet it wasn't enough.

Not nearly enough.

But he pulled back, just enough to hold her gaze, his thumb brushing the curve of her jaw. "More?" he asked, his voice rough with restraint.

Her eyes were wide, her chest rising and falling with rapid breaths, but she still didn't pull away. Instead, she smiled—a soft, teasing curve of her lips that hinted at endless mischief. "Always."

For a heartbeat, he could only stare. Damn her. She knew exactly what she was doing. And if he wasn't careful, he'd be the one undone. Who was he fooling?

I already am.

WHEN IT CAME to teasing, Lady Ashley knew how to wield her charm like a finely honed blade. But with him—Linsey—every smile, every word, every touch felt like more than a game. It was a dangerous thrill, a breathless dance at the edge of something supremely perilous. And she needed to be careful, for already she could feel a slight shift in power, leaving her wondering just who was truly in control.

She couldn't let it be him.

So, when he leaned in for another kiss, she blocked her lips with a hand and laughed at his momentarily befuddled expression. "Always doesn't mean right now."

"Now you are just teasing me."

She arched an amused brow. "I believe we have both been doing just that."

He grinned, leaning back on his arms. "Quite right."

Ashley stared at the rogue across from her and felt a tantalizing ripple carry down her spine. It suddenly occurred to her. What better way to tease a man's heart—and steal it—than in the stables he loved so much, amongst the hay and sighs of the horses below them. Quite frankly, it should have occurred to her earlier, which was oddly disturbing in itself, but she'd merely followed the mood before. Now, she deliberately inched closer, their noses almost touching, their *lips* almost brushing before she pulled away again.

"And I'm thoroughly losing," he said gruffly.

"Then we complement each other," Ashley said breezily. "For I love winning. Otherwise, why play?"

"You think this is a game?" His voice was soft. Raspy.

"Anything can be turned into a game if the stakes are right." She cocked her head to the side. "Much like horse racing."

"Someone is rather competitive," he said, his voice smooth and sultry. If a man could purr, it would sound like this.

"You almost sound as if you are intrigued by this."

"I might be."

"Really?" Ashley laughed. "I seem like the opposite of what you would want for a wife."

"And yet since the first moment we met, I could not keep my mind from wandering over to you no matter how much I tried to rein it in."

The hairs on the back of her neck raised. She wouldn't lose at her own game.

"In all of the two days since we've met?" She refused to lose. Yet statements like these unnerved her in a way that made her second-guess her carefully crafted confidence, igniting a flicker of uncertainty that danced just beneath her surface, tempting her to reconsider what she thought she knew about herself—and him. No.

No.

There was no second guessing anything!

"Losing is not fun," he agreed. "But sometimes it's necessary."

"How could it be necessary?" Ashley asked, watching the light dance in his eyes. Fascinating. She couldn't fathom giving in to this man, didn't want to, mainly because it meant...well, it meant something she wasn't ready to contemplate. For the first time in her life, Ashley wondered if she'd been wrong in acting *before* overthinking. "You mean, so that there's a winner?"

"We learn from losing," the earl said, drawing her back into the moment. Their proximity. "We don't learn from succeeding."

Nonsense! She'd gain nothing from losing. Nothing she wanted. "We also learn *to* succeed if we succeed."

"Through failing, yes." He shrugged. "Otherwise, what standard do we have to measure failure against victory."

Ashley ignored the uncomfortable pinch in her breast. "Wise words. But I dare say, I still prefer winning, and I don't believe I can lose in this game." In more ways than one.

That thumb—that naughty thumb—returned to her lower lip, caressing, his touch sending a jolt of electricity down her spine. "Are you sure?"

Ashley's breath caught at his challenge. This was no game of teasing any longer. This was a battle of wills. A test of mettle.

A thrill shot through her. "Weren't you the one preaching we learn through losing? So why not start now?"

He chuckled. "Very good, Lady Ashley, very good." He took a swallow of wine. "But when it comes to you, I find I don't want to lose."

"Well, what do you know. Neither do I."

"Then shall we both win?"

Impossible. "I suppose that all depends on what's at stake."

She mirrored his earlier actions once more, but instead of her thumb, she used the tip of her finger to trace his lips more boldly this time. She wasn't certain what she expected from him either, perhaps a manly gasp, maybe a jerk of his body. Instead, his tongue darted out and flicked over her finger right before he nipped at her thumb, his teeth grazing her skin.

She snatched her hand back, and to her dismay, his head fell back, and laughter spilled from his lips.

Splendid.

She had amused him. Drat. She wanted to *tempt* him, not make herself the source of this mirth. The man understood the art of teasing as much as she did. Perhaps even more. But then, amusement and mirth were not bad either.

She filed his trick away for later use.

She'd semi-failed this round. So, she would learn.

This is dangerous, Ashley.

Yes, but she felt herself coming alive with the thrill.

She was accustomed to being the one in control, the one who dictated the terms of any engagement involving her. But with the earl, it was different. He matched her step for step, leaving her breathless and slightly bewildered. And *that* bewilderment, beneath these awkward yet playful moments, unsettled her. It was as if, with each playful exchange, he was peeling back her layers, revealing vulnerabilities she wasn't ready to confront. Almost as if her body were privy to information her mind had yet to grasp, she found herself responding to him.

She couldn't shake the feeling that there was more to the earl than met the eye, that there were depths to him she had yet to uncover. The question remained: Did she want to uncover this depth? Did it serve her purpose? Did it matter?

You're losing yet again.

No.

She wouldn't lose.

Not in this.

She was a bold woman. She claimed what she wanted. And she wasn't averse to learning. That night, she'd learned. While he could tease and set her pulse leaping, he did it in the most subtle way. Not her. She didn't do subtle. She did bold. And bold she would do! Her lips stretched into a grin, widening when he blinked twice at her sudden change, and she leaned into him. Not a little. A lot. So much so that her bosom pressed into his chest.

She delighted in his gasp.

He leaned backward, but she refused to let him escape so easily. She followed him down, her gaze never leaving his.

"You are not playing fair."

"How is this not fair?" Ashley questioned. "This is called claiming the moment."

His eyes narrowed to slits. "This is called cheating."

She raised an eyebrow, her lips curling in challenge. "By whose standards? Yours?"

"Yes," he breathed.

"Then let us raise them higher, no?"

He swallowed. "So confident. I can't help but admire your pluck."

He carried a blend of spices and something uniquely his own, an essence that drew her in. She couldn't let it distract her. "Like I said, Linsey, I don't like losing. I'm also a quick learner. Are you?"

"I thought I was." His gaze dropped to her lips. "Now, I'm not so sure."

She held his gaze. "Time will tell, I suppose."

He nodded slowly, then cleared his throat. "Are you done? I can humbly say you won this round."

"Really? But what if I'm not done yet?"

"You're not?" The question was filled with question marks.

She didn't answer; she just kissed him. It didn't matter who started the kiss. It wouldn't matter who ended it. It was blazing hot. All-consuming in a way that burned through her veins. If the frantic waltz of their tongues proved anything, it was that she was in danger of losing her wits in the presence of this man. That she ran the risk of falling into her own trap.

She pulled away from him, finally putting distance between them.

You are in trouble, Ashley.

Chapter Ten

THOMAS RECLINED, FROZEN, the lingering heat of her kiss still burning on his lips. She had taken control in a way he hadn't anticipated, leaving him both dazed and befuddled. He was a man accustomed to dictating the pace, always holding the reins, yet with her, everything shifted. Paisley had once viciously tugged at his control, making him fight to keep it, but with her, it was different.

Every look, every touch, subtly pulled at his grip, and he felt as though he was losing ground in a battle he hadn't realized he was engaged in. Desire warred with his need for dictating the pace of his life, and he struggled to reconcile the man he thought he was with the one who was slowly unraveling under her influence.

"Where did you learn to kiss like that?" Ashley asked, tucking her blonde tresses behind her ears and seemingly trying to catch her breath as she settled into the bed of hay again. Hell, he could still feel her pressed up against him. What a heavenly feeling.

Where did he learn to kiss like that?

Did one *learn* this?

His gaze drifted down to her lips, still slightly parted from the kiss, and he had to stop himself from leaning in again. Instead, he reached out, almost absentmindedly, and pulled one of those loose tresses of hair back out from behind her ear. He let it fall, then ran his fingers through it, stroking a silky tendril. It was impossibly soft, like a foal's first tufts of mane, and she smelled of crisp bloom and fresh morning dew, a scent that seemed to wrap around him, intoxicating his senses.

"Why do I feel I shall regret answering that question?" he finally replied, stretching out his legs to find a more comfortable position.

She raised an eyebrow at him, her lips quirking into a small smile. "You think I can't handle hearing how many women my betrothed has kissed? Do you want my number?"

Her words hit him like a blow.

His blood curdled at the thought of her kissing another man. Jealousy, sharp and immediate, surged within him. He tried to tamp it down, but it lingered, gnawing at his insides. The idea of Ashley kissing someone else—anyone else—was unbearable. Yes. He wanted her number, every detail, every name, so he could snuff them out of existence.

Did he want to know? Yes. "No." He scowled. "How many men have you kissed?"

Her smile only grew.

Come to think of it, he thought bitterly, given her boldness and how she kissed him, he could not have been her first.

"I have kissed only one man the way I've kissed you."

He stilled. He was her first? A tightness in his chest that he hadn't realized he was holding onto eased, and he silently cursed himself for caring. Of course, he cared. How could he not? His whole body hummed with want for her. He wanted nothing more than to lay her down in the hay, kiss every inch of her, and rip her bodice off with his teeth. His hands clenched into fists, grasping the brittle blades of hay beneath him. Just like his restraint, they cracked and crumbled under the pressure.

"What about you?" Ashley asked, her smile never faltering. There was a lightness in her tone, as though she already knew the answer but was merely curious how he would respond.

He grunted, shifting his weight uncomfortably.

The question irked him, not because he was ashamed of his past, but because, suddenly, he found himself wanting her to believe she was different from any other. That she meant more. But to admit that... He wasn't sure he was ready to admit that to himself, let alone to her. This certainly wasn't the perfect moment for such an admission.

"What man keeps count?" he practically grumbled.

Ashley laughed, the sound bright and infectious, filling the small space between them with warmth. It disarmed him in a way that nothing else could.

"You're impossible, you know that?" She nudged him playfully with her foot. "But I suppose that's part of your charm."

Charm.

He felt he had less charm than a rock, hard as he was. But the fact that she said he had charm made him ridiculously pleased. "It's hot in here," he said, unbuttoning his shirt and pulling off his boots. "Time to settle down." Before he truly crossed a line he'd rather cross at home.

"Ah, yes, sleeping together. In a bed of hay. Here."

Thomas chuckled, taking his shirt off.

"Why are you taking off your shirt?"

He caught her gaze flicker to his chest, and he felt a surge of confidence. "Because I turn into a furnace at night."

"Is *that* really the reason?" Her disbelief made him laugh.

He flexed his pecs.

She laughed, settling into her side of the bed. "I do believe you are right; we *should* turn in for the night."

"You don't have any curiosity?"

"Curiosity over...?"

He scooted forward and took her hand. She let him guide her over his chest. He knew he was in good shape—he spent so much time outside riding, and he'd always had to use his strength for his horses. "This?"

She blinked, then dug her fingers in his flesh, scoffing lightly. "Are you trying to seduce me?"

"Never."

Her brow shot upward. *"Never?"*

Thomas cleared his throat and allowed her hand to fall away. "Not tonight." Damn it, what the hell was he doing?

Her gaze fell to his chest again. "By the by, why are your muscles so visible?"

"Strain makes them bulky."

She shot him a deadpan look. "Strain?"

He laughed. "I am jesting." It was his attempt to block the temptation of the moment. He didn't just want to lose himself in her; he wanted to discover who they could be together, outside of the confines of this hasty marriage that he did not want to be of convenience. He still wanted love. Hers. It was a bold notion, a reckless one, but he still felt a thrill of hope.

Maybe, just maybe, they could rewrite not just the rules.

But everything.

⇶⇷

ASHLEY JERKED AS their carriage hit another rock on the road.

She hadn't slept a wink last night. How could she, when the man—her enemy with ambiguously blurred lines—held her, his hard, unforgettably chiseled—and thoroughly naked—chest pressed up against her back. But not only that, rather a certain hardness that sprang forth just as sleep was about to claim her, only to banish any hope of rest altogether.

And she had never thought she'd love hay.

She had welcomed the prickly straw poking through the blanket, a distraction from the temptation to lean into that warm, solid form behind her. Otherwise, she might have *leaned* into that chest. Even worse, a man she had never thought would be a master at flirtation. And speaking about flirtation, she'd grossly underestimated the degree to which he'd take it.

Jordan had never taken a kiss that far. He had always preferred to press his lips to her cheek or forehead, and she had never questioned it. And she had never been overcome with a sense of boldness with him. It hadn't been necessary.

Right?

She kept her eyes shut, refusing to look at the tempting devil.

Last night had put so much in perspective.

He was *good*.

So good.

At bewildering a woman's mind.

She had to be more careful if she wanted to stay in control of her plan of retribution. She couldn't allow it to become an afterthought, like having her mind trail all the paths of how they were different.

He was—could she admit it?—a bit handsomer than Jordan, a bit taller, and a bit sturdier. His smile was certainly brighter and made his eyes sparkle, even in the dim light.

No.

Let's stop the comparison there.

What she couldn't stop was the undeniable seed that had taken root in her mind, sprouting and blooming with every passing moment. The more time went by, the more Jordan's once vibrant, laughing face faded. Merely faded.

She patted her chest for the brooch he gifted her and came off short.

The brooch!

Oh. She glanced at the simple baluster of the hayloft. She had attached it to the coat she'd carelessly draped over one of the wooden beams. But how had she had forgotten about the trinket? She hadn't thought of it, nor touched it, for a long time.

What a confounding predicament!

What had once been clear and sharp had become blurred, distorted—until only a vague impression of the man she once thought was her whole world remained.

She peeked at Linsey.

His brows were scrunched as he stared out of the window.

Her slippered foot nudged closer, tapping his boot.

She stilled, waiting.

He turned slowly, eyes flicking down to her foot, then back up to meet her gaze. He smiled, and she smiled back. His smiles were so frustratingly infectious!

"You slept quite deeply last night."

He blinked twice. "You did not?"

"I kicked you; you didn't wake."

"You did not."

This man! "So, you were also awake?"

"Wild dreams couldn't pull me under."

Sturdy liar. He snored. Urgh, but even those snores sounded—she wanted to say seductive, but that wasn't quite the word. Snores weren't seductive! But the man snoring and the boyish face he had when he was relaxed tugged at her heart.

Was she going crazy?

Those snores felt like a breeze against her back. Except that she didn't even have a cat! Why did it sound like a lion's purr?

And then…and then! This morning he'd acted as though nothing had happened! As though they hadn't had a whirlwind flirtation filled with the bulge in his breeches he could hide as much as the Tower of London.

Don't think about it.

Ashley put her hands on her cheeks, hoping she didn't blush. Thomas had woken up so handsomely disheveled—glistening muscles on display—rubbed his hands through his hair, and pulled on a shirt as though a new day had dawned without the memories of the previous one.

As dawn's gentle light seeped into the hayloft, Ashley shivered when the cool morning air replaced the comforting warmth of the night—the comforting warmth of the handsome blond earl. The scent of crushed hay mingled with the remnants of their picnic—a bottle of claret, half-eaten bread, and cheese—scattered like the echoes of their shared escape.

Thomas moved with quiet purpose, gathering the remnants of their secret meal. His presence was a steadfast anchor in the morning light, yet Ashley's heart fluttered with nerves, a persistent reminder of the night etched into her memory. Her fingers trembled as she folded the blanket, a simple task now heavy with whispered confessions and stolen glances.

As they prepared to leave the hayloft's secluded embrace, Ashley's pulse quickened. The ladder stood before her; each rung felt like she was descending back to reality. Thomas reached out, his hands firm on her waist. His touch sent a shiver through her, both grounding and unsettling. As she placed her foot on the first rung, her balance faltered. Thomas's grip tightened, steadying her effortlessly before she fell off the ladder.

"Thank you," she croaked before he let her go, and she felt the ground melting away from under her feet as he held her. Being in his arms was…it was just so…as if he could make her fly.

"Since you'll be my wife soon, it is my duty to keep you safe. It doesn't matter if from a mouse in a hayloft or splinters on a wooden ladder."

Ashley wanted to smile, lean against him, and feel the warmth of his lips and that strange but addictive tingle he sent through her.

No!

"And as your wife you'll tell me those secrets, will you not?"

"My number?"

That, too. "And, you know, secrets like the wager that made you rush into marriage with me."

"With time comes all secrets. I'm also afraid that the more I get to know you, the more insufficient my haste is, Lady Ashley." He stepped closer, the hard middle of his body as solid as a large oak leaving Ashley in his shadow. The morning light coming through the open stable doors made him glow like a golden trophy and Ashley had a choice:

One, she could wrap her arms around him and let him press her against the wooden wall, splinters or not. It played out in her head just like in a forbidden book: fast, quick, and there'd be the haste he'd mentioned.

Two, she could follow the advice from the handbook.

Just when you think you captured his interest, let him fight for it. Be the challenge that preoccupies his thoughts.

Ashley inhaled sharply, the silence around them thick with unspoken words. Thomas moved closer, oh so deliciously close that she only had to tilt her head and let him kiss her. She yearned to surrender to his embrace, to let herself truly fall. But it wasn't she who was supposed to fall, rather it was he who should fall—on her sword.

Whoosh!

She slipped down and he leaned with his muscular arms against the ladder. She took a big step back and turned around, securing her bonnet and she only heard him growl.

Ashley sucked in her lower lip. She'd escaped the kiss—or had she missed out? Well, either way, it had worked. If she wasn't mistaken, he'd kicked a hay bale and groaned in frustration. That was exactly where she wanted him, wasn't it?

But Ashley began to wonder if the wisdom in her plan had accounted for the price she'd pay? In the abstract, it had all sounded easy. Could Charlene be right and she was making a mistake?

When her feet touched the wet ground outside the stables, her resolve wavered. She was ankle-deep in the muddy road that would take her to Thomas's estate. Truth be told, Ashley didn't know exactly what she'd gotten herself into. Charlene's warnings echoed in her mind, caution she had too easily dismissed.

Then he emerged from the stables, sleeves rolled down and in his coat. He looked like the earl again, leaving the less composed and much hotter Thomas behind.

I see you now...both sides, Linsey.

Her gaze met Linsey's, reading a question in his eyes—a plea for something. A kiss? She wasn't ready to respond. Not yet.

The world outside awaited, unchanged by the night's secrets, but Ashley felt transformed as their carriage rumbled along the soggy road. Whether a mistake or destiny, the path she had chosen lay before her, and it seemed a lot more slippery than she'd expected. As they left the hayloft behind, Ashley felt a pang of sentimentality—it may not have been the most elegant first night, but it was certainly the most memorable. Side by side but worlds apart, she felt the weight of her decision settle on her like a cloak, both soft and unyielding. Much like the path on the horizon, there was a fork in her path, and she didn't know which way was right. Vengeance and lust were like power and submission—they didn't overlap. Neither did the choice she had to make.

She would let him off for now, the handsome fiend. "How far until we reach your estate?" She certainly didn't want to think about those wild dreams.

He pulled the curtain aside and peeked out the window again. "Not long now."

Splendid.

There would be space on an estate. Grounds to recoup her wits! Also, her bottom was beginning to go numb, and her bones were starting to feel restless, too. She needed to move. Dance. Run. Point a sword at someone. She required a breath of...

Not him.

Ashley composed herself as well as she could, tried to tame her hair, and pinched her cheeks to get some color that she was sure had drained from her while staring at him.

Minutes later, the carriage rocked again, jolting Ashley from her thoughts. She shifted in her seat, trying to ease the ache in her muscles. She flexed her toes. Just a bit more. Because between the bumpy ride and the lingering discomfort of an altogether *hay-bed* night, she wasn't sure what felt worse—her body or her mind!

"I suppose it's too late to warn you, I live a rather simple life. Nothing like the whirlwind one would call London."

She'd already estimated as much. "Well, I suppose I should warn *you*. Now that you've let me into your life, that might change." *Change? Inevitable. For us both.*

Thomas lifted a curious brow. "Should I look forward to this remarkable statement?"

No. She couldn't help her gaze being drawn in by his. "You should...try to..." Why was she hesitating? "Protect what you are best at protecting." *Like your horses.* "So then, it has never occurred to you that I might bring mayhem into your simple life?"

"It occurs to me every day."

Good. It should. "I don't know how to respond to that since it's been all of three days since you made my acquaintance."

"You're counting?" His grin came. "Every single day?"

Well, hadn't she dug the proverbial shovel into the ground with that answer. She had a feeling that the shovel was only going to dig deeper. But the ground was muddy, and she felt like she was getting her hands dirty.

But it was *her* battleground.

She had come with a purpose, after all. Every step she took was a calculated move, each moment another skirmish in the greater war she waged against her own restless heart. It was the way his presence unsettled her, the way a simple glance from him could send that strange flutter trembling through her stomach. She drew in a breath, steadying herself, and her hand lifted instinctively to her chest where her brooch should have been.

But of course, it wasn't there.

Ashley's fingers hovered for a moment before she dropped her hand, her lips pressing together in a faint grimace. She had noticed its absence earlier but had resolved not to think on it. And yet, the loss lingered at the edge of her thoughts, sharp and nagging. That brooch had always been her anchor, pinned over her heart like a shield. To have it gone now felt careless and wrong, as though she had already surrendered something vital. Her frown deepened. When had she last seen it? Why hadn't she been more careful?

She pushed the thought away. There was nothing to be done about it now, and she had far larger battles ahead.

Later, Ashley.

Yes, she could think about it later.

At that moment, she had to focus. She couldn't let herself be swayed by the allure of the earl and whatever charm that clung to him. She had come here with a plan, and she would see it through.

Chapter Eleven

THOMAS PARTED THE curtain and peered out of the carriage window, his grin widening at the sight of his estate sprawling across Elysian Fields. Every time the carriage crested the hill and wound down the familiar lane toward Fort Balmore, that same rush of pride hit him. It was his—the land, the house, the stables—all the product of years of hard work and a dash of stubborn determination. If nothing else in his life made sense, this estate did. It had been his favorite place since boyhood, and now, he was bringing *her* into it.

Home.

He couldn't believe it—he was bringing a fiancée *home*. Somehow, he'd always imagined it differently. His parents and his grandfather would have been alive to welcome the love of his life when he first brought her to see their family pride. He'd introduce her to the staff, people who had been in his life for as long as he could remember.

But he was the only one left and there wasn't enough time before the Ascot. And it was too soon to know whether Ashley was the love of his life, wasn't it? He'd never been in this situation, so how could he know?

Thomas pondered how he had ended up in this position while he stared at the beauty who was eyeing his estate. Of course it wasn't something he could hide, but he felt vulnerable showing her.

Marrying to save his horses.

A wager had started it, but as the days passed, it had become more than that. Those horses were more than just prized possessions—they were his father's legacy. The thought of losing them—it wasn't just the value or prestige at stake. They were the last real connection he had to his father and grandfather, to the men who'd instilled in him every bit of honor and pride he held. They were also his pride, the product of years of effort, a symbol of who he was beyond the estate and titles. The title and the horses belonged together, and Thomas wanted nothing more than to be worthy of both.

Thomas glanced at Lady Ashley, who sat quietly across from him, her gaze fixed out the window. He wondered if she realized just how she was saving him. A wave of gratitude washed over him. He was—Thomas gripped the edge of the upholstered cabin seat—happy. Happy that Ashley was with him. That she was coming home with him.

His brow furrowed as the realization settled in. She'd been uncharacteristically silent since their night in the barn. Uncannily so. In fact, it was unlike her. He wished he could peer into her mind. After yesterday, the truth was as clear as the dawn light. Oh, how he wanted her. Not just for fleeting moments, not just for the convenience of marriage, but wholly—heart and soul. In every way possible.

He wanted Lady Ashley to be his in every sense of the word.

And if that meant getting crafty? Well, he wasn't above using every charming, sneaky, or underhanded trick in the book to win her heart. And it was a beautiful day—perfect for plotting ways to steal her heart, if he did say so himself. But he'd never truly tried to woo a lady, especially not one who'd agreed to marry him for some other reason. What was her secret?

Ah, it's hot again.

He opened the window of the cabin as they reached the path that followed the creek. He loved its sound, which, despite the constant noise, brought him a quiet peace.

"It's quite impressive." Her voice filled the carriage. "Your home. I can see why you wouldn't want to part with any of it—even if it's just a few horses."

Well, they aren't just any horses. He sent her a small smile. "I'm glad you like it since this is your home now, too." He pointed out the window. "Over there, by the tangled willows, is where my grandfather put me on a horse for the first time." He couldn't hide the nostalgia in his voice.

"Willows?" Lady Ashley frowned, squinting out the window. "All I see are naked trees with frost on them."

Thomas shot her a look. "Such a city girl, aren't you?"

She shrugged. "All trees without leaves look the same to me."

He let out a short laugh. "A tree doesn't need leaves to be recognizable."

Lady Ashley tilted her head with a playful smirk. "Is this also where you break in your wild beasts? There are rumors about you and the wild horses in London, you know. I hope you don't have any plans to treat me like livestock."

Thomas chuckled. *Ah. Yes. His soon-to-be wife might be harder to tame than the wild Normandy stallion he'd acquired last year.* But he didn't want her tamed. He liked her wild—bold.

"I would never dare," Thomas drawled with a smile. "Horses of this caliber, Lady Ashley, are not livestock. I do, however, own livestock—chickens, cows, a few sheep. They're useful animals, but none of them come close to the beauty of a horse. Would you like to see them, Lady Ashley?"

"The horses or your chickens?"

He shot her a pointed look and she laughed. "I would very much like to meet the very animals responsible for this engagement of ours."

"Excellent." He rapped on the carriage roof and called out, "To the stables first."

"You truly are a country boy!"

Thomas grinned. "Aren't we the pair?" Odd that his heart lurched when he'd said it. He was one half of a pair now and he felt responsible for her. Plus, he was eager to show her, and to discover himself, what it felt like to be with him. The Earl of Linsey with his Countess…

"Some might consider it bad."

"Why?" Thomas challenged. "Opposites attract in all sorts of ways."

"Indeed."

When the carriage pulled to a stop, Thomas wasted no time to leap out of the carriage, turning to offer Lady Ashley a hand. She placed her fingers in his palm, and a jolt raced down his spine. His body didn't even spare him such a simple touch.

"Come," he said gruffly, clasping her hand and pulling her toward the stables.

"Does your staff always wave to you?" Lady Ashley asked curiously. Thomas tilted his head, a faint smile playing on his lips. What would Lady Ashley say if she were to see him working alongside his men in dirty breeches come spring? The thought amused him more than it should, and he suddenly couldn't wait for that moment.

"Oh!"

Thomas followed Lady Ashley's gaze.

A beautiful brown mare trotted into view, her chestnut coat shimmering like polished mahogany in the sunlight. Her muscles rippled with every graceful stride. She was the finest horse he owned, a testament to his care and patience. And she'd win for him at Ascot—there was no doubt.

He grinned as he reached for the mare, who tossed her mane with a playful flick. Her ears twitched, and she leaned into him, nuzzling his hand in a gesture of familiar affection.

Lady Ashley jerked her head back and crinkled her nose. "Is the horse kissing you?"

"She's saying hello."

"But the horse touched your mouth." Ashley's face was crinkled like a dried prune, and he laughed.

"This is Lady Stradivarius," he introduced the mare, beaming with pride.

"As in the violin?"

"Yes, she's an Italian thoroughbred, and the color of a Stradivarius. I got her as a foal last year. Isn't she magnificent?"

"Well, I suppose…"

The horse flicked her ears and blew gently, inclining her head toward Ashley. She hesitated, but only briefly, before she pulled off her gloves and tentatively stroked the mare's forelock, her touch delicate but firm.

Thomas watched, transfixed.

He'd lamented Paisley all through his time in London, but now he couldn't help but feel grateful. He would not only win this wager, but he would keep so much more than just six horses.

⇶⇶

ASHLEY HAD A secret.

She didn't care for horses. Well, she cared in the sense that she could admire their beauty and all, but she kept her distance because they were big. And a bit scary. Perhaps because they were so big. They also kicked. And they bit. But she had come this far, and she wouldn't back down now.

That didn't mean she didn't jerk at the slightest movement of the horse.

One.

Two.

Three.

She slowly retracted her hand.

It hadn't bitten her. Certainly not like that nasty one from the fair when she was six.

She had to admit, this one was beautiful. Her mane, dark as the night sky, flowed freely, dancing with the wind as it cascaded down her arched neck. The mare's equally dark forelock tumbled forward, framing her expressive eyes—pools of dark chocolate filled with intelligence and a hint of mischief, just like Linsey. The most striking feature, however, was the unique white patch gracing her forehead.

"Her star is gorgeous," Ashley murmured.

"You know horses?"

"A little." She smiled at him. "Does that surprise you?"

He shrugged. "Not by much. What about riding? You can ride?"

"As much as any lady ought to." Did she mention she had a secret? And within that secret was another. She couldn't really ride like a lady ought to. Perhaps like a four-year-old child. She didn't even own a riding habit. Winning his heart, however, might mean mucking about the stables and climbing atop a horse.

She could do that.

"Then we should go riding."

What? Ashley inwardly grimaced. She could think of nothing worse, but her head was bobbing up and down before she knew it. "Shall we do it tomorrow?" The longer she could hold this off, the better. "I'm a bit weary from the trip. I'd also like to go into town sometime."

He smiled. "I shall escort you."

That wouldn't do. She had to go purchase a riding habit. Her gaze fell on a riding crop beyond him hanging on the wall of the stables. Was that...?

He followed her gaze, and then glanced back at her again. "Don't laugh."

"It's colorful."

He strode over to the pink and yellow riding crop, tracing a finger over the leather. "I badgered my riding instructor to let me make my own when I was a child. This was the result."

"Pink?"

"It was once red. It's faded."

Ashley laughed. "Well, at least it wasn't meant to be pink, then. I suspect the yellow was meant to be orange?" It would coincide with the colors of the Linsey family crest.

He arched a brow. "Is there something wrong with pink?"

She tilted her head, considering him. "It just doesn't suit the overall picture of you in my head."

He folded his arms, leaning casually against the stable door. "And what picture is that?"

"A country gentleman who loves horses."

He chuckled "Descriptive."

Ashley smiled, brushing a loose strand of hair behind her ear. "I am detail-oriented that way."

"Oh? Then what color would you associate with a country man that loves horses and country?"

"Blue," she said without hesitation, striding over to take a closer look at the peculiar riding crop. "Like the sky. And maybe a bit of green. Perhaps brown boots and a belt?"

"These are the colors I attribute to the country, quite right."

Ashley grinned, her gaze flicking back to him. "Your riding crop has become the summer sun with a pink sunset."

"How generous. I shall take that as a compliment."

Generous? In fact, Ashley wasn't generous at all. She always called things exactly the way she saw them. Which was what Jordan had loved about her even when no one else, perhaps with the exception of her father, had.

Especially not her mother.

Her mother loathed her directness. She couldn't stand when Ashley spoke her mind. She would always call for the smelling salts. As though that alone would make Ashley keep her mouth closed and her opinions to herself.

Even the way she poured tea vexed her mother. In fact, little did not. "Why don't you hold the spout? Be careful that the lid of the pot doesn't slide into the cup!" Ashley rolled her eyes.

She often wondered if her mother even loved her.

Ashley's gaze flicked back to the horse and over the stables. It was a lot different than the stables they had slept in. They were bigger, but clean. She could tell the owner of these stables took great pride in them.

These stables were loved.

And this man who loved the stables, the horses, and even behaved freely with the staff was supposed to fall in love with her. He would love her, think that she'd be the mistress of all he held dear, and then... Ashley looked at him and blinked.

He was magnificent.

That's a complication.

The truth was, she hadn't been entirely silent on that journey because of the fatigue she'd claimed when they set forth that day. No, it was because every time she closed her eyes, she could still feel the solid warmth of his back pressed against hers. The sensation left her flustered, making her crave a little distance to regain her composure. She had felt a bit lighter after penning a note to her friends, inviting them to join her at Linsey's estate. Once they arrived, they could serve as a barrier and a reminder that she mustn't fall into her own trap.

"What are you thinking?" he asked, pulling her from her thoughts.

She blinked, realizing she had been staring. "I...about how clean you are."

"What?"

Yes, what? Why had she just said that?

Her face flushed. "I mean, how clean your stables are. In correlation to you."

His brows drew together in confusion.

Drat. She was making it worse. "I just mean your stables are clean, and so are you."

His laughter rumbled through the stable. "Was that what caught your attention about me? That I was *clean*?"

Your appearance, yes. Your dealings, not so much.

"Well, all women like cleanliness."

"I love how we discuss cleanliness like strangers talking about the weather," Linsey said, chuckling.

"Well, since we aren't strangers, we might go a bit deeper than the topic of the weather," Ashley replied, wishing she could just find a hole to crawl into.

"True enough. My father always said that a clean environment reflects the character of its caretaker."

"He sounds like a wise man."

The earl nodded absentmindedly. "He was." His gaze swept the stables. "Many of these horses are his legacy."

Ah, so that was why.

"If they are his legacy, why wager on them in the first place?"

Linsey rubbed his temples. "I never thought I could lose."

"How delightfully arrogant."

He nodded. "You are right, of course. I haven't always made the best choices."

With that, Ashley could agree. She wanted to ask what other reckless wagers he entered and what their dire consequences might have been, but she simply cleared her throat, dispelling the awkward tightening in her chest.

It wasn't yet time.

It was almost amusing how blind he was to the chaos he'd created in her life. But now that arrogance would serve her purpose. She could use it to her advantage, to ensnare him in a web of her own making, a tangled trap that would lead to his downfall.

He might have won the wager he made with Jordan, but he would lose the gamble he'd taken on her.

Chapter Twelve

THOMAS WALKED TO the back of the estate. Lady Ashley had been shown to her chambers, and he had ordered a bath for her as well. She might need time to rest and get used to the new surroundings. He wasn't sure what a woman needed but he thought that he'd give her some space. The largest room had been made up for her in a dash. It used to be his mother's private chamber with the most elegant, polished furniture. It was the most feminine place in all of Fort Balmore.

While Thomas bathed and changed out of his stuffy London clothes, he couldn't stop imagining what Ashley might do in the bath, how she might be toweling dry her delicate naked body…the butler stopped his daydreams with a message.

"Lord Cambridge has arrived. He's been where he always is."

Thomas should have known his friend would be too curious not to visit. Minutes later, he stepped into the brewery, his eyes adjusting to the dim light filtering through high windows. The air was thick with the scent of malt and hops, a robust aroma that enveloped him, grounding him in familiarity. Large barrels lined the walls, their dark wood stained from years of use, each marked with chalk for identification. The cool, slightly damp stone floor beneath his feet bore evidence of the day's earlier cleaning.

Good. Everyone had continued their work in his absence.

In the center of the room stood a massive brewing vat, its copper surface gleaming under the soft light—a testament to the care taken in its maintenance. Nearby, a stack of fresh barley awaited its turn to be transformed, the grains golden and promising.

Sebastian was at the far end of the room, perched on a wooden stool beside a small, rustic table. He had an array of glasses in front of him, each filled with beer of varying shades—from pale gold to deep amber. His attention was focused, his expression one of concentration as he took a sip from one glass, then scribbled notes onto a piece of parchment beside him. Sebastian wasn't just tasting; he was savoring, searching for the perfect balance of flavors that would satisfy the discerning palate. Exactly as Grandfather had taught them both since they'd been wee lads.

The bubbling from a smaller kettle in the corner drew his attention. Steam rose from it, carrying the fresh scent of hops, which mixed with the underlying sweetness of malt dominating the room.

Thomas cleared his throat.

His friend glanced up. "There you are. I had wondered when you were going to show your face. Thought you might have eloped."

Eloped? The thought hadn't even crossed his mind. It wasn't the worst one. "Anything worth tasting?" Thomas asked, settling across from Sebastian and placing both hands on the rough wooden table.

"Besides your bride?"

Thomas sucked in his lips and gave Sebastian a stern look.

"Oh, so this is rather serious then, you coming to the rescue of her reputation."

"Seb," Thomas warned him.

His friend was teasing him, testing. And until Thomas knew his heart, he wasn't sure how to answer. But one thing was for certain: His bride was not a joking matter. She was real, natural, and a force in his life he'd never want to let go.

"I'm trying to make something lighter for the spring," Sabastian said thoughtfully, pushing a yellow-orange glass toward Thomas.

Beer. Good idea.

He took a sip, then licked his upper lip. "The foam is too dense. Tastes like honey."

Sebastian looked up, his eyes lighting up as he gestured for Thomas to try another. "Try this then," he said, pushing a different glass forward. "It's a new recipe I've been working on. I think it might just be the best yet."

Thomas tried it, noting the hint of lemon and something else sweeter and tart in an aromatic way—grape, perhaps? He licked his lips, the aroma of the deeper malt note still dancing in the air. "This is amazing. Do you have enough to serve it at my wedding?"

Sebastian nearly dropped the glass he was holding. "I must have misheard; did you say beheading?"

Leaning back on the stool until its wobbly leg screeched, Thomas folded his hands on the table. "You heard right. Wedding."

Sebastian was silent for a moment. "So, she said yes."

Thomas grinned. "She did."

"You look awfully happy for a man's wedding because of a deuced wager he entered with a diabolical duke."

"I have hope."

"I have suspicions," Sebastian shot back. "Why would she agree to wed a man she just met?"

"Why not? It's the way of our society. Chaswick agreed as well."

"Now, I'm even more suspicious," his friend muttered. "Wait, Chaswick?"

Thomas laughed. "Cheer up, old friend. This is a time for celebration, not depression. You shall meet her later."

"The Earl of Chaswick's daughter is here?" Sebastian rose, his stool falling to the floor. "Are you mad?"

Thomas got up as well, his brows drawing together. "Are you not happy for me? It's in time for the wager. She's an earl's daughter.

Beautiful. Bold. I could do much worse."

"Do much worse? How?"

"I beg your pardon?"

"You don't know?" Sebastian's voice came as though he'd been cornered into speaking words he'd wished could remain undiscovered.

Thomas narrowed his eyes on his friend. "Know what?"

Sebastian shook his head. "You don't spend enough time in town." Sebastian combed his hand through his hair. "Chaswick."

"What about him?"

"No, not him! His heir!"

"There's none. She's his only…" He paused at his friend's expression. "*Oh*."

"Yes, there's an *oh*." Sebastian walked around the table. The shingle floor had dried, and the air seemed to have drained from the room as Thomas began to understand. "It's rumored that the *oh* is about to come out of the shadows. I happened to be at White's and the gentlemen couldn't stop gossiping about it. Her family will be mired in scandal soon." Sebastian waved grandly in the air.

Was that why she wished to marry speedily?

Was that why Chaswick allowed him to take her to the country without lifting a brow?

Thomas rubbed his temples. "Who's the *oh*?"

"So, I watched from a distance when the Lord Chancellor suggested to Paisley that Chaswick's daughter was growing rounder by the day. Rumors of pregnancy are floating about. A man by the name of Clyde Sheffield stormed toward him, grabbed him, and—"

"Clyde Sheffield? From geometry class at Eton?" The one he'd seen again a few times at Oxford. It couldn't be that one, he was so kind. Blond, blue eyed…like Ashley, but different. Thomas tried to place the name, but he'd never heard of it other than his old classmate.

"Lady Katharine Sheffield's son. Illegitimately so." Sebastian shook his head. "But at least he stood up to defend his sister's honor. But more rumors sprouted because of that."

"I don't think Lady Ashley has a brother."

"Or does she not know he exists? Or is she leading you on perhaps?"

Thomas swallowed hard. "She's not that devious."

"Perhaps not. But Paisley knows." Sebastian pursed his lips. "You should sit."

"I'd rather stand."

"Sit down, Thomas. You won't like what I'm going to tell you now."

"It doesn't matter. We are already betrothed. She is willing; so am I."

"Willingness is one thing, Thomas," Sebastian said, shaking his head. "But you must think of the long term. What will you do if you discover she's not who you thought?"

Thomas frowned, leaning forward, a fire igniting within him. "Then I will face it as it comes. I won't hide behind caution and lose my chance at happiness. Plus, she's still an earl's daughter, isn't she? Why would that be bad for me?" Scandal only mattered until they married, in London, but what Thomas pictured for a happy life was something else entirely.

Sebastian sighed, his shoulders sagging. "You're playing with fire, my friend."

"Perhaps," Thomas said, straightening his back. "But I've always found warmth far more comforting than cold caution."

Sebastian stared at him, clearly unconvinced. "Then I can only hope you don't get burned by your bewitching new fiancée or the secret brother of hers."

So did he.

A LADY IN want of gossip need look no further than the kitchen, Ashley thought when she took it upon herself to tour the castle. The kitchen maids were the undervalued, forgotten staff of society, remembered only when there was a mishap with the food—and even that was rare. Recipes were easily followed once one mastered the skill, and yet, for all their simplicity in the culinary arts, the kitchen staff were the most outspoken of all the servants.

That was what Ashley had learned over the years.

She didn't gossip all that much with hers, not like Charlene. She loved instead to converse with the staff. She often dressed up as them and did chores around the house to see if she could fool her family.

So, Ashley breezed into the kitchen with a bright smile. "My apologies for the intrusion. I'm Lady Ashley, a guest of the earl." Should she say betrothed? No. That might seem a bit too arrogant! "I'm wondering about his normal appetite." After all, the book of her mother had a note that a man's heart could be thawed with food. Not that she dared cook. She didn't want anyone to die. But knowledge was power, as they said.

The staff cast her a sidelong glance before flicking their gazes to the cook, who was currently kneading dough. Ashley kept a smile perched firmly on her lips, determined to charm her way into their gossip.

"I'm Mrs. White," the woman said, and after a pause, added, "He doesn't like green beans."

Ashley's nose wrinkled in mock distaste. "Who does? They should just stop growing them altogether. England would be a much happier place without them."

"England would also be riddled with more illness," Mrs. White replied, her hands busy shaping dough into surprisingly even lumps as she spoke.

Ashley arched a brow in amusement. "Are you telling me green beans will save the world? The people of England would disagree."

Mrs. White shrugged. "That doesn't make them less good for your body. Keeps you regular."

Ashley jerked her head back. "Agreed." And now that the ice was broken with the cook... "Very well, what about what the earl's favorite food?" Ashley's asked, suddenly curious.

Mrs. White gave a thoughtful pause. "None which come to mind."

"Mrs. White!" Surely the woman was teasing her! "Did I just catch you in a lie?"

The woman laughed. "My allegiance lies with the earl." The woman gave her a once over. "And I question your presence in my kitchen."

"What's to question? I'm here for gossip. I shall not deny it. I know all the good stuff is brewed in the kitchen."

The staff snickered, and Cook shook her head, but her lips still quirked upward before she sent the staff a scolding look, and they swiveled to go about their tasks, mouths clamped shut.

Ashley laughed.

She leaned against the door with a smile. "What about love interests?" Her voice dropped to a conspiratorial whisper. "Are there any women woefully in love with the earl his future wife might need to be wary of?"

"Lady Catrina."

Ashley's back shot straight. Linsey really did have a love interest. Mmm. She was probably a pretty country girl who danced in fields of flowers and rode horses in green pastures.

What on earth are you thinking, Ashley?

She cleared her throat. "Who is Lady Catrina? Does she live on a neighboring estate?" Distance matters.

Just look at her and Jordan.

Forget about him.

Just for a moment. Just for this stretch of time where she was engaged to Linsey. Afterward she would think about that rascal again.

"No, no, she lives on the estate," Mrs. White announced.

The estate? As in this house? She would have to ask him later. "What about him? Is he fond of Lady Catrina?"

"Exceedingly fond," the cook said, relentless in her kneading of the dough. "They often go for morning rides and evening strolls."

Both morning and evening? That was rather troubling.

"What's the matter?" Mrs. White asked, "Didn't you wish for the latest gossip, my lady?"

The staff snickered again, and Ashley scowled. "If he is so fond of her, why does he not ask for her hand in marriage?" Ashley muttered.

"How could the earl do that? Lady Catrina has hooves, not hands."

Ashley's face went deadpan even as the hairs on the back her neck shot straight. Ashley made a mental note never to mess with Mrs. White. "Catrina is a horse." *Of course, Catrina is a horse.* Why did he keep including titles to his horses? It was a recipe for misunderstanding! He could at least have named it after a cello.

The staff burst out laughing now.

Ashley sighed, but in the end, she couldn't help chuckling along.

I can live here.

The thought came so suddenly, so unexpected, that Ashley's laughter caught in her throat. She could really? Was it too presumptuous to think such a thing just because she enjoyed a silly conversation with the kitchen staff?

It wasn't just the kitchen, though. It was the estate, the house, even the stables—it all felt so warm, so...*warm.*

And then, of course, there was the man himself: Linsey.

He wasn't just warm; he was blazing hot compared to everything else. Which tempted Ashley to want to get to the bottom of who he was at the core all the more. But temptation was a dangerous game, one she wasn't sure she could afford to play. It threatened to pull her in, like a moth to a flame, whispering that the heat would be worth the burn.

It wasn't.

Couldn't be.

"Well, you certainly had me there, Mrs. White," she said with a shake of her head, a rueful smile tugging at her lips.

Mrs. White smiled. "Our employer is a good man, my lady, but no man is without his faults. It's up to you to discover them, along with all the good things, too. He is your best resource."

Truer words have never been spoken.

Only, Ashley didn't know how much time she had left with the earl. Their whole relationship started on a quest for revenge. No good ever came from such a start. Then there was the man himself, who had his own reasons for procuring a wife—a wager over his horses. And she to make sure that didn't happen.

This certainly was no love match. But it was no less intriguing.

In fact, she didn't need a love match, if she were completely honest with herself. She didn't even know if her affections for Jordan had run that deep. But she was deprived of the chance to discover that. Besides that, all she wanted was to be seen. Understood. She wanted someone to discover all her faults too and accept them, too. Someone who wasn't like her mother and would offer her a marriage that didn't leave her as lonely as her father.

It certainly wasn't easy to find such a match.

Perhaps the earl had the right of it. Focus on horses. They were easy. They didn't care about a man's faults. They accepted. They loved. Perhaps, if they were particularly bright, they would *see* as well.

There you go again, Ashley.

Chasing absurd thoughts.

So long as she only chased them in her head.

Chapter Thirteen

THOMAS TOOK A swig of beer. The smell of hops and malt hung thick in the air, and he felt a sense of timelessness. This place, like his stables, was a part of his legacy. And here, amidst the barrels and brews, was the shared passion that bound him and his friend, Sebastian, together. They had spent a lifetime chasing the perfect ale, as well as a lifetime of friendship. If Thomas had a brother, it would have been Sebastian.

He hoped, with all his heart, that Ashley would like his estate because he was no longer willing to let her out of his sight. There was no question anymore—there never really had been—but now, it was settled in his mind: his marriage to Ashley had to happen. And the sooner, the better for his comfort. The rest would fall into place.

All his life, he had tried to do the right thing. The dutiful thing. The peaceful thing. But this wager with Paisley...something about it unsettled him. The looming deadline to marry or lose his horses weighed on him every moment. It had turned into something deeply uncomfortable and disturbed his peace. And that wasn't even counting the unexpected, but thrilling, variable that was Ashley.

That she had an illegitimate brother?

Thomas still couldn't fathom how that might influence his—their—future life. But he had always been a man who accepted people as they were, flaws and all. And it wasn't Ashley's fault that an illegitimate child had been sired.

She was innocent in all of this.

Even without the wager hanging over his head, he could no more toss her to the wolves than he could abandon a newborn foal. He'd already questioned her motives at the start, judged her too quickly. He wouldn't make that mistake again.

His desire for Ashley was no longer just about fulfilling a wager. Well, it was, but it also wasn't. It was about winning her heart, about proving to himself that he could be the man she deserved. But his goal remained: to marry her before his birthday and secure his future. That didn't change. It couldn't. The tension between his duty—this promise to his father and the wager he made years ago—and his desire to truly earn her love was like a lead anchor weighing him down to one immovable spot.

He wanted it all to be over.

And another thing. She knew the reason he had to wed hastily, but she didn't seem to care all that much. He couldn't decipher what she might be thinking. What happened *after* they wed? Did she plan to stay with him? According to his recollection, Chaswick's wife was never home, choosing to travel all over the country.

He took another, heavier swallow, allowing the beer to burn down his throat.

"I'm sorry you had to learn of it this way," Sebastian said, running both hands through his hair. "But Paisley might show up at your door."

"No, no." Thomas replied. "I'd rather have you tell me than run into Paisley and have him surprise me. But let me make sure that I understand this correctly." He tapped his glass with a finger. "Paisley already bet on my horses as the stakes with this Sheffield?"

"Yes."

"So, he thinks I won't marry Ashley."

"Paisley can't let you marry Ashley because then he cannot repay his debt to Sheffield."

Thomas narrowed his eyes. "That's rather convenient." And bloody dishonorable. "But he was the one that took me to Almack's.

Sebastian shook his head. "An interesting move. I doubt he wanted you to suspect anything, or he just wanted to see you cringe. With that man, you never know."

"Then I must do everything in my power to ensure this wedding goes forward as soon as possible," Thomas said as the thought formed in his mind. Why did Sheffield have to be Ashley's brother?

This complicated matters all the more, but it also wouldn't touch them all that much. Unless this marriage did not happen…

"It takes two, though. What if she finds out about the wager?"

"I told her."

"And you told her that if the wedding doesn't happen before your birthday, you'll be left with nothing? That you're marrying her *because* of a wager?"

"Even if I don't have a penny to my name, I still have my title."

"That's rather vain of you," Sebastian retorted.

"It's a fact." Thomas grinned at his friend, leaning back into his chair and crossing his ankles over each other. "And it doesn't matter if I'm penniless. We are both the sort of people that will rise through any occasion."

Sebastian arched his brow. "Until the moment you tell her she can't go out and shop."

"Oh, stop it. None of this will come to pass anyway. My more pressing concern is why Paisley would wager with a deed not yet in his name."

"I agree," Sebastian said. "It's unlike him to act so rashly."

"Yes, something must have happened."

Sebastian's expression darkened. "I've never liked the duke. You're too soft when it comes to people who approach you. Just like Lady Ashley. She approached you first, didn't she?"

Thomas arched a brow. "What makes you say that?"

"This entire affair is just too smooth. What if she and Paisley are working together?"

Thomas furrowed his brows. He'd had the same thought at the start, but ultimately dismissed it. However, now that her brother was involved, could he truly, recklessly dismiss the possibility? *Yes.* "I don't believe that is true."

"Can you be sure?" Sebastian challenged. "Would you stake your entire stables on the fact that she's not working with Paisley to keep you from winning the wager?"

Would he? Could he? Thomas hesitated, but not for long.

"Absolutely. I already did," he said, his voice firm. Ashley wasn't part of some conspiracy; he was certain of that. He had seen the honesty in her eyes, the genuine way she carried herself. She wasn't someone who would betray him or work with a scoundrel like Paisley. She couldn't be. And more than that, Thomas realized with a startling clarity that he didn't want to believe otherwise. He needed her to be exactly who he thought she was, because the alternative was too painful to even consider.

She held the power to break his heart.

ASHLEY HAD TO get back to her original plan: Breaking the earl's heart. And she had to dress for the task.

"I need to get into town."

Without Linsey finding out.

Her mind whirred with ideas on how to slip away without alerting him. If only she had the skill to handle a horse herself—then she could simply borrow one. After all, countrymen rose early, did they not? She'd have to slip away when he went on a drive or after he went.

Probably after.

Hopefully, she could be back before he noticed her absence.

It's just a riding habit, Ashley.

Yes, but he might question why she didn't bring one to the country, and she didn't want that.

Her ears perked up at the sound of approaching voices and laughter. Linsey's familiar tone mixed with another she didn't recognize.

Two men. The earl, and a gentleman.

They were walking in her direction, yet to notice her. As their conversation became clearer, Ashley's eyes narrowed.

"So, when am I going to meet this vain creature who asked to marry you and who is about to be penniless?" the unknown man quipped.

Ashley stepped into the hallway, her chin lifting as she faced the two men. "How about now?"

Linsey and his friend came to an abrupt halt, both men staring at her with wide eyes like startled deer. She might have laughed at their expressions if the word "vain" hadn't lodged in her throat.

"Lady Ashley," Linsey began, looking as though he'd rather be anywhere else at that moment. She inwardly scoffed. His friend, however, bowed gracefully, seemingly unfazed.

"Sebastian Moore, Marquess of Cambridge, at your service, my lady," the man introduced himself with a slight bow. "Thomas has spoken much about you."

Ashley's lips twitched. "So I heard."

Sebastian glanced at Linsey before offering an unapologetic grin. "You may place the blame on me, my lady. It was I who commented that like attracts like."

Her gaze slid between the two men, eyes narrowed. "Is that so?"

Linsey nodded, looking somewhat embarrassed.

Ashley raised a brow. "Like attracts like…" she said, thankful her voice remained steady. "You seem to have formed some mistaken views about me, Lord Cambridge, as well as your friend. And allow me to point something out—I did not ask to marry Linsey. I asked him to marry me. A minor difference, perhaps, but a difference, nonetheless. I also don't consider myself vain, though I suppose I'm not without vanity. We women are complicated in that way. And as for being penniless—well, I'm afraid you've been grossly misinformed."

Lord Cambridge's eyes narrowed slightly, suspicion flickering in his gaze, but Ashley met him head-on. She would not be intimidated by the likes of any man, but she did so enjoy their effort once in a while.

This friend, however—she could feel doubt dripping off him.

No matter.

He couldn't possibly know about her initial plans. He could only suspect her sudden proposal, which Linsey had found suspicious as well but said yes anyway.

They all had their reasons.

Linsey suddenly cleared his throat. "Shall we go riding later today?" His question broke the rising tension that filled the space between her and his friend.

Ashley stiffened inwardly.

No! Not today.

She needed to get into town, commission riding habits, and stop by the bookshop. How else could she learn about horses and appear more refined than her current clumsy state? And with Lord Cambridge's hawk-like eyes on her, there would be no hiding her lack of skill. He'd be watching her every move, no doubt scrutinizing her.

What a bother!

"I'm afraid I'm too tired for a ride today," she said smoothly, feigning weariness. "Perhaps tomorrow afternoon?"

"What about tomorrow morning?" Lord Cambridge countered with a challenging smile.

Ashley forced a gracious smile. "Forgive me, but I cannot say with confidence that I shall be awake at the early hours to which you country folk are accustomed."

Lord Cambridge's eyes gleamed with amusement, but his jaw remained tight. "A true city girl," he mumbled into a hand feigning a cough, but Ashley heard him.

"I'm afraid so," Ashley replied, her smile unwavering.

"So why, if I may ask," he continued, his tone suddenly sharp, "are you marrying a countryman?"

"Seb." Linsey's voice carried a warning, but Ashley had already squared her shoulders, hands on her hips. She didn't need him to fight her battles.

"I can marry whomever I please, Lord Cambridge," she said sweetly.

"Will you be happy in the country?" he pressed.

What sort of question was this? "I can be happy wherever I put my heart."

"And what of your duties?" he asked, his eyes narrowing.

What a disappointing quip! "What duties would those be?"

"Washing the horses," he deadpanned, his expression perfectly serious.

Ashley blinked, momentarily thrown off by the absurdity of the remark. Was this a trick question? "Aren't there stable hands for that?"

The marquess shrugged nonchalantly. "Thomas always mentioned how his ideal wife would rub down his horses."

Ashley rolled her eyes. "And I always imagined my ideal husband would rub my feet and feed me grapes." She turned to Linsey, arching an expectant brow.

Linsey cleared his throat, looking both amused and flustered. "I said those things when I was a boy. No need to pay attention to Sebastian."

"Not a foot man, I see," she teased, but before Linsey could reply, Lord Cambridge interjected again.

"He also mentioned he wanted to marry a black-haired beauty,"

Lord Cambridge was clearly intent on stirring trouble.

Ashley's fingers dug into her waist. "Is that so?"

"Sebastian." Thomas's tone had turned into a deep growl that resonated in her stomach in a way she couldn't afford to pay attention to, if she were to best his friend.

"It's quite all right," she said, her tone sweet and smile in place. In her mind, however, she kicked Lord Cambridge where she knew it would hurt. "Your friend is simply looking out for you. Our engagement was sudden, yes, but I'm sure he is unaware of how quickly such things often transpire within the Ton, being your *friend* and all."

Linsey groaned softly.

Lord Cambridge tilted his head, studying her with a hint of admiration. "You're quite the feisty one, Lady Ashley."

"Thank you," she said coolly. "And you are quite the outdated one, Lord Cambridge."

Linsey winced, but to her surprise, Lord Cambridge merely chuckled. "Touché."

The earl offered a sheepish smile. "Forgive him, Lady Ashley. As you said, he's just looking out for me. We also had a bit of beer, though that is not an excuse."

Ashley's eyes lit up. Lord Cambridge instantly flew from her mind. Why hold a grudge against a man who was looking out for his friend? "Beer, you say? Did you go into town for it?"

Lindsey shook his head. "I have a brewery on the estate."

Ashley's interest piqued instantly. "How marvelous! You must take me on a tour sometime."

Linsey's face visibly relaxed at that, his lips quirking up in a slight smile. "Of course. You're welcome to sample the beer as well."

"That sounds delightful," Ashley replied. "But for now, gentlemen, I must excuse myself. The journey has been long, and this city girl is in need of rest."

With a small curtsy, she left them behind, heart pounding as she retreated to her room. What was this strange tightness in her chest?

She pressed a hand to her ribs, but the feeling lingered. Was it the conversation with Lord Cambridge, his probing questions, or something far more unsettling? The walls seemed to close in as doubt crept over her. She had thought this engagement would be a simple arrangement—a matter of revenge.

But now, for the first time, she wasn't sure what game she was truly playing, or if she had already lost her best card—her heart.

Chapter Fourteen

THE NEXT DAY, Ashley awoke with the single-minded determination to get that trump card, her heart, back in the game. And getting to the bookshop had been easier than Ashley anticipated. Once she'd confirmed that Linsey was out on his morning ride—which would last roughly two hours—she demanded a carriage be readied. Many things could be accomplished without question, she realized, if done with confidence. Therefore, after she had demanded with confidence, the stable hands had scurried to prepare her drive into town.

Truthfully, she hadn't felt all that confident. Her fingers had trembled even as she held her head high.

She had half expected Linsey to leap from a stall and prevent her escape—ahem—excursion, of course. She wasn't a prisoner, even if she felt shackled already.

Linsey would no doubt question her later. She had alluded to keeping city hours, but she also required a riding habit. It wouldn't be long before he discovered she didn't have one. That, too, would require some creative explanations, wouldn't it?

She plucked a book from the shelf and flipped it open to a random page. So far, none of the books had offered any helpful riding tips. They were going riding, and though she knew the basics—how could she not, having learned from her father at a young age—she hadn't ridden in years. She lacked confidence now, which, ironically, was the very thing she was there trying to find in a small stuffy shop, with a rather small selection, compared what she was used to from Regent Street.

"Find anything you like?"

Ashley froze, lifting her gaze to meet the sharp, hawkish eyes of a familiar face—the Duke of Paisley. He stood so close, she immediately caught his scent, and an uncomfortable itch spread across her skin. He smelled exactly like the chickenpox tincture she remembered from years ago. She suppressed a shudder.

"Your Grace," she greeted, forcing a smile. "What brings you to the bookshop?"

"I saw you enter and became curious," he replied smoothly. "Linsey did not accompany you?"

That's because he doesn't know. She wondered if the duke had guessed as much. He seemed the sort of man who saw far more than he let on and merely asked stupid questions to lull you into security. Snake.

She tilted her head, smiling. This, at least, she excelled at—facing opponents with hidden intentions and eyes that revealed nothing. But his eyes. There was something unsettling in them. A flash of something that didn't fit the moment. He might be a shapely man, but there was something chilling about him that overshadowed the glint of handsomeness at first glance.

"I didn't wish to disturb him," she said.

"Is that so…" Paisley rubbed his chin with his shiny gloved hand.

His tone made her instantly wary.

"Yes," she lifted her chin a notch. "His morning ride is most precious to him."

He nodded, his gaze dropping to her hands. "What book are you looking for? Perhaps I can help you search for it."

Ashley froze. She couldn't very well tell a friend of Linsey that she was looking for a book about horses! She shut the book she still held in her hand and placed it back on the shelf. "I'm merely browsing."

He just smiled, observing her, like a hawk who had spotted a rabbit.

"Well, then," she said, stepping back. "I shall be on my way."

"I'll go with you."

"No need." The quicker she escaped this awkward moment, the better. Every instinct told her to leave. And Ashley usually trusted her instincts. It was only with Linsey that she dared to be stubborn.

He lazily leaned against the bookshelf. "Are you sure? It's dangerous for a lady to be alone."

Dangerous? In the countryside? She nearly snorted. *The only danger I sense is from you.* She paused. Wait. Did that mean it *was* dangerous in the countryside?

Focus, Ashley.

She forced her smile wider. "Rest assured, I can handle myself perfectly well."

He laughed suddenly. "Funnily enough, I believe you, my lady."

"As you should, Your Grace."

His head tilted, his eyes narrowing. "Why did you agree to marry Linsey?"

The question was so abrupt, Ashley blinked. "I beg your pardon?" Why on earth would he ask her such a thing?

"You don't have to answer if you don't wish," he said, shrugging casually.

"It's not about whether I wish to answer. It's whether or not it's your business." She eyed him coolly. "And why do you care?"

His smile deepened, though it held no warmth. "Do you know why *he* asked you to marry him?"

Ashley narrowed her eyes. "Can you ask me that without knowing why *I* agreed?"

"Point taken."

"Why are you so interested, Your Grace? Concerned for your friend?" she asked, testing the waters, knowing it couldn't be that simple. But his reaction would speak volumes.

"More confused than concerned."

Ashley arched a brow. What was he getting at?

He must have noticed her suspicion, for he said, "Weren't you attached to Jordan Critton? The third son of Baron Critton—"

"What?" Her heart plummeted to her shoes.

He knew.

He knew about Jordan.

It shouldn't have come as a surprise. Their attachment hadn't been a secret, but it also hadn't been formally announced. The fact that the duke knew and had said nothing to Linsey was…odd.

Very odd.

So odd that she took a step back.

"From your reaction, I take it Linsey doesn't know."

Ashley forced herself to gather her composure, squaring her shoulders. "What is there to know? I'm engaged to Linsey, not Mr. Critton."

"Didn't Critton have a wager with Linsey?" Was that a question or a threat? One couldn't know from Paisley's tone.

"I cannot say. Men never talk to women about such things." *Good job, Ashley. You said that with a straight face.*

"Has there been much talking since your first dance at Almack's?" Paisley gave her a condescending look that made her blood boil.

"The appropriate amount," she snapped. Raising her chin, she turned to leave, not willing to give him a second more of her time.

But the duke moved swiftly, taking a large sideways step to block her path. "The conversation is not finished."

"It is." Ashley's voice was cold, sharp. She knew how to be curt when necessary and never shied away from giving a man exactly what he deserved. And the duke certainly deserved no more of her time.

"You dare cut me?"

Ashley glared at him. His eyes held no good intentions. Unlike a certain earl. Her thoughts turned suddenly to Linsey—honorable, stronger, kinder.

And much more handsome.

"Ashley?" A deep voice echoed through the bookshop, confusion lacing her name. "Paisley?"

Ashley whirled around, her eyes widening at the man now standing in the doorway. Linsey. His gaze was narrowed, dangerously, at both of them.

Speak of the devil…and he shall appear.

Ashley had never felt such relief in her life.

And such trepidation.

HE NEVER IMAGINED a throb could spread so widely through his chest. Thomas didn't know what to think at the sight that met him after he entered the bookshop. When he returned from the post, after he'd sent the Archbishop of Canterbury a note, though he didn't expect his family friend to deny him a special license, he thought a note with his seal could smooth the path since he hadn't had time to visit him in person while in London. He thought of that word again: elopement.

He should have insisted on eloping.

Was Lady Ashley truly in cahoots with Paisley as Seb had alluded? It couldn't be. And yet the sight of them standing side by side. Conversing in hushed voices…

No, do not lose your calm.

Calm and steady, just like facing two wild stallions.

Thomas strode over to the pair with long, purposeful steps and took a wide stance next to her, extending his arm. "Lady Ashley," he said more firmly. The breath he hadn't realized he'd been holding escaped in a soft rush when she placed her gloved hand in his.

Her fingers squeezed his lightly.

Was that a squeeze of thanks? He glanced down at her and caught a fleeting vulnerability behind the bold exterior she presented to the world—to him. It was a crack, but enough to show there was something more beneath her composed façade. Something more delicate. Had Paisley said something to her?

Could that be it?

They weren't in cahoots, but Paisley wanted to win the wager.

His eyes narrowed on the man.

"Linsey, what a coincidence to see you on such a lovely morning," Paisley drawled through a smile that didn't quite reach his eyes "Shouldn't you be training a racehorse or taming another—"

Thomas's jaw tightened. "I could say the same about you, Paisley. It's rather magnificent to run into you in town, in a bookshop...with *my* lady. Lady Ashley."

He felt her head whip to him but didn't take his gaze off Paisley, whose grin widened. "Ah, a mere coincidence, I assure you. When I saw *your* Lady Ashley enter, I thought you wouldn't be far behind."

Bastard. Thomas barely restrained the snarl curling in his throat.

He suddenly knew for certain; Ashley was not in cahoots with this man. Paisley had approached her with no good intention.

Paisley shrugged, his eyes flicking back to Ashley. "I was hoping to catch up with you, perhaps discuss inventory..."

Thomas's back stiffened, his gaze locked on the duke. "We're done here." His tone left no room for argument. He cast one final look at Paisley, silently promising to settle things later.

Paisley's parting shot stung like a hornet's sting. "Does she know she's risking her reputation for a man who might not give her the life she expects?"

Thomas's stomach churned.

What the hell was Paisley on about?

Was he purposely trying to provoke him with nonsense? He looked down at Ashley, but her chin lifted slightly higher. He gave her fingers a reassuring squeeze, letting her know he wasn't shying away from this fight.

"Don't expect a wedding invitation," Thomas bit out, his hand pressing against her lower back. "Let's go."

Ashley nodded. Her entire posture screamed *good riddance*, and she followed without a backward glance.

"I'll have to come back and finalize our transaction!" Paisley called after them.

Thomas flinched but didn't stop. *Damn that man.* He didn't take his wager lightly, but if Paisley thought he'd allow Paisley to chase Ashley away from him…

I'll ruin him before that happens.

A wager was a wager, but approaching his bride?

Should he just ask to be let off? No, Paisley would never let him off and would only take grim satisfaction in his plea. And it was matter of honor. Plus, Paisley was not like Thomas, who had recently let a man off a wager after he had fallen to his knees before him in a pitiful sight.

"Mark my words, Thomas, your racing mares will be mine!"

You've already gambled your pride away, Paisley. I'm not going to forfeit my birthright to satisfy your idiotic gambling habit.

And certainly not Ashley.

"Let's go," he said and led Ashley away, gently tugging her hand.

Thomas slammed the door shut behind them with a sharp crack that echoed through the street. He led her around the corner, toward the stables, his thoughts racing.

Thomas felt the slight tug on his arm, a gentle resistance that slowed his steps. Ashley's hand was warm in his, yet there was a hesitance in her grip, fingers loosely entwined with his own. As they moved down the narrow path, he noticed the soft scuffing sound of her feet against the gravel, a deliberate reluctance in each step.

He glanced at her. Not even the bright morning sun covering her in a crown of light could match the way her presence illuminated everything in him. The soft, silky ringlets escaping her coiffure framed her face in a halo of gold, making her look almost ethereal. *Had he always found her this beautiful?*

His thoughts spun in a swirl of poetic nonsense, and he cursed himself for it. *He was hopelessly falling.* Especially when she smiled up at him—those eyes, the same startling blue as the dress that clung to her figure in all the right places—he was lost.

Completely, utterly lost.

Until now, Thomas had regarded Ashley as suitable, agreeable, and—most importantly—available. A match that made perfect sense on paper. But right at that moment, something shifted. She wasn't just suitable. She wasn't just agreeable. She was a prize, a treasure he hadn't realized he wanted so badly.

I truly fancy her.

He'd never been sentimental about his feelings, but realizing the depth of them in a bookshop, after catching her in the company of another man, felt like a cruel joke. *Why hadn't she told him she was going shopping?*

She's not a captive, Thomas. But still…

"Linsey?" Her voice cut through his thoughts, soft but pointed.

He suddenly stopped. "My apologies. Did you want a book from the bookstore?"

She shook her head.

Lady Ashley was more than he had ever hoped for, and he vowed, then and there, to protect her at all costs. What's more, in her presence, he felt a sense of completion, a promise of a future filled with shared adventures.

He nodded and marched on. Her strides matched his now, but her voice softened. "Though I may be a mere transaction, my legs aren't as long as yours."

Thomas stopped in his tracks, turning to face her. "That…" he trailed off, searching for the right words. "Don't take what he said to heart. You are *not* a transaction."

Ashley glanced up at him, her posture resolute, but her eyes...her eyes told a different story. "But I am," she said quietly. "Let's not pretend otherwise. So are you, strictly speaking. However, our start is our start."

Our start is our start.

He couldn't deny that. In fact, he loved that.

And that cursed Paisley. He'd ruin the mood, but damn it, he wanted her to see his sincerity, his hope for their future. His hope for them.

"Ashley."

Her gaze flickered with hesitation. "What he said about—"

Thomas stepped closer, cutting her off by placing a finger over her lips, his voice low. "Forget what Paisley said. Don't pay him any heed."

"But..." Her lips parted as if she wanted to say more, but the words didn't come.

"No buts," he said with a soft smile. "You promised me a ride."

He would get her to his horses, bring his two loves together and away from Paisley.

No matter what.

Chapter Fifteen

SHE HAD PROMISED him a ride today, yes.
My Ashley.

The words still echoed in her ears, sending shivers through her whole body, wreaking havoc on her heart.

Why was she so affected by this earl who had nearly ruined her life? Very well, perhaps *ruined* was a bit strong, but he had certainly complicated things with Jordan—if not entirely severed that thread. And yet, despite her reasons for approaching him, never had she expected that anything he did or said could make her pulse flutter so erratically.

And then there was his confrontation with the duke…how could one man make her feel so relieved, vexed, and utterly amused all at once? The male species!

Ashley simply couldn't understand them.

She had thought she had, at least to some extent, figured them out. She'd read the whole handbook after all. A man's mind couldn't juggle too many things at once, surely—three, at most, in her estimation.

Duty. Procreation. Pleasure.

Nothing too complicated. Except, perhaps, for the last one—pleasure. The specifics of what brought each individual man joy differed. One look at the Duke of Paisley, and she knew that his twisted version of pleasure came from other people's suffering.

Perhaps Thomas could keep honor right there with duty. The way he'd come to her rescue certainly brought no other thought besides honor to mind.

The events in the bookshop had proven as much.

But Paisley clearly wasn't above getting his hands dirty if it meant winning. The bitter taste of that realization still clung to her tongue, sharp and lingering. Strange, really, because in another world, she and the duke could have been allies. He wanted Linsey's horses, and she wanted him to lose them.

Yet somehow, the mere notion of aligning herself with the duke sharpened the bitter taste in her mouth. *And* he knew about Jordan. Funny, she had once called him *her* Jordan, but that didn't feel true anymore.

My Ashley.

Drat. The words unsettled her more than she imagined, clouding her thoughts. She didn't know what to feel or think anymore, couldn't focus. So, she shoved those two words—and the loathsome duke—out of her mind, forcing herself to concentrate on the man standing before her. She had a more immediate challenge to face.

He smiled at her, and—oh, his smile. *Stop it, Ashley.* "You should have told me you wanted to come into town," he said, his voice low, concerned. "I would have escorted you."

Ashley looked away for a moment, steeling herself before meeting his gaze again. The tension between him and the duke still lingered in the air, thick and undeniable. And yet, the way he looked at her now was far too gentle for words.

"I'm sorry," she offered simply.

His brow furrowed. "There's no need to apologize. Did you need something in town other than visiting the bookshop?"

Ashley sighed, her shoulders sinking. "A riding habit. Or habits."

His blink of surprise was almost comical. "You didn't bring one with you?"

I don't own any. "I don't often ride, so it never occurred to me." That, at least, was true. While *he* loved horses, it hadn't seemed like something that mattered to her.

"Ah, well, shall we commission some for you?"

"No need. I already did before entering the bookshop."

He nodded. "Is there anything else you require?"

She shook her head, searching his gaze. "Are you all right?"

Linsey dragged a hand through his hair, mussing the strands in frustration. "Paisley. He's gone too far."

Ashley shrugged, more to hide her uncertainty than indifference. Everyone had their reasons. He wanted to marry her to save his horses, the duke wanted the horses, and she wanted to stop him from having—in diabolical terms—all he held dear.

But meeting Paisley today…

She inwardly shuddered. Did that make her any better than the duke? The thought thoroughly unsettled her. Her gaze dropped to the cobblestone beneath her boots, her heart heavy with doubt. Could she even follow through with her plan? And if she didn't? Did that mean she lost? She glanced up at the tall, handsome man beside her. Even if she abandoned her revenge plot, she couldn't marry Linsey.

There was no way to make this work.

Setting Jordan aside, their entire engagement was built on a lie. She sighed softly. No matter her intentions, it seemed inevitable that Linsey would be hurt.

Then don't hurt him.

She jolted at the intrusion of that thought. Don't hurt him?

But that would mean marrying him.

Could she do that?

No, no. That would be madness. Wouldn't it? But…they were already engaged, after all.

But Jordan…

He left, Ashley. And he hasn't sent so much as a note after he'd disappeared.

Fine. But what if Linsey found out the truth? Would he hate her? Would he look at her the way he had just looked at Paisley—with distaste, anger, disdain?

Her motives had been impure, and she feared that would taint, well, everything!

Her chest tightened at the thought.

"Ashley?"

She blinked, Linsey's face coming back into focus. "I'm sorry. I was lost in thought."

"So where did your thoughts wander to?" he asked, his tone soft yet searching.

She smiled. "It's a secret." Her heart wasn't ready to bare the truth. "Now tell me—what brought you to town?"

"You," he said simply, before glancing over his shoulders. "Oh, right, I almost forgot. I thought we could visit the stationer's while we are here."

"The stationer's?"

"To send word to *The Times* for our engagement announcement." He waved grandly and then grinned. "Or for our wedding invitations."

Engagement announcement. Wedding invitations.

The world seemed to close in around her, her pulse roaring in her ears. Yes, she knew they were engaged, but hearing it, talking about wedding invitations, made it all too real.

"I...ahem..."

He arched a brow. "We need wedding invitations, you know."

"Isn't it too soon?" she asked, her voice wavering.

"You know about my wager," he reminded her gently, "so there's no reason to mince words. I need to marry, or Paisley wins."

She understood that, but...ah, criminy. Why did her heart throb at his answer? He could look at her so sweetly and still utter those words with a straight face. Yet she knew the truth. She'd always known.

Paisley must have truly thrown her off her game.

"You are also the one who asked me to marry you, remember.

There must be a reason you did that, wasn't there?"

Yes... "There is..." *Say it, Ashley. Now is the time.* 'Tis no time to clear the air like the present. Confess and put an end to it all. "I..." She couldn't do it. To confess would mean revealing all her flaws. All her imperfections. But for as long as she could, she wanted to be that other Ashley in his eyes, the one he'd somehow drawn out. So she just couldn't do it. She shook her head, smiling. "I couldn't stand spinsterhood looming."

That, at least, was also the truth.

He chuckled, offering his arm. "Now, that I believe but it seems too soon." He shrugged and offered his elbow. "Shall we, then?"

Ashley nodded, slipping her hand through his arm, one question echoing louder than the rest—what on earth was she going to do next?

※

THOMAS STEPPED INTO the stationer's shop behind Ashley, the tinkling bell above the door announcing their arrival. Shelves lined the walls, displaying an assortment of crisp paper rolls in various sizes, while a polished window display showcased sleek fountain pens, their barrels gleaming in the sunlight. A small sign boasted that they were the latest imports from Switzerland, equipped with barrels to hold ink—a symbol of elegance and practicality. The air also carried the comforting scent of fresh paper, wax, and ink, immediately easing his nerves that tensed in the bookshop.

He moved closer, brushing his fingers over the surface of one pen. Nearby sat corked bottles of ink, sealed with wax, their contents a rich, permanent black. Thomas sighed, hoping the invitations he was about to commission would carry the same sense of permanence. A corner of the shop was dedicated to wax seals, intricate designs carved into each stamp, alongside sticks of vibrant sealing wax in hues of red, gold, and blue.

He wanted the best for them.

He also just wanted to elope.

Damn Paisley.

The stationer, a gentleman with keen eyes and a welcoming smile, approached Thomas, clearly recognizing him. "Good day, my lord. How may I assist you today?"

Thomas gestured toward Ashley, who stood distantly, inspecting stationery in the far corner. "I'm here for wedding invitations. They need to befit the occasion, embossed with my family crest in gold."

He sensed Ashley's gaze with the last.

A slow smile crept across the old man's face, and his gaze softened as it flicked to Ashley. "If I may, my lord—on behalf of my family and staff, we extend our heartfelt congratulations."

It was the first time anyone had congratulated him so wholeheartedly, and Thomas couldn't help but smile brightly. "Thank you."

"I have some splendid choices for you," the stationer said, guiding him to a polished oak table where samples were spread out like treasures. Thomas cast a quick glance at Ashley, who still lingered off to the side, before he turned back to the man, who presented a variety of heavyweight papers, each one more exquisite than the last, their surfaces smooth and inviting to the touch. "For such a distinguished request, I recommend our finest vellum. It has a subtle sheen that will beautifully complement the gold embossing of your crest, my lord."

Had Paisley's words affected her more than she led on?

He distractedly examined fonts and layouts with the stationer, the man offering expert advice on achieving the perfect balance of elegance and legibility. He couldn't follow the man, but a sample of gold embossing caught the light, casting a regal shimmer across the crest, left Thomas certain it was the right choice.

Yet, despite the weight of this decision, Ashley remained distant, only casting him brief glances from her corner of the shop.

He wanted the input of his betrothed. After all, this wasn't just any order; it was the first announcement of their future together. Yet she had distanced herself from the selection process, and without Ashley's engagement, it felt a bit incomplete.

He cursed Paisley again.

Even so, the stationer's attentiveness reassured him that the invitations would not merely announce a wedding; they would declare his commitment and devotion to the world. He strode over to Ashley. If she didn't come to him, he would go to her. "What do you think about this one?"

Her gaze skimmed over the design. "It's very pretty."

"Then you like it?"

She nodded again. "I am fine with whatever you choose."

Thomas furrowed his brows. "Are you all right?" She did seem fine moments ago, or had he imagined that?

Her smile seemed a bit forced. "I'm just a bit overwhelmed. I believe I need a touch of fresh air."

Thomas nodded. She did look a bit pale all of a sudden. "Let's step outside for a moment." He returned to the stationer and nodded his approval. They could settle any other details later. They stepped from the shop. "Shall we return in the carriage or on horseback?"

"Do you mind if we walk back? A stroll would be nice, and your estate isn't that far."

With a nod, Thomas guided her to the carriage used and instructed the carriage driver to take the horses back to the estate. As he turned toward Ashley, a gentle breeze stirred the air, carrying with it the scent of freshly cut grass and the faintest trace of distant rain.

Perhaps this was what they needed at the moment.

He led her to the path that ran to his home. Fields of green stretched out on either side, framed by tall hedgerows that swayed gently in the breeze. The soft glow of the morning sun kissed the tops of the trees, creating long shadows that stretched across the road. Thomas glanced at Ashley beside him, her eyes fixed ahead, lost in her own thoughts.

He averted his gaze again.

She'd been fine up till the moment they entered the shop. Could it truly be meeting Paisley, or did it have to do with the wedding invitations? Was she having doubts?

He tugged at his cravat.

Oh, right.

He wasn't wearing one except when he was in London.

His estate loomed in the distance, the spires of its roof barely visible beyond the rows of trees. It was a familiar sight, but today it felt different somehow. Thomas felt it in the quiet tension, in the way Ashley's fingers lightly grazed his arm before falling away.

Thomas's pulse quickened.

How to get their playful mood of the past few days back?

He wanted to reach for her hand, to close the distance between them, but something held him back—perhaps the unspoken doubts that had clouded their morning. Instead, they walked side by side, the silence between them not entirely uncomfortable, but heavy with unspoken words.

"I never thought I'd enjoy a country stroll so much," Ashley remarked suddenly, her voice breaking through the silence between them.

"You're such a city girl," Thomas teased lightly, grasping the statement that felt more like a lifeline.

She smiled wider. "You've said as much, and you are still right."

"Does it bother you?" he asked, glancing at her. "That I'm not?"

She pursed her lips thoughtfully. "No. You wouldn't be you otherwise."

Thomas nodded, relieved by her answer, and before he knew it, he leaned in and pressed a brief kiss to her cheek—a soft, sweet peck.

Ashley blinked in surprise but didn't pull away, and for a moment, the world felt steady again. Thomas grinned, entranced by the sudden closeness, weaving the spell. "Are you still up for a ride?"

Ashley held his gaze, her smile fading into something more unreadable, her eyes shining with the same unanswered question hanging between them.

"Always," she whispered, a promise that lingered in the air between them. But good or bad, he still couldn't tell.

Chapter Sixteen

A SHLEY SHIFTED UNSTEADILY on her mare.
When it came to moods, Ashley had never struggled to rally from the depths of her spirits. She had mastered the talent for changing her outlook, swapping despondent thoughts for brighter ones. Whether it was the sting of rejection or the weight of expectation, she always found a way to rise above, wrapping herself in laughter and a sunny disposition.

Or revenge.

But she wasn't ready to dwell on that sentiment again—not right now.

Thomas's excitement over the upcoming wedding, the way he had spoken of the invitations with such pride, had made her heart twist with a pang of guilt she hadn't been prepared for. She wasn't sure why, but something inside her recoiled at the thought of not being able to match his enthusiasm. And it had taken the entirety of their walk back to the stables to pull herself back into liveliness, a task that began the moment Linsey had pressed that quick, unexpected kiss to her cheek, which should have deepened her guilt, but left her breathless instead.

Now, on horseback, Ashley felt unsteady and rattled in numerous ways she wouldn't even bother to count. With the horse's rhythmic stride beneath her thighs, Ashley's newfound composure was at risk again. If ever there was something to dread about attempting to impress a man who adored horses, this was it.

Riding.

On a horse.

All ladylike and graceful.

Was she riding ladylike? Ashley wasn't quite sure. She was doing her best in her new habit shirt. The collar was entirely too high and scratched her chin, so high was it. And the weighted hem of her dress might have been draped elegantly over the horse's back, but she couldn't remember ever being so uncomfortable or immodest in sitting that way…how did Thomas make it look so natural? However, clothing was only a small part of riding. The fashion part. However, spine straight? Accounted. Shoulders lowered? Accounted. Chin up? Accounted.

Elegance is confidence, she reminded herself.

Reins held properly? Accounted. Smile? Accounted. Legs? Her gaze flicked down, then back up again. Accounted. Nerves? Oh, very much accounted for.

Her neck sent a jolt of pain through her spine as if her bones complained about being on horseback.

Come on, Ashley. You can do this.

Her grip tightened on the reins as she lifted her chin another notch. This was an exploration, was it not?

Confidence is elegance.

"This horse rides smoothly," she announced. Oh dear, why did she say "this horse"? And smoothly? So many better words she could have chosen!

A warm laugh drifted across the space between her and Thomas who was too far away for her comfort. "Lady Catrina is a smooth-riding horse."

She inwardly grimaced as she recalled the cook's bland teasing. "Indeed."

"What is your dream, Lady Ashley?" Linsey asked, his question as sudden as a sharp gust of wind. Her head snapped toward him.

"My dream? Do you mean...what I dreamed last night?"

He shot her a look. "That's not quite what I meant. I want to know your dreams. What do you think about when you're alone? What do you long for?"

She'd suspected he'd meant that, but no one had ever asked her this question. It caught her off guard. "I suppose..." What should she answer? "To wed and raise a family. You know, *not* to become a spinster." She scrunched her brows. "Though, I suppose that isn't much of a dream, is it?"

"It is if that is what you long for."

She glanced at him. "I suppose." She hadn't quite thought about her dreams. She'd always known what was required of her. There was no mystery, nothing to fight for or fight against. It was the way of their world. Until she found a measure of purpose in her mission for revenge.

However.

It wasn't the kind of purpose she had ever expected to cling to, but it had given her direction, a way to channel the anger and hurt that simmered beneath her calm exterior. It was easier, sometimes, to focus on settling old scores than to admit she didn't know what her own future should look like. Dreams had always seemed too fragile, too uncertain, and it was proven with Linsey and Jordan's wager. But revenge? That was tangible, something she could control. It gave her focus, a sense of reason when everything else felt uncertain.

But even then, it wasn't a future.

No, what she wanted—what she had always wanted—was acceptance.

Her mother had often despaired over her outspokenness, the way Ashley spoke her mind in a world that demanded women remain silent and proper. "You'll never find a man with that sharp tongue of yours," her mother had said countless times, her disapproval seeping into every conversation like an ever-present shadow. For years, those words had weighed on her, planting a seed of self-doubt she could never fully shake.

But her father had been different. He had always been patient, never quick to reprimand her for speaking her mind. He had made her feel heard, accepted, even when she feared her voice was too much for the world to bear. It was that kind of man she sought—someone with the patience of a saint, like her father, who could understand that she wasn't trying to defy society for the sake of rebellion; rather it was because she couldn't be anything less than herself.

It wasn't love she craved. It was someone who would look at her, with all her edges and faults, and simply…stay. Not because he had to but because he wanted to despite and because of everything that she couldn't change about herself—or didn't care to change because she wouldn't be herself anymore. Perhaps that *was* love. Or was love a requirement for such a commitment?

She glanced at Linsey again.

Was he that man? Could he be? Or would he be like so many others, charmed by her spirit but, in time, worn down by it?

Stow that thought!

She was not here for that.

Ashley felt the familiar grip of her leather gloves as she released the reins with one hand, the supple material allowing her to move with confidence. The veil of her riding hat teased her nose, a persistent tickle that demanded attention. As she reached up to adjust the hat, a sudden gust sent her tilting sideways. Her heart lurched as her body shifted unexpectedly, the world briefly tilting with her. Instinctively, she tightened her hold on the reins, her muscles tensing to stabilize her precarious position. With a sharp inhale, she centered herself again, the horse's steady rhythm beneath her gradually calming her racing pulse.

"What I long for?" she finally murmured. "I don't know…" *Anymore.* She cocked her head, studying him. Perhaps it was time to probe.

"Tell me, Linsey, have you ever run anyone out of England?"

"Please, call me Thomas, and what do you mean have I ever run anyone out of England?" He turned to look at her. "That's quite a specific question." Amusement still lit his tone. A smidgeon of uncertainty. The latter perhaps of where the conversation was going.

"No. I have not. Have *you*?" he countered.

She considered him. "Does my mother count?"

He chuckled, and she averted her gaze, focusing on the shadows playing off the trees. It wasn't a lie—her mother had made it quite clear she hadn't wanted a daughter like her. So, she had left to travel with her friends most of her childhood. Of course, Ashley knew now that it wasn't all because of her.

"Whatever happened with your mother," Linsey suddenly said. "You're not at fault. A child could never be at fault."

She glanced at him. "Bold words." For a man that just lied to her, and for a man that would surely point a finger straight at her the moment he learned about her connection to Jordan, as well as her plot. How low had she stooped in this, she didn't know yet, but she'd fall even lower—once Thomas found out about her motives—that she'd hit the hot center of the earth.

Yes, hot.

Ashley fanned herself with her left hand again and slipped a little again.

So she couldn't move but the horse was shaking her up and that was called a leisurely strut? Why did Linsey like horses?

"Perhaps I'm merely trying to match your spirit."

"Well, if that is the case, how can I complain? If only everyone could attempt to match it, the world would be a delightfully interesting place," she said wistfully.

His laughter prickled across her skin. "Bold is for the bold." He paused. "Sometimes it's easier for people to run away than stay. It's not in everyone's character to face the truth and work to correct it."

Ashley's lips twitched into a grin.

"What?" he asked when he caught it. "That's a terrifying look. What are you thinking?"

"Just that you are right. It's easy to run away." She cast him a small smile. "I practically ran away with you, didn't I?"

He stared at her a moment before clearing his throat. "Yes, well, I do like running."

A sense of foreboding crept up on her.

"I'll race you back to the stables." His grin turned wicked. "The winner gets to demand anything from the loser."

A race? Demand anything from the loser? That loser would undoubtedly be her!

Before she could protest, Thomas spurred his horse into a gallop, leaving her in a cloud of dust. But he'd sent her that ravishing smile over his broad shoulders that she couldn't deny the pleasure of following him.

Oh well, if she was going to fall, she'd better make it fast.

She urged her horse into motion, her heart pounding. It wasn't that she couldn't ride, but there was something she had never told anyone. Not even her father when he taught her to ride. Another little secret.

Heights.

She was terrified of heights. And she'd forgotten how high horses were. Even getting this far had been a miracle.

But she couldn't let go now. She couldn't lose, not like this. Determined, she pushed herself forward, gripping the reins tighter.

Her body slid precariously to the side.

Dear heavens, she was going to fall!

No! *I refuse to fall! I refuse to be humiliated to such a degree.* Fear surged through her, a primal instinct kicking in, screaming for survival.

Don't let me fall, Lady Catrina!

But no matter how hard she held on, her body continued to slip.

She hadn't ridden in years. She didn't know what to do. Despite her desperate grip, she felt her body sliding, inch by inch, an unstoppable descent fueled by years without practice. The rough texture of the saddle seemed to push her away, and panic rose in her chest, sharp and insistent. Her father had never taught her how to handle it.

Her heart pounded louder than the horse's hooves, and she squeezed her eyes shut, the world becoming a blur of sound and sensation. Wildflowers blurred into streaks of color as she braced herself for the fall. Her hands, slick with sweat, lost their hold, and she felt the terrifying rush of inevitability.

Ashley squeezed her eyes shut, bracing for the inevitable—preparing to meet the ground, wildflowers and all. For all her best efforts, for slipping out to the town, trying her best to showcase her talent, it still ended this way. With her in the dirt!

This couldn't be how it ended.

Not like this.

Please, not like this!

THOMAS HAD KNOWN fear in his life, but nothing to this degree. He'd been distracted for barely a moment, and that had been enough for disaster to unfold. He'd wanted to race, had set off at a neck-breaking pace, but something had nagged at the back of his mind. Intuition, perhaps. He had turned back just in time to witness the chaos.

And there she was—Lady Ashley, slipping from her mare, Lady Catrina!

She bobbed helplessly, making strange noises atop the horse's back. If it weren't so dangerous, it would have been amusing.

Pure instinct took over.

By all that was dear, he couldn't let her fall.

"Are you all right?" he called, urging his stallion forward with a firm press of his legs. "Ashley?"

Swish! She slid to the side, her hands clinging to the reins as her skirts fluttered up, revealing her boots.

"Pull yourself up!" The mare was moving too fast for her to dismount safely, and if she wasn't careful, her legs might tangle with the horse's. Thomas clenched his jaw. No. He wouldn't allow it.

His heart pounded in his chest as he edged his stallion closer to her. The trees blurred into a whirlwind of green as hooves pounded against the earth. He could see the panic in Ashley's posture, her grip on the reins frantic and unsteady. Her mare, feeding off her tension, only accelerated, turning an already precarious situation into a full-blown crisis.

"Steady," he muttered, more to himself than the horses, calculating the distance and timing of his next move. His stallion responded to his unspoken command, matching the mare's speed with precision.

Thomas didn't hesitate.

Thomas scanned the path ahead, his eyes flicking over the landscape with practiced speed, confirming the way was clear. The wind howled in his ears, blending with the pounding of hooves against the earth, a chaotic symphony urging him to act. With a deep breath, he released the reins, feeling the familiar leather slip through his fingers. It was a reckless move, one born out of sheer necessity.

Muscles coiled, he pushed against the saddle, the powerful surge of his horse beneath him providing the momentum he needed. The world slowed as he launched himself into the air, his legs splaying in a daring arc. Gravity tugged at him, but adrenaline sharpened his focus, every second stretching into an eternity. He was weightless, suspended between the two beasts, the ground a blur below.

The impact jolted through him as he landed on Lady Catrina, his hands gripping the saddle with fierce determination. The transition was seamless yet jarring, her powerful stride absorbing the force of his leap. Thomas steadied himself, the thrill of the daring feat coursing through his veins, his only thought now on reaching Ashley and pulling her back to safety.

He landed hard behind Ashley, the impact shaking them both.

But there was no time to waste. His arm wrapped around her waist, pulling her firmly against his chest. With his other hand, he reached for the reins. "I've got you," he said, his voice steady despite the chaos.

His stallion galloped alongside them, as if it too was part of the rescue.

Thomas gently tugged the reins, his hands coaxing the mare to slow. Bit by bit, the horse responded, easing from a wild gallop to a more manageable trot.

Relief washed over him, but his awareness of Ashley, pressed so closely against him, flooded his senses. Her breath, ragged and uneven, began to sync with the slowing pace of the horse. His arms, still securely around her, tightened ever so slightly.

She felt like heaven in his arms.

"I had her under control," Ashley said between breaths.

Thomas bit back a curse, but he decided to play along. "Yes, I could see that. Straight as an arrow."

She nodded, her head brushing against the arm holding onto her. "I was."

"Pointing toward disaster, Ashley." He shifted, taking both reins in one hand while the other wrapped more snugly around her waist. "You scared me to death."

"Me, too."

Was that a moment of vulnerable honesty he'd spotted?

He buried his face in her hair for a moment, the scent of jasmine filling his lungs. The thought of what could have happened, of losing her—no, he couldn't bear it. "Why didn't you tell me you can't ride?"

She twisted to face him, her gaze meeting his. "I didn't think there was much to it. Besides, it's not that I can't ride…it's just that I haven't ridden in years."

"How many years?"

She hesitated. "Twelve. Maybe thirteen."

"Thirteen years!" By Jove! That's...*horrifying*. "You could have been seriously hurt."

She shrugged, the motion causing her to rub against him, sparking all sorts of sensations. "I got on the horse. I sat. How hard could it be?"

Thomas groaned. "You have to sit astride properly." He guided her to lean forward slightly, his hands shifting her position. She stiffened, still tense with fear—or perhaps, he dared hope, from his proximity.

She nodded.

He rested his chin briefly on her shoulder. "Relax your grip on the reins," he murmured, covering her hands to show her how to hold them without strangling the leather. "Feel the horse's rhythm. She's calm now, so should we be."

But calm was the last thing he felt with Ashley's body pressed against his. His crotch tightened painfully. "You're doing wonderfully," he said, adjusting her leg position so she was balanced more securely. Her body fit perfectly onto his.

Ashley scoffed, but there was a smile in her voice. "I'm practically sitting in your lap."

"That, too," he teased. "I'll teach you the rest."

That didn't come out right. "Riding, I mean."

"And the rest?" She turned her head, and her eyes met his for a flicker of a second.

Thomas swallowed hard. "Anything," he croaked.

She snorted. "It's rather...distracting."

Thomas grinned. Oh, it was. All thoughts of his earlier frustrations vanished as they rode together, their bodies moving in sync with the horse. He hadn't just saved her from a fall; he had somehow fallen himself—hard and fast. He didn't think he could ever return to a life without her.

She shifted against him again. Thomas pinched his eyes shut for a moment as they rode toward a patch of woodlands in the distance. The sun filtered through the trees, dappling their path with soft shadows. Shade, he needed that cool air.

As they approached a cluster of tall oaks, he gently squeezed the mare's sides. "Easy now," he murmured, though his words were more for himself than the horse.

"Are you speaking to me?" she asked, and he tensed when she leaned back against him slightly to cast a quick glance his way. Every time she did that his heart leapt.

He chuckled. "I meant the horse, but it applies to you too. We'll stop in the shade."

Following his lead, Ashley held the reins and guided the mare toward the trees. Thomas placed his hands on her thighs, ready for anything. She shifted in response, her body molding against his as her skirts hiked up even more, revealing more of her legs.

"Hah! We are here!" Ashley's voice held a note of triumph as the mare finally eased to a slow walk. His pulse raced at the excitement that lit her face as she turned to him again. His arms encircled her, fingers lightly resting on her waist.

"We are."

Her eyes dropped to his lips, and Thomas felt the beat in his chest start to hammer. He couldn't help himself. If that wasn't an invitation, he didn't know what was. Her lips so close, her breath feathering over his chin, and he captured them in a heart-thundering kiss.

The world around Thomas seemed to still.

He brushed her lips—a gentle exploration at first, a question posed and answered with equal softness, a tentative warmth that coaxed an answering flutter deep inside. But as her lips parted slightly, the kiss deepened, grew more urgent. Thomas's hand moved from her waist to cradle her neck, and he ventured further, fingers threading through her hair, securing her to him as if afraid she might slip away.

So sweet.

His hands, previously a shield around her waist, now became agents of a different kind of care, one that sought connection and intimacy.

The air around them was charged with the electricity of their bodies, every sense heightened. The scent of her hair, a mix of jasmine and the fresh, earthy outdoors, filled his nostrils, anchoring him to her in a way he couldn't even begin to understand, but neither did he want to. He just wanted more.

The sensation of her lips sent jolts of pleasure through him, as if she were lighting him on fire, a warmth that dwarfed the sun's rays on his skin. Her taste was an elixir that promised endless discoveries. The world outside their embrace ceased to exist; there was only the steady shift of the mare beneath them, the breeze stirring the leaves, and the quiet echoes of their shared breath.

Yet, he slowly relinquished her lips.

Thomas sensed something profound had shifted between them. This kiss was not just an expression of desire, but a declaration, a forging of a bond that neither time nor circumstance could easily unravel.

He was unraveling.

At a speed much faster than any horse on the race field.

Thomas took the reins from her, his fingers brushing hers, slowing Lady Catrina to a halt. Dismounting, his focus shifted entirely to Ashley. Her eyes followed his every move, lips swollen, cheeks flushed—everything about her begged for the kiss to continue.

"Why did we stop?"

"I thought we could use a reprieve." He certainly could. The kiss had nearly undone him.

She gave a faint nod, and his hands wrapped around her waist, the touch reverent, as if he were holding something far more precious than he'd ever known. With gentle care, he lifted her down, her body melting against him for the briefest of moments, as if his arms were the only place she belonged.

When her feet met the ground, the space between them felt fragile, neither willing to step away. Thomas's hands lingered on her waist. Only when he was sure she stood steady on the soft moss did he finally pull back, though the warmth of her remained imprinted on his palms. "How are you feeling?"

"Breathless."

He smiled, feeling much the same. He moved to secure the horses to the closest tree, his own having followed them. Returning to her, he offered his hand. "Shall we take a stroll?"

Her hand slipped into his, her fingers intertwining with his as though they'd done it a thousand times before. As though they'd always known the way. Maybe they had. He almost laughed at the thought. He couldn't deny that he was a sentimental man, but with her, it seemed, his sentimentality reached unprecedented heights.

Leading her toward a grand oak, he tugged at the collar of his shirt.

"Do you enjoy walks in nature?" she asked as they approached the tree's sturdy base.

"Of course. Don't you?"

She wrinkled her nose slightly. "It's not the nature I mind, but the insects that come with it."

He chuckled, stealing a glance at her. "They are just bugs. They are everywhere, even indoors."

"Still...there are *fewer* indoors."

His thumb brushed lightly over the back of her hand, a casual gesture that sent sparks up his arm. "I'll do my best to keep them away from you."

She scoffed. "You think rather highly of yourself if you believe you can swat away every bug that comes my way."

"I do. Just like with mice in haylofts."

She arched a brow. "Are you sure that's within your power, oh gallant bug-slayer?"

He grinned, stepping closer to guide her to lean against the tree's rough bark. "I hope so, because I don't want to leave yet. Trying is better than not trying at all."

Her gaze softened, amusement flickering in her eyes as she leaned back against the sturdy oak. "Then I suppose I'll have to put up with your heroics a little longer."

"In that case," he murmured, stepping into her space again, his hand sliding up to rest just above her waist, "I'll try not to disappoint."

"I have a feeling," she whispered, "disappointment isn't your specialty."

Thomas glanced at her lips again, fighting the urge to close the space between them. Every nerve in his body hummed with the temptation to kiss her, to pull her close and abandon all caution.

She looked up at him, her eyes filled with mischief. "You're thinking too much." Her teasing tone did nothing to calm the fire in his chest.

He laughed softly, though it came out rougher than intended. "And you think not enough."

She tilted her head, a smile playing on her lips. "What's wrong with thinking a little less?"

His heart pounded at the challenge, a thrill running through him. She was dangerous. "Careful," he warned, his fingers twitching. "You may be shocked at what happens if I stop thinking."

But even as he said the words, he knew he was dangerously close to doing just that. He didn't want to think anymore.

And by the look in her eyes, he wasn't the only one.

With a deep breath, he forced himself to take a step back, the pull between them almost unbearable. "Let's walk some more before I forget myself entirely."

He'd rather not ravage his intended in the woods where bugs reigned supreme.

Although, he wouldn't mind.

Chapter Seventeen

ASHLEY WOULDN'T MIND if she could stop thinking at that point. About everything.

She couldn't make up her mind anyway, and her heart—that was a lost cause.

Especially after Linsey's breathtakingly bone-melting kisses. The man truly *had* taken a page from her *bold* book. And she hadn't held back either. But in her defense, she'd been so grateful that he'd saved her from a tumble, she hadn't thought to resist or keep any safe distance. That seemed to be the theme with him. Whenever in his presence, she forgot about her plot for revenge.

All of that seemed to belong to a distant past, and even now, Ashley found it difficult to summon the same determination that had fueled her at the start.

This is all part of the plan.

She inwardly scoffed at herself.

They kissed. Again.

Her feet grew heavy, her arms were cold, and her heart was racing. Trouble.

Now they were alone in the woods. Bug-laden woods. The crisp, fresh scent of nature filled the air, but it wasn't enough to calm her racing heart. If anything, it only kept it at a galloping speed.

Her cheeks flushed with heat, and she was acutely aware of it.

The man's flirting could be considered on par with his kissing. Lethal.

Ashley took in the breathtaking meadow, where sunlight danced over a carpet of yellow and white flowers, each bloom a gentle burst of color against the emerald sea of grass. The trees stood like silent guardians, their branches arching gracefully over the clearing, creating a sanctuary of tranquility and renewal. It was as if the earth itself had awoken from its wintry slumber, stretching and unfurling under the tender warmth of spring.

In this vibrant picture, Ashley felt a kinship with the landscape, sensing her own heart mirrored in its revival. Once dormant and untouched by the chill of solitude, she now felt herself unfurling, each petal of her being opening to embrace the new warmth Thomas had brought into her life. His arrival in her life, however jaded it may sound, had melted the frost from her spirit, igniting a bloom within her that echoed the meadow's own awakening. Here, amid the fragrant air and the gentle rustle of leaves, she understood that her heart had been a garden waiting for its spring, and Thomas had been the sun coaxing it to life—coaxing her to life.

"This is quite the secluded spot." She blinked at the warmth of the spring's sun and inhaled the crisp air. It was invigorating, just like the man holding her.

He followed her gaze before his eyes landed back on her. "I found it while out exploring the lands."

"We seem to have that in common."

"Exploring lands?" he asked, his lips curving into a smile, yet his arched brow announced his skepticism.

She laughed softly. "Exploring."

He arched a brow, something wicked flashing in his gaze. "Ah." He leaned in closer, their faces mere inches apart. "Is that why you didn't confess you hadn't ridden in years? And years, and years and years? You were exploring whether those few training classes you might have had would save you?"

She shrugged, trying to play it off, though the proximity was making her pulse erratic. "I didn't want to disappoint you."

His smile softened, but the gleam in his gaze did not. "Well, I'm not disappointed. If anything, I'm impressed."

"You are?" How unexpected.

He nodded, cocking his head to the side, studying her. "I'm impressed you had the courage to even attempt such a thing. I'm also impressed you didn't burst into tears when I came to your rescue."

"Well, I'm not moved to tears easily."

The corner of his lips lifted in that dangerously irresistible way. "Somehow, I believe that."

"What else do you believe?"

His gaze dropped. "I believe your lips taste sweeter than all the dewy nectar on this field."

She raised a brow, touching her mouth. "That can't be true. Lips don't have a taste."

His fingers caught hers, gently brushing them aside. "Yours do. And I can't seem to get enough of them. Of you."

For a moment, Ashley lost her speech, then slowly murmured with narrowed eyes, "Is that your way of telling me you wish to kiss me again?" A grin formed on her lips. "Well, well, Linsey. *Thomas.* I do believe I have corrupted your pure soul."

"I never knew this about myself, but it seems I am, when it's the right person, exceedingly corruptible." His voice dipped low, sending a thrill through her.

The right person.

Heat rushed to her face, her boldness faltering for a moment. "Well, I do try."

He chuckled, shaking his head. "I truly find myself defenseless against your charm."

Her charm?

"Why do you look so surprised?" he murmured, eyes tracing her features with a kind of reverence.

"I suppose I didn't think I had a thing such as charm." Her mother certainly didn't believe she had.

"How can that be?" His expression turned curious, genuine. "You don't believe boldness can be charming?"

"People don't usually find it so," she said, thinking of all the times her forwardness had been a source of criticism.

He nodded thoughtfully. "I didn't, either."

Ashley arched a brow. "You've suddenly changed your mind?"

His thumb brushed across her knuckles. "I've been changed…ahem, my mind…" Oh drat, she lost all sense of coherent thoughts.

She caught her breath, her heart skipping as his words sank into her bones. No one had ever truly liked that trait of hers. No one except her father and Jordan. "My mother would call you a miracle."

"Well, we do live in a world filled with them."

She smiled, pushing thoughts of everyone else away. She didn't want to think about either Jordan, her mother, or her father right now. She didn't want anyone intruding on this singular moment. She had a man to charm, for purposes that appeared to have become as obscured as the dappled sunlight filtering through the canopy, fading into something far less clear, far more dangerous.

Her hands smoothed over his lapels. "Then I suppose I'll have to work hard to be converted to a country girl, too."

"You've not been already?" His voice lowered, sending a shiver down her spine. "That is rather problematic for me."

"Is that so?"

"Yes," he murmured, stepping closer, the space between them vanishing. "I can't have a wife who hasn't been converted to the countryside."

Wife.

His wife.

The word hit her like a physical force, her heart stumbling over itself.

It's not real.

This was not her moment. Not truthfully.

Remember that, Ashley

And yet, no matter how much she told herself that, there, alone in the woods, where the countryside seemed all too alluring, she could pretend otherwise.

Just for a moment.

All the reasons that had brought her to this point—her plan for revenge, her resentment, even Jordan—scattered like flowers in the meadow. She reached up, yanking him down to her, her boldness surging once again.

"Then convert me," she whispered, and kissed him.

This kiss wasn't like the ones before. It was deeper, more urgent. She suddenly understood what he meant when he said she tasted sweet. He tasted of malt and fresh air. Crisp, earthy, and yet utterly intoxicating.

Even though it was brazen, this kiss wasn't born of recklessness. It was an exploration—a discovery of him, of them. Of this strange pull that drew her closer and closer to him.

The confusion.

The attraction.

And the fear of what it might mean.

Would it consume her? Or would it destroy her? She didn't know. But at that moment, she didn't care.

⇶⇷

CONVERT ME.

Bloody hell, what those words did to him!

Thomas abruptly surfaced from the depths of those words, a sense of awakening washing over him as if he were coming up for air after being submerged in the most intoxicating of dreams. Ashley's back still pressed against the tree, one of his hands resting there too, the rough bark a stark contrast to the softness of her touch. Dappled shadows danced across her features, softening the light, adding a gut-wrenching quality to her beauty that left him utterly spellbound.

His insides hurt.

It hurt so much to feel all these *feelings* and not show it.

Yes, he had fallen for this woman. Hard.

And he wanted—no, needed—to express his feelings, lest he perish on the spot. But how? He didn't want to scare her away, yet he couldn't live without her. He had to have her now, even if only a little more than a shared kiss.

He stared down at her.

Her lips, swollen from their kiss, bore the flush of passion. Her eyes, wide and luminous, met his with a vulnerability and desire that mirrored his own. So damn beautiful. And perhaps he was moving too fast, but Thomas needed her in a way he couldn't quite comprehend himself.

His hands, which had found a home at her waist, still marveled at the curve of her body, the way she fit so perfectly against him. The warmth of her skin seeped through the fabric of her dress, igniting a longing that only closeness could quench.

"I'm ready," she whispered onto his mouth.

"That's a dangerous statement, love."

"I'm quite fond of danger."

He traced the line of her jaw with the pad of his thumb, awe washing over him for the woman who had, in such a short time, become the focal point of his every thought. He still couldn't quite fathom it. *Love?*

Her scent had become a sensory tether that grounded him to the undeniable reality of her presence, shifting his world since the moment she'd brazenly asked him to dance. What had only occurred a few days ago now felt like the inevitable steps of a lifetime destined to bring them to this moment.

"*You.*" Thomas smiled, brushing a lock of hair from her face unable to gather words. "A danger in itself."

"Is that what you were thinking so hard about?" Ashley asked, her voice soft but teasing.

"That and how you've bewitched me."

"Oh?" Her lips quirked in amusement. "I didn't even try."

"That's the worst part," he murmured, voice low. "You didn't have to."

"Then I must be a witch, no?"

He laughed softly, averting his gaze, struggling to find the right words, but his feelings were too much to contain. If he could express them the way he felt them, he'd take the wildest horse and ride at breakneck speed along the coast, letting the hooves splash in the salty waves. He'd throw his arms out and scream at the top of his lungs. But here, under the spring buds, and birds chirping overhead, he could find nothing better than, "My heart is all yours."

Her eyes widened. "It *is*?"

"Yes, I have fallen deeply in affection with you, Ashley."

Her head jerked back, her mouth slightly open, then her eyes wide.

"I like it when you call me *love* instead of Ashley. Nobody else ever did." Her voice was a mere whisper.

His heart pounded. "I...that's not what I thought you'd say." He released her waist, only holding her hand between his, drawing strength from her touch. He searched her face. "It's so fast, I know. We'd agreed to marry soon, but I just didn't know yet when I proposed..."

"Know what?" she whispered.

"How much you would come to mean to me in such a short

amount of time. I want to show you pleasure, love, everything that comes with being my wife."

She swallowed, blinking at him, her lips parted as though to speak, but no words came. Didn't it please her to hear these words? Wasn't a declaration of love what women wanted? She looked away, then back at him, and away again.

"Ashley? It's all right; you don't have to say anything." He could be patient and woo her. He might not need to convince her to marry him, but he needed to convince her that he was trustworthy, earnest, and that she was his world. "I know it's new, sudden, but I'd like to show you."

"I..." Her gaze fixed on him again, and he could tell she'd made some sort of decision. "How will you show me?"

He pressed her gently against the rough bark, feeling the heat of his desire clash violently with the caution in his mind. His body, especially the lower part, burned with an intensity that left him breathless, a thin sheen of sweat collecting at his brow. Every fiber of his being ached to hold her, to draw her close and let their hearts beat as one. He longed for the soft brush of her lips, the arch of her neck, her whole body if she would allow it—anything to ease the desperate yearning that consumed him.

But he held back, knowing that if this was to work, it couldn't just be about desire. It had to be about trust, about love.

He suddenly grinned at her. "Do I still need to convince you that I'm the right man for you? How much conversation do you need?"

"I..." She inhaled a deep breath, then nodded, that familiar glint entering her gaze. "More."

This was all Thomas needed to hear. His grin widened. "Good." Without waiting, he cupped her face, leaning in. "I'll let my actions speak for themselves."

His lips claimed hers with a fierceness that made her gasp, but she met him halfway, her fingers curling into his shirt. Thomas pressed against her, the feel of her body melting into his, igniting something primal within him.

Ashley hesitated for a heartbeat, but then her lips parted fully, inviting him to deepen the kiss. He obliged, and the world outside their little haven disappeared, the only thing that mattered was her—soft, responsive, and his.

Every brush of her lips, every touch stoked the fire.

"Thomas..." She whispered his name against his mouth, breathless.

"I won't stop," he murmured, his words a promise. "Not until you're convinced."

"Then convince me. I'll help you."

He didn't know what exactly she meant by that, but he kissed her with the force of a blazing fire, making every single kiss from before seem like child's play. Holding her head, he drank her in and yet nothing was enough. When a moan escaped her, she pressed her left leg against him and her hand came to his middle. She felt for the length of him.

Thomas froze.

So, that was what she meant.

She would be the death of him yet.

Just when he thought her boldness had reached its peak, she surprised him. But just like that, her hand moved up again.

Teasing minx!

They didn't venture beyond the bounds of the fabric that shielded them. His riding breeches had never been more uncomfortably tight down there, but he wasn't going to defile his bride.

But oh, the pleasure he would show her.

His hands itched to explore the curves of her body, to elicit sighs of contentment and whispers of desire. He envisioned her eyes fluttering closed in ecstasy, her lips parting with breathless anticipation. With one hand, she grabbed the back of his head and pulled him closer, opening her mouth even more. Her tongue met his in a dance of deliciousness and then she did the unspeakable.

She lifted her leg higher, wrapping it around his waist, pulling him closer until their bodies were flush. Her hips pressed firmly into him, sending a jolt of heat between them as her hands roamed over his back, anchoring him to her as if she couldn't get close enough.

I love it when you want to take control. I love you, Ashley.

Thomas reached for her thigh.

She wore her new riding shirt with a day dress and layers underneath, but when he looked down, the fabric had bunched up and her bare leg, in nothing but a garter and a thin stocking, clamped him to her. He'd never seen anything more erotic and pressed further against her, stabilizing her against the trunk, so that he bore her weight. She was light and he'd hold her for the rest of his days—for as long as she'd wish.

Thomas held her thigh up with one hand, gently stroking the underside. Up and down, along her soft skin and over the lace band of her garter, his hand trailed back. And when he found his way up, only inches from the apex of her legs, he froze. It was a threshold he couldn't cross without further invitation. Not *the* threshold, but still. She was an innocent. And like a wild mare drawn to the promise of freedom, she needed to be approached with care, only willing to yield when she felt truly ready.

"Thomas." She breathed heavily, her chest falling and rising, and slowly drew back to melt into his gaze.

"I promise I won't—"

"Stop promising what you won't do." She heaved for air and tensed her leg. "I want *more*." Her voice was barely above a panting whisper.

Hell and damnation, how could he hold back after that brazen demand. With practiced ease and yet mesmerized like a green boy, he found her soft folds with his free hand. He felt her breath hitch when he ventured to her opening with his right index finger. At first, she twitched. But instead of stopping him, she looked down. Expecting something...did she know?

"Have you ever done this yourself?"

She nodded, her gazed fixed down.

Then she arched into his hand.

She felt so warm, so good, in a way that made Thomas lightheaded. "Lie down," he said, supporting her as she slid down the tree and onto the soft moss. He removed his riding coat, rolled it up, and placed it behind her neck. He brushed a few stray hairs out of her face and took in her beauty. Slowly, he traced the curve of her cheek and the dip of her neck. He watched the rise and fall of her chest as if it were the most beautiful sunrise on the horizon of his future.

There was nothing more precious he could imagine.

Nothing.

He skimmed her sides, then trailed his hand over her flat stomach. Reaching under the layers of her skirt, his fingers danced lightly over her skin, leaving a visible trail of goosebumps in their wake. As his hand ventured higher, he felt her breath hitch and saw her eyelids flutter.

"Should I stop?" he asked.

"After coming this far?" she shot back, but her voice came out breathless.

Thomas chuckled. Right. Plucky and smart. *My Ashley.*

The fabric of her gown bunched as he pushed it up, revealing the softness beneath.

He leaned in, inhaling the scent that clung to her skin, their lips meeting in a tentative kiss. When she sucked his lower lip, he slid his index finger to her opening. Pausing, he opened his eyes to gauge her reaction. She blinked back at him, mouth slightly open and lips swollen, waiting.

He pushed into her softness, exploring thoroughly as her tongue mimicked the movements of his finger. His free hand roamed boldly, tracing the shape of her body while he discovered what she liked. He wanted to learn what she enjoyed.

Thomas loved every moment.

Each touch whispered promises of devotion, and she melted against him, clutching his shirt and pulling him closer. He chuckled against her lips. "Relax."

"I'm not on horseback," she replied, eyes narrowing. "I won't fall."

Oh, yes, you will. This time, it wouldn't be gravity but pleasure, heat, and a desire he vowed to cultivate for life. When his middle finger slid inside her, a gasp escaped her lips. "You'll fall deeply, but I'll catch you and make you fall again, love."

She was so tight, so soft. Her muscles clenched around him. He was not just offering her pleasure but taking on the responsibility of making her happy—now and always. Their eyes met for a moment, and he inserted his ring finger. She arched her back with a moan, surrendering once more.

He was in charge of this moment.

But she was in charge of him.

Finding a rhythm, he held her close as she softened in his arms. He leaned in to kiss her, and though she clung to him at first, his thumb teasing her pearl made her forget to kiss. Her fingers grasped the grass as her breathing grew strained.

She was close.

And he was…

Utterly lost.

Chapter Eighteen

PLEASURE CAME IN many forms. The joy of a friend's company, the approval of one's parents, the thrill of a waltz with a rogue. But this was something else entirely. The pleasure of flesh.

Not that Ashley had known much about it firsthand, but she'd heard enough gossip to wonder. When Thomas's fingers moved within her, she finally understood. Pleasure wove through her body, flooding her limbs in waves, intense and unrelenting, like the force of a cannon blast. And Thomas—the gunpowder that ignited it all.

Slowly, he drew his hand back, his touch trailing down her thigh as he settled beside her, her breaths slowing. The silence between them was thick, almost tangible, thrumming with what she could only describe as something close to…magic. Her heart thundered as she lay there, catching her breath, staring up at the canopy of trees above. If this was what ruination felt like, no wonder parents tried to shield their daughters. Once found, there was no chance to not wish to repeat it.

Her lips parted and inhaled to speak, but it took a moment for her voice to return. "Thomas, that…"

He kissed her softly. "Was perfect."

Perfect. She couldn't deny it, but it was earth-shattering too, fracturing her carefully constructed convictions. She fought down the rush of emotion clawing to break free, gripping his hand just a little tighter.

"What happens now?" The question slipped out before she could stop it.

"Now we stay a little longer. Or we return home, if that's what you want."

Home. His home.

She swallowed, the weight of her decision settling over her. "Stay a bit longer…" Her mind was too muddled to move, much less to choose.

He gathered her in his arms, both of them lying back. Ashley lay nestled against the soft moss, her gaze fixed on the leafy canopy above. The spring leaves wove an intricate pattern, their edges shimmering as the sun filtered through. Where the leaves overlapped, shadows deepened the greens, painting a darker, richer hue, yet elsewhere, the light danced freely, casting sparkles almost at odds with the heavy feeling in her chest.

Beside her, Thomas stretched out, his presence a comforting warmth against the cool earth. His blond hair caught the dappled sunlight, each strand glowing with a brilliance that seemed to capture the very essence of spring. She watched as the light played over his features, rendering him almost ethereal, his hair gleaming like spun gold amid the muted tones of the countryside. So different from the man she'd her sights on at Almack's.

She'd come so far toward her goal and yet felt never further removed from the truth.

Ashley breathed in the fresh scent of the earth and blossoms, a stark contrast to the smoky, bustling air of London. Here, everything felt alive, every rustle of leaves and distant bird call a reminder of the world's vibrancy. Yet, beneath this lively exterior, a quiet melancholy scraped at her, a gentle ache that refused to be ignored.

Despite this, Thomas's presence steadied her, his proximity both exhilarating and soothing. She turned her head slightly, taking in the slight rise and fall of his chest, the peacefulness etched on his face.

Nature here was a living, breathing entity, different from the manicured gardens of the city, offering a raw beauty and an unfamiliar sense of freedom. She'd miscalculated Thomas just like she'd underestimated nature. Not just the countryside but even her own. She was out of her depth.

Her heart caught in a delicate balance between mental longing and physical contentment. The countryside, with its untamed charm, seemed to promise new beginnings, and perhaps a different path for her heart to follow.

"It's pretty," Ashley said, breaking the silence to quiet the persistent echo of *What have I done* in her mind.

He tightened his hold. "Yes, you are."

She nudged him, half-smiling. "Oh, stop."

He chuckled, his hand trailing gently along her arm. "I tell no lies."

"Look there," she said, pointing at a leaf that dangled above. "That one looks like a horse. Or maybe a donkey." She paused, realizing, "Where's yours?"

"Lord Chesterton will find his way back to the stables." His fingers traced slow circles on her arm. "He's quite capable."

"Lord Chesterton?" She raised a brow. "I can't believe you put titles in front of all your horses."

"They deserve them," he replied with an earnestness that made her laugh.

"You must hold them in high esteem."

"They're a passion of mine. And I believe every passion deserves the highest importance. Don't you?"

She stilled. Revenge had been her passion when she'd learned of Linsey's arrival in town. But that fire felt dulled now, softened by spending time with this man. What she held onto now was fleeting—this moment, this connection, however long it lasted. She needed to savor it, while she still had it.

His words from earlier flashed through her mind.

My heart is yours.

It worked. Her revenge. She could walk away right this moment, and he would feel her loss. A surge of emotion clenched her heart. She'd set a trap for him, one designed to end in heartbreak, yet here she was, teetering on the edge, caught just as much as he was. She pinched the bridge of her nose, battling the growing feeling she couldn't shake. "Not all passions are equal."

"Perhaps," he said softly, "but all passions are meaningful."

Ashley laughed, almost too sharply, as if to deflect his words. "Remember that, Linsey."

"Thomas," he corrected, his eyes gleaming. "Call me Thomas. Or love, or darling, I don't mind."

"How about *Lord* Linsey?"

"Please, no." He laughed, and she managed a smile, though her mind was in chaos. She trusted him—at least in this moment. But beyond that? There was so much he didn't know. And if he ever discovered the truth...

His words kept replaying in her mind: *My heart is yours.*

The thought gnawed at her, reminding her of the supposed wedding looming ahead. None of this was ever supposed to happen. What about the sword she told Charlene about? Was she wielding it and falling on it at the same time?

She felt like she was being pulled into something beyond her control. She wasn't ready for this, to leave or to stay. Lying there with him... In that moment, nothing mattered; in the grand scheme of things, *everything* mattered.

"I think I might be falling in love with you," she wanted to say, but the words stuck in her throat. She needed time. Time to think, to decide what this meant, and to figure out what she wanted—no, needed—to do next.

Quite frankly, Ashley didn't know how to feel.

Her body thrummed. Her mind thrummed. Her heart thrummed.

This could be a trick of her own heart.

She couldn't make any sort of decision in this state.

"You're quiet," he murmured, brushing a lock of her hair back. "Is your mind racing, love?"

She arched a brow. "You can tell?"

He gave her a soft smile. "I'm good at races, especially reading them."

"Reading?" She laughed. "No one reads a race. One places bets."

He nodded, amused. "Only after you've weighed every factor—considered all you know about the horses."

She jabbed him playfully. "Are you saying I'm like one of your horses?"

Catching her hand, he grinned. "Not quite. I'm saying I know you well enough now to tell when your mind's running ahead."

She bit her lip. "Am I really that transparent?"

"Always have been," he teased, his gaze steady.

Her lips parted. No... "I am not *that* transparent."

He shook his head, amused. "Your boldness, your honesty—that's what drew me to you. I don't mind that there aren't many secrets between us."

Again, his words settled uncomfortably in her chest. He was wrong. She had a secret—a deep one that wasn't mere undiscovered knowledge. It was intentional, something she'd kept hidden from the start. She didn't know if she could bear to reveal it, to shatter this moment.

I have to tell him.

She had always prided herself on her strength and independence, yet here she was, on the brink of surrendering to something far more powerful than she'd ever imagined. It frightened her, this burgeoning affection, because it meant relinquishing control. But even as her mind rebelled, her heart whispered a different truth: that perhaps, in letting go she might find something even more profound than she had ever dared to dream.

So, she had to tell him.

She couldn't wait until that horrid duke blurted out her secret like he thought he had done to Linsey. That was no action of a friend, and she, who was just an obstacle to the duke, what would he do to her?

He'd wait for a pivotal moment to announce *her* wrongs.

That's probably why he spared her secret in the bookshop.

"We all have our secrets," she muttered.

He lifted her chin. "I quite like that there aren't any between us. There are only things we don't know about each other yet."

Well, that was certainly one way to put it. "By that definition a secret is only undiscovered knowledge."

"I can't dispute that, but secrets also have an intention behind them. An intention not to share, where undiscovered knowledge is that waiting to be discovered."

"Well, you certainly have an interesting point of view on the matter." And not a wrong one.

Tell him.

If she didn't, the knowledge of her deceit would fall upon him like a hammer. Yet admitting it now felt like leaping into an abyss, knowing there was no soft landing. Would he hate her? Would his affection crumble the moment he realized her intentions hadn't been pure? She hadn't been a different person, but her motives had been dark, and now they risked tainting everything between them.

Ashley didn't want to break his heart. Not anymore. But she couldn't help feeling that it was too late for that sentiment.

She would tell him. But not today.

Maybe tomorrow. Or the day after.

For now, she still had a bit of time.

THERE CAME A time in every man's life when he needed advice—the kind of advice that no friend with a pint in hand could provide, nor could any well-meaning lordly acquaintance. No, this was advice best dispensed by a woman, someone who understood matters of the heart with an insight that men simply…didn't. Unfortunately, Thomas had no sisters or mothers or aunts nearby, only the household staff.

Which was why he found himself slipping into the bustling kitchen.

He glanced around, blinking at the flurry of activity: copper pots clanged, meats sizzled on spits, and steam billowed up in fragrant clouds from pots boiling over the stoves. The air smelled rich and hearty, but Thomas still hesitated, feeling a bit like a misplaced cravat at a country fair.

Then Mrs. White, the head cook—a tall, formidable woman with hair tucked beneath her cap and a rolling pin in one hand and a ladle in the other—turned toward him, giving him a look sharp enough to slice bread.

"Lord Linsey," she said, arching an eyebrow as if his presence were some breach of kitchen law. "What brings you here?" But her eyes betrayed that she already knew.

She'd known him since he was a boy and read him like an open cookbook.

Thomas cleared his throat. "I, uh…I need some advice."

"Advice?" Mrs. White dusted off her hands on an already flour-dusted apron. "On what, pray tell?"

"Well, you see," Thomas began, glancing around to make sure no prying ears would overhear, "I've taken quite an interest in a lady. And I thought, given your…experience with certain spices and recipes…"

Mrs. White chuckled. "So, you came to me for advice on how to cook up a romance? Well, I suppose I can't fault you for recognizing talent," she said, gesturing to a wooden stool. "Sit, then, and let's see what can be done for you."

As Thomas gingerly took his seat, Sebastian strolled into the kitchen, freezing at the doorway when he saw his friend sitting beside the cook's worktable.

"Oh, this is rich. A love-struck lord seeking advice from Mrs. White of all people? I didn't believe your valet when he told me so. Continue. I'm just watching," he said, leaning against the doorway with a wicked grin.

Thomas gave him a deadpan look. "I thought you'd already left for town."

Sebastian shrugged. "Changed my mind. And, frankly, I wouldn't miss this for the world. Go on."

Mrs. White gave a loud cluck of her tongue, snapping Thomas back to attention. "If you do not want advice, I am a busy woman," she said, fixing her steely eyes on him. "Is this about the young lady you brought back? The one you are already betrothed to?"

"Just because we are betrothed doesn't mean I hold her heart." He had admitted he held affection for her, but she hadn't returned his sentiment.

It bothered him more than he cared to admit.

"Then, you'll need finesse. Romance is like a well-baked pie, my lord. You need to get the filling right, or it'll all fall to pieces. The crust on the outside isn't everything," Mrs. White said, dipping her ladle into a pot and stirring. "You want her to open up to you, yes? You need a warm atmosphere, and a gentle approach. Something sweet, but not too bold."

"She thrives on boldness," Thomas muttered, thinking back to their passionate encounter.

"The heart thrives on both. There is a balance to things. Always."

Sebastian snorted. "A pie, Thomas. You must woo your woman like a pie."

Mrs. White swatted at Sebastian's hand as he tried to reach for a tart cooling on the counter just like she used to when they were boys.

"Hush, you. Listen and learn, or leave." An earl and a marquess were nothing in Mrs. White's humble kitchen. She was the reigning queen here and Thomas was glad for it. Sebastian held up his hands in mock surrender, and Mrs. White continued. "Now, a lady needs to feel special. Do something small, unexpected. But personal." She eyed Thomas. "Anything of note she fancies?"

Thomas thought for a moment, picturing Ashley's reactions to different things. "She likes..." Oh boy, had he ever asked what she liked? "I suppose she likes to be surprised." At least, he sensed she did.

"Then that's what you use," Mrs. White said, nodding approvingly. "Surprise her."

Sebastian gave an exaggerated sigh. "Surprise her? That is rather anticlimactic. Really, Mrs. White? Our friend here needs a list with clear instructions."

"Then he must write them himself. It will do our *friend* good to figure out some recipes by himself," Mrs. White replied, unfazed. "And, Lord Linsey, you must speak to her heart. Ladies love to feel understood, to know that you see them truly. You do it well with me."

"What?" Seb grimaced.

"You see me for who I am, a woman older than you, perhaps wiser, and certainly one who holds you as dear as your grandfather knew I did. You see me beyond our differences in standing. Go and see your sweetheart and let her know who you are deep in your heart." She gave him a warm smile that nearly made Thomas choke, especially in combination with the memories of his grandfather. He'd gone in and out of Mrs. White's kitchen as if they'd been old friends. "Tell her what you like about her."

Thomas nodded, his mind racing. Well, he'd certainly done that much. "I've told her that I admire her boldness."

"Is that all you admire about her?" Mrs. White asked, pausing to add, "You should dig a bit deeper, my lord, and make sure what you say is true."

At that, Sebastian stifled a laugh. "This is Linsey we're talking about. Our man here might melt if he attempted that level of sincerity."

"Oh, Seb," Thomas replied, managing a grin. "I can be sincere. I *am* sincere."

Mrs. White gave them both a measuring look. "Whatever you do, keep it simple," she added, ladling a spoonful of something warm and savory, offering it to Thomas.

Thomas tasted the soup absentmindedly, nodding. "I can do that," he said, wiping his mouth. "Surprise her, keep it simple." A flash of insight lit his head. "A ring. I can surprise her with a ring."

Everyone in the kitchen fell silent, heads whipping to him.

"What?" he asked hesitatingly, feeling like he'd been caught with his hand in the sweets jar.

"You haven't given her a ring yet?" Sebastian asked. "No token of affection?"

"No, not yet. It's not typically done. Everything happened so fast, I thought I'd do it later."

"Aye," his friend mocked. "Your sincerity is palpable. Your resourcefulness, however..."

Mrs. White cleared her throat. "I would start with that, if I were you, my lord."

Thomas dragged a hand through his hair.

A hand clamped down on his shoulder. "Don't worry, old chap. Your lady doesn't mind penniless, so I daresay she doesn't mind a stingy husband either."

Thomas cursed.

Mrs. White handed Thomas a warm pastry. "Gentlemen, love may be as simple as bread and butter, or as complicated as a French pastry. Just be sure you're worth it."

You're worth it.

His cook certainly didn't mince words.

Him? He couldn't say. But she? She certainly was.

Chapter Nineteen

Two days later

Thomas enjoyed the late afternoon sun that cast a golden hue over his estate as he and Sebastian walked side by side, leading their horses back to the stables. "Something is wrong."

"What do you mean?" Sebastian asked, shooting him a quick glance.

"Lady Ashley is avoiding me," Thomas confessed, an edge of frustration creeping into his voice.

Sebastian arched a brow. "I haven't noticed anything. She's been her outspoken self at all the meals."

"At all the meals, yes, but she's been fleeing to her chamber afterward," Thomas said, absently patting his horse's neck as they approached the stable entrance. His steps slowed, the familiar environment feeling suddenly foreign.

"We've been training Lady Maude for two days, so don't read into things that might not be there," Sebastian reassured him.

Thomas frowned and shook his head. "No, she's definitely avoiding me." He handed the reins of his horse to a stable hand who had come to meet them. "On the outside, she's still all teasing grins and flirty words, but the moment we're alone, she makes an excuse and flees. It's as if...as if she's afraid to be alone with me." The memory of their shared moment beneath the tree played in his mind. Had he been too hasty?

Sebastian, having handed off his own horse, turned to face him fully, a thoughtful expression crossing his face. "Afraid? Of you?" he asked, skepticism lacing his words. "I find that hard to believe."

Thomas groaned, running a hand through his hair. "It's been like this since that afternoon. I was perhaps a touch too…" His voice trailed off as he leaned against the stable door, staring off into the distance.

"Are you not a bit too quick to imagine the worst? I still believe you're seeing something that isn't there." Sebastian crossed his arms, leaning casually against the stable wall.

Thomas let out a frustrated sigh.

"You've known her for a week," Sebastian pointed out.

"It's more than that," Thomas insisted.

Sebastian arched an eyebrow, clearly unconvinced.

"Don't look at me like that," Thomas muttered.

"Maybe she's just playing a game," Sebastian suggested with a shrug, his tone light. "Women enjoy keeping us on our toes, after all."

"A game?" Thomas echoed, his brow furrowing in confusion. "What kind of game?"

Sebastian smirked, pushing off the wall and taking a step closer. "Oh, you know, the kind where they test your patience, make you question everything you thought you knew about them. It's all part of their charm, really."

Thomas rolled his eyes, though a small smile tugged at the corners of his lips. "The thrill of uncertainty? You sound like a bad poet. Lady Ashley is not like that."

"All women are like that."

"You don't know many women, do you, old friend?"

"And you do?" Sebastian shot back, a challenge in his tone.

"More than you, apparently."

Sebastian grinned, clapping Thomas on the shoulder. "Perhaps you do, but it doesn't make me any less right. Lady Ashley seems to be a force to be reckoned with. If she's pulling away, it might not be because of anything you've done—it might be because she wants you to notice. She wants you to wonder, to question, to—"

"To drive me mad?" Thomas cut in, feeling exasperated. She'd been doing that from the very start.

"Precisely," Sebastian replied, his eyes sparkling with mischief. "And from the looks of it, she's succeeding admirably."

Thomas let out a heavy sigh, some of the tension in his shoulders finally starting to ease. But a strange feeling still churned in his gut. He was a man accustomed to action, to solving problems with a directness that had served him well dealing with matters of business. But this—this was a different kind of matter altogether, one that left him feeling utterly powerless. "You're enjoying this far too much," he muttered, though there was no real heat in his voice.

"Of course I am," Sebastian admitted with a broad grin. "It's not every day I get to see the great Earl of Linsey, renowned for his cool head and steady hand, brought to his knees by a mere slip of a woman."

"Careful, Seb," Thomas warned. "Lest I remind you of the time you were rendered speechless by that French duchess."

Sebastian winced, raising his hands in mock surrender. "Touché. But in all seriousness, Thomas, if you're truly concerned, then talk to her. Confront her—gently, of course. Find out what's on her mind."

"She's not a shy fawn. She's a lady."

"Show her your respect then. While you are at it, give the chit a jewel. Perhaps a ring."

Right. A *ring*.

He'd forgotten about it again.

But only because he'd been dwelling on her avoidance.

And it's not like he hadn't approached her with the intention of probing her mind. However, whenever they did converse, his thoughts tended to drift toward other matters, like her lips, and she wasn't much help either. Was it even possible to have a serious conversation when she set her mind to teasing him? Or flashed that impish smile of hers?

He felt utterly powerless in the face of that smile. But he had to at least try, or he would be endlessly plagued with worry.

"Tomorrow, maybe," he said to Sebastian. Tonight, he wanted to spend time in the stables. He wasn't going to get any sleep anyway. And one of the mares was about to give birth at any moment. If he were to speak to her, he would have to do it when he was clearer of mind.

Lady Ashley was unlike any woman he had ever known—fierce, independent, and utterly unpredictable. And it was precisely these qualities that made her so captivating...and so impossible to read. Which was why he had decided to name this foal after her.

Lady Ash.

That would be his surprise.

Whatever her reasons for avoiding him, he had to get to the bottom of it. He had to.

As he contemplated his next steps, a stable hand hurried toward him, waving a letter. "This just arrived, my lord."

Thomas frowned, taking the note, his heart sinking as he recognized the crest on the bright red seal. "It's from Paisley."

Sebastian leaned in, curiosity sparking in his gaze. "What does it say?"

Thomas broke the seal and unfolded the note, his hand tightening around the paper as he read the arrogant scrawl. "It's not what he says," he murmured, his voice tense as he glanced up, expression grave. "It's what he asks."

Sebastian's brow furrowed, his head tilting.

"What does he ask?" Thomas's grip tightened further.

At the upcoming Ascot's, I shall be accompanied by an esteemed acquaintance, one well-versed in the finer points of thoroughbreds. Our meeting will undoubtedly lead to the discussion of the fine horses that are destined to become my own as my companion possesses some rather enlightening insights regarding Lady Ashley Chaswick—insights that will surely tilt the scales of fortune in my favor concerning our little wager. Rest assured, this revelation will secure my triumph.

Regards,
Richard Ballard, the Duke of Paisley

"Who's this companion?" Thomas grimaced. "Is he attached?"

"Paisley attached? To his mirror image perhaps. A man without a heart can't give it. Also can't let a woman break it."

"How very Shakespeare of you, Seb. But better to love and l—" yet he couldn't get himself to say the words. "It has something to do with the wager, not women."

"What if it's not one or the other?" Sebastian asked. "I have started to ask some questions about Lady Ashley."

"Seb, this is awfully kind of you, but I trust her."

"You do perhaps. I, however, am your friend and it is my duty to look out for you."

"She's not a threat, Seb. She's wonderful."

"Wonderfully cunning if she knows and wonderfully naive if she doesn't."

Thomas didn't appreciate the insinuation. "Tread carefully when you speak about my future wife."

Sebastian cocked his head. "I'm just saying that there are some dark secrets in her family. Be careful."

"Just tell me what you know and let me decide what to do with it."

"All right. Sit." Sebastian started. "How well do you know your fiancée?"

My heart is all yours.

Those five words haunted her every waking hour.

At the start, she'd wanted him to lose everything he cherished, which at the time had been the horses he had held dear. But now, because of those five words, she didn't need to go that far. Couldn't bear to go that far.

So, why haven't you walked away yet?

No matter how tempting it might be to forget all that had happened between them, to let herself be swept up in the dangerous game they were playing, she wouldn't falter.

Not yet.

Not until she had what she came for.

And yet.

Thomas.

His name echoed in her mind like a lament.

Ashley peered out her window to where Thomas trained his horses with Sebastian. His jacket was draped carelessly over a fence post, his sleeves rolled up to reveal arms that, even from this distance, looked well-defined and powerful. She had a perfect vantage point from her chamber, shielded behind lace curtains that veiled her from the world outside. The sun was beginning its descent, casting a warm glow over the fields, though Thomas looked anything but relaxed.

Handsome.

No. *No, no, no!*

She couldn't think of him as handsome. But neither could she deny it. Handsome was hardly a strong enough word; the man was breathtaking. Truly dashing. Anyone who claimed otherwise was simply lying—to the world or to themselves. Fine, so he was perfect. But did he have to look so unbearably handsome while training a horse? He should have been a sweaty mess, but instead, he took her breath away.

Ashley sighed, pressing a hand to her chest. She'd been avoiding him for the past two days, struggling to clear her mind. She had to decide what to do next. A familiar carriage caught her eye as it rolled up the drive.

Her heart skipped—she recognized it instantly.

A wide grin broke across Ashley's face. Without a second thought, she dashed from her chamber, her skirts fluttering as she hurried down the stairs. By the time she reached the foyer, the footman had just opened the door, and her two friends were stepping down from the carriage that had halted before the castle.

"Charlene! Sera!"

"Ashley!" Charlene replied with a bright smile, sweeping forward with Sera by her side. She laughed as they gathered each other into a spirited group hug.

Ashley pulled back, surprised but delighted. "I didn't think you'd arrive so quickly after I sent the note!"

"Yes, well, we've been waiting on pins and needles ever since you left," Sera said, a knowing smile lighting her face.

Ashley could hardly contain her happiness. She hadn't seen her friends in ages! Well, not so long ago, perhaps, but it certainly felt like ages upon ages. So much had happened since they last had tea together the day—Ashley swallowed hard—Thomas proposed.

Sera suddenly laughed. "I believe we've rendered our friend speechless, Char!"

Quite right. So much had happened that Ashley wasn't sure whether to blurt it all out at once or order tea and reveal it bit by bit.

"Speechless, indeed! And here I was thinking you might have forgotten us altogether. Did you know that we had to find out about your engagement from *The Times*?"

"You did not." Ashley tilted her head.

"But your mother did, and she was seething. Told mine all about it," Charlene said over her shoulder.

"I'm afraid she will pay your betrothed her respects," Sera said with the look a doctor had when delivering the news of a fatal diagnosis. "You should insist your father accompany her."

"He hasn't been able to control her in a long time." Never actually. But Ashley didn't have time to worry about her parents now.

Charlene's gaze swept over the estate grounds. "So, where is your betrothed?"

"You mean my *foe*," Ashley muttered, unsure how best to refer to the earl in front of her friends.

Charlene and Sera exchanged a knowing look, and Sera remarked, "That is not the look one gives one's foe."

No, of course not. It was the look one gave to a foe turned—well, not quite a lover, but something else that couldn't yet be explained.

Ashley sighed. "It's hard to explain."

"Do not tell me you've fallen for the earl's charm?" Sera asked, amusement dancing in her eyes.

Charlene looked back with astonishment. "The earl has charm?"

Ashley crossed her arms, feigning indignation. "I haven't fallen for *anything*." *Just everything*.

"Ashley!" Sera's tone was gentle but firm. "You do remember why you approached him, don't you?"

"As if I could forget." She could practically feel the weight of it, a cloud looming overhead that refused to blow away, despite the breezes sweeping the estate grounds.

"Then it's good we arrived when we did." Charlene raised a brow. "What happened?"

Ashley swallowed and braced herself. "We kissed."

Both her friends' eyes widened in shock. "You kissed?" Charlene asked, her voice just above a whisper.

We did more than that, Ashley thought, though she couldn't bring herself to say it aloud. She felt half miserable about the entire affair since she felt like her heart had become a fickle mess, and she had started to question her heart ever since she met Linsey.

Sera's narrow watchful gaze didn't miss a beat. "And what else happened?" She always had a way of seeing right through her.

Ashley's cheeks flushed, and she glanced around before saying, "We...may have done a bit more than that, but nothing that would ruin me!" she quickly added, seeing both their expressions turn wider than teacup saucers. *Though, that part might not be entirely true.* From the moment she met him, Thomas had been unraveling her carefully built defenses. Slowly, persistently, and undeniably.

"You left in a carriage alone with him. That would do the trick of ruination," Sera said.

Well, the night in the hayloft would, too. But Ashley decided not to dwell on the exact time it had happened. "So what, then I am ruined. It's a very fragile matter this virtue and all."

Sera didn't seem as phased as Charlene, who took a step back as if ruination were contagious.

"What happened to the handsome Mr. Critton? And what about your revenge?" Charlene asked, her voice hushed. "Heaven knows, after all we did to get you introduced!"

"Things are a bit more complicated than they seem."

"How so?" Sera prompted.

Ashley exhaled, glancing at the grassy path. "I asked him if he'd ever run anyone out of town, and he denied it."

"And you believe him?" Charlene asked, her brows drawn together.

"Well...I *want* to. He's rather honest, in both words and actions."

"But you can't know for certain," Sera said, her tone edged with doubt.

"No, I can't. Honestly, I don't know what to do."

"Break off the engagement," Sera suggested.

Ashley's head snapped back. "What?"

"Think about it, Ashley." Sera's tone softened as she placed a hand on Ashley's arm. "The only reason you became engaged to him was because you thought he drove Jordan away. If he didn't, then you're engaged to him for nothing."

"And got ruined for nothing," Charlene added, her mouth a flat line of resignation.

"Well, not, erm, *nothing*," Ashley muttered under her breath.

"Unless you suddenly *want* to marry him?" Charlene asked, brow raised. "In which case, I'd have to question your sanity."

Ashley chuckled dryly. She was questioning it herself already.

"He doesn't know about Jordan, does he?" Sera asked.

Ashley shook her head. "I have to tell him, though."

Charlene nodded decisively. "Yes, you do. And I'd suggest being as direct as you were that night at the ball."

Without warning, Ashley blurted, "He confessed his heart." She wrung her hands.

Both friends' eyes widened again. "He did *what*?" they exclaimed in unison.

Ashley nodded, a small smile tugging at her lips despite herself.

"What did you do?" Charlene demanded. "Wait—did you use that book? Does it work?" She glanced back toward the carriage. "Where's the chapter on making men fall in love?"

Ashley shrugged, wrapping her arms around herself. "The book and my charm don't exactly get along." And also, she'd forgotten about it. She didn't even know what she'd done to deserve his heart, which only left her questioning everything between them.

"Well," Sera said, folding her arms with a grin, "it's a good thing we are here to help you through this."

Through love? Ashley didn't know if anyone but Thomas could help her and yet she couldn't face him alone.

"We'll help you with whatever decision you need to make. But it seems clear you should tell him soon," Sera added. Such a good friend.

Innocent and clueless, but so dear.

Ashley tipped her head back, sighing. These days, all her boldness, which she'd had since the moment she'd approached him at that ball, seemed to vanish whenever he was near.

Charlene glanced over her shoulder toward the stables. "And who's that man I saw at the stables when we passed?" She shaded her eyes. "Handsome, isn't he?"

Ah, she must be referring to Linsey's friend Sebastian. Handsome, certainly. *And just as annoying,* Ashley thought, recalling that overheard conversation when they'd first met. But at least Thomas would have a friend at his side when she told him the truth—just as she now had hers.

She glanced back toward the stables, steadying herself. *I should wait for him to return from the stables.*

Then she would confess.

Chapter Twenty

THE SKY WAS awash in tender dawn hues as Thomas emerged from the stall where the mare had given birth. As he stood there, the crisp morning air wrapped around him, carrying the faint scent of fresh hay mingled with the earthy aroma of the stable. The warmth of the newborn foal brushing against his hand lingered, a reminder of life's perpetual cycle. It was an event he'd witnessed countless times, yet today it stirred something deeper within him. Watching the foal struggle to stand on wobbly legs, he couldn't ignore the parallel to his own life.

His line would not continue with horses alone. For years, they had been his sole focus, the creatures understanding his unspoken words and sharing his quiet moments. But now, with Ashley's laughter echoing faintly from the house, he realized his priorities were shifting. Not away from the horses—no, they were a part of him—but it was as if there was suddenly room for more.

Ashley's presence in his life had awakened a desire for something beyond the realm of races and thoroughbreds. He imagined a future where her laughter filled not just fleeting mornings but entire days, a life where their bond grew as naturally as the foal finding its feet. The thought warmed him more than the rising sun ever could.

Standing there, surrounded by the gentle sounds of the waking world, Thomas felt an unfamiliar but welcome sense of expansion within his chest. There was space now for dreams he'd never dared to dream and for a life where Ashley was by his side, sharing in both the quiet and the chaos of his days.

Don't be too greedy.

But he was. He wanted it all.

The crisp air filled his lungs, keeping him grounded to some extent. He'd spent the night with the foal, carefully watching over the baby and its mother. Yet, despite the magic of newborn life, it was Ashley who filled his thoughts, gnawing at him with questions he couldn't shake. What else would this spring bring besides this new wave of feelings?

He dipped a cloth into the bucket left by one of the stable hands, the cold water jolting his senses as he splashed it over his face and bare torso, hoping to cool the pang of pressing impatience that wouldn't let him be. Had he crossed some invisible line? Been too open, too eager?

Greedy, greedy, greedy.

He thought of Paisley's ominous note. Damn bastard. He didn't believe it was any more than a tactic to rattle him.

He forced himself to focus on the task at hand, though it was impossible to shake the persistent image of her face from his mind. But as if the mere thought had conjured her, she appeared just beyond the stable doors in a frilly blue dress the color of the little forget-me-nots dotting his estate. Just like the flowers, he wanted Ashley everywhere. He'd lay his estate at her feet if it meant wooing her, for he didn't know how to bare his heart more than he had. He didn't understand but wanted to, for her gaze held an expression he couldn't quite recognize, something he'd never seen from her before.

Yet still breathtaking.

"Ashley." Her name slipped from his lips, his pulse quickening.

"Did you sleep in the stables?" Her gaze flickered over his torso, lingering a bit before lifting back to meet his eyes.

His lips almost twitched.

"I've been occupied. My apologies if I've been a poor host," he said, snatching up a towel and slinging it over his shoulder.

"You haven't," she replied softly, her eyes locking onto his, unwavering. "You've allowed me time to welcome my friends."

"That's a generous way to put it. But as the future countess, you may well entertain whomever you wish." Did that sound as haughty and stupid to her as it had in his head?

Do better, Thomas.

He took a careful step forward, inhaling deeply. Communicate—that had been one of the pieces of advice from his cook, hadn't it? It was worth a try. "Have I made you uncomfortable in any way?" He hoped he didn't sound too insecure because he felt like a green boy out of his depth.

"Why would you ask me that?"

He arched a brow. "It seems that you've been avoiding me, unless I've misunderstood." Thomas combed a hand through his hair, studying her, and hoping he had misunderstood.

Her lip caught in hesitation before she shook her head, a hint of a smile breaking through. "You've not misunderstood, and yet I sense you have also misunderstood."

Thomas stilled, thrown by the contradiction. "So...you *have* been avoiding me?"

"I won't deny it," she said simply. "But I can assure you that you've misunderstood the reason."

Thomas took a step closer. "And what is this reason?"

She brushed a fingertip over her nose, then tilted her head, her gaze steady on him. "The pace at which we're moving."

Thomas stilled. "Is it too fast?"

"It's both too fast and too slow," she said, her voice growing softer, but no less certain.

Bloody hell. What was he supposed to make of that? "Well, that's...quite the conundrum," he said, his voice low, as if to contain the feelings that were stirring dangerously close to the surface. He wanted to get closer, to feel her near. He wanted to *possess*. He wanted to be as greedy as she allowed.

"Conundrum?" She laughed. "Interesting that you would use this word."

"How so?"

"It's the word I've attached to you."

She had? What made her believe him to be a conundrum? Because of the pace? "Well, I don't see a problem with this conundrum."

"Oh?" Her breath hitched, the single syllable laden with curiosity and something else—something that made his pulse quicken.

He reached out, his fingers brushing a stray lock of her hair, tucking it gently behind her ear. "Ashley, love, I feel exactly the same way."

You do? flashed in her widened eyes. "You mean we're moving both too fast and too slow?"

"Yes." He couldn't hold back his grin.

She laughed, then shook her head as if baffled by him. "Now I'm a little uncertain of what to say next."

He smiled, tipping his head. "Somehow, I doubt that's true."

She cocked her head to the side. "Why does it feel like you're in the mood for a faster pace at the moment?"

Mrs. White had said to keep it simple. Honesty was the simplest form of communication, wasn't it?

"Because I am." His eyes bore into hers. He wanted to bridge the distance he sensed between them. "I'm in the mood to be greedy."

"Greedy?"

He studied her, the morning light catching the brilliant blue of her eyes. "Have you ever been so greedy that you wanted to think only of yourself and no one else? Even for just a moment," he said, his voice growing more intense. He cupped her cheek. "Or a morning?"

"I have." No hesitation. "I feel that way right now."

"Then shall we both be greedy?" Thomas held his breath, waiting.

She glanced over her shoulder to the stable yard and back to him, as if considering the likelihood of watchful eyes. But she seemed to dismiss the thought as quickly as it had come, and, just for a second, tilted her cheek into his palm.

"This greediness…would it include something between what we've done already and something that we have yet to do?" Her voice dropped, filled with curiosity that seemed to mirror his. The spark he'd come to love entered her eyes again.

"You sound as if you might want to test those boundaries."

She looked up, lips twitching. "And if I did?"

He chuckled, feeling his pulse thunder in response. "Then trust me," he said simply, his hand finding hers, their fingers interlacing as naturally as breathing. "Trust that I will always cherish you, always respect the boundaries we set together. Trust that my admiration for you is vast enough to wait. Or not. I am at the mercy of your pace."

"Trust…" Her voice softened, as if testing the sound of it in her mind. For a moment, she hesitated, but then determination settled her features as she squeezed his hand, her eyes shimmering. "What if you should not trust me?"

"What if I shouldn't trust clouds from blocking the sun and pouring rain over the lands? I don't live in terms of what-ifs, love. Why not just enjoy the moment?"

"Then…" A bright smile spread across her face. "Then let's be greedy."

Bloody hell, yes.

Thomas leaned in, his lips ghosting over hers in the lightest of kisses. The day was waking up, and so, it seemed, was his heart.

ASHLEY'S LIPS TINGLED with warmth and anticipation as Linsey kissed her. *I am doing it again,* she thought fleetingly. She hadn't come here for this—but with this man, her resolve seemed to shatter like glass with the barest touch.

Not the *barest* touch.

All night, she had paced the floor of her chamber, waiting for him to return from the stables. She had listened for any sound in the hall, her eyes fixed on the stable yard, where a lone flickering light had betrayed his vigil. When the dawn broke in a sliver on the horizon, she made up her mind: if he wouldn't come to her, she'd find him.

But before entering the stables, her purpose had nearly flown right out of her mind. There he was, splashing cold water over his face and chest, looking like some ancient, sculpted Adonis brought to life, oblivious to the torment that had kept her awake.

And what a sight.

Her annoyance with him, so calm and unbothered while she'd been in turmoil, coiled tighter in her chest. Yet her heart still fluttered at the sight of him, so real and so maddeningly at ease. So when he spoke of being greedy, of wanting to be selfish just this once, it felt like her carefully guarded restraint incinerated. *Poof!*

Whatever purpose she'd come with seemed to dissolve in the heat between them. She reached up, pushing her hands into his already tousled hair, and pulled him closer.

It wasn't their first kiss, but holy saints, it was the first time her whole body felt *this* on fire. Every inch of her absorbed the feel of him, all solid muscle and intensity. She'd never expected to like this man, let alone be so thoroughly swept away by him.

You are in so much trouble, Ashley.

But oh, trouble had never felt this good.

And the man could *kiss*.

His mouth claimed hers with a hunger that made her toes curl, as though they were the last two people left in the world. As though nothing mattered except for them, this moment. Even the snorting of the horses and the sharp scent of hay couldn't pierce the spell. She felt completely, deliciously lost.

He drew back, his lips hovering close to hers, his voice a low murmur. "Do you wish to slow the pace?"

"Just keep kissing me," she managed, breathless.

Let's be greedy.

She'd come to tell him the truth, to warn him before the Duke of Paisley could twist it to his advantage. But that need was smothered in the heat of his touch, her body, perhaps even a bit of her heart, screaming louder than her mind. Her hands left his hair to explore the bare muscles of his back, her fingertips grazing the strong lines beneath his skin, cherishing every inch she could reach.

Tendons rippled beneath her fingers.

She suddenly found herself being lifted. With a gasp, her arms circled his neck as he carried her to a bundle of hay, sitting down with her cradling his lap, lips never leaving hers as he continued to devour her.

He gathered her closer, pressing her flush against him. Ah, his skin. So warm. So solid. She could feel his desire growing, and a shred of reason sparked in her mind. Pulling back just enough to meet his gaze, she inhaled deeply. "Breathing is important, you know."

"Nothing is more important than you," he whispered, his eyes flashing. "No time for breathing on my end."

She laughed softly. "I'd rather not be the death of you. Tell me, is this where the pace slows just before ruin?"

"There's much more." He groaned, shifting slightly. "But if we go much further, I might not stop. And just so that you are aware, love, there is no ruin in my arms."

Oh, but that was precisely where her ruin lay. "Kissing is such a temptation for you?"

He gritted his teeth. "It's already testing my control."

Her grin turned wicked. "Men, so easily undone."

"And how would you know?" His hands tightened around her, his tone low.

"It's the glint in your eyes," she teased, tracing her fingers lightly along his neck.

A deep, shaky breath escaped him. "You enjoy playing with fire."

"I enjoy you," she replied, her voice a soft purr. She rested her hands on his shoulders, bracing herself. "We can slow the pace, if that's what you'd prefer... A more mellow pace."

His gaze darkened. "Isn't this what you came here for?" She glanced at the cold-water pump.

She had come for a conversation, yes, but the meaning of it had slipped further from her grasp with each embrace. "Talking requires, well, it requires distance." She shifted slightly, smirking. "Hard to manage that here."

He leaned against the trough and she was all but on his lap. "Do you want to leave?"

"No," she murmured, nestling closer. "This is rather comfortable, yet also a bit uncomfortable."

"Full of contradictions today, aren't you?"

"It's a special talent for us women."

A low chuckle rumbled from him. "You're set on snapping my control, aren't you?"

She laughed. "And what gives you that impression?"

"Your eyes," he replied, his tone softening. "No man could mistake the glint of mischief in them."

Her smile turned impish, and a perceptible note of said mischievousness rose in her. "Men are so easily unstrung."

His hands spanned her waist, giving a gentle squeeze. "There it is again. *Men,* as if I'm not here."

"Women too."

"Then why don't I believe you're just like them?"

"Do I seem like a marble statue to you? Even those shatter when they fall."

"No, indeed. I only mean that I see a strength in you that's rare."

Her grin widened. "Well, I am one of a kind."

"That, you are."

She leaned in close, their noses almost touching. "Why aren't you kissing me anymore?"

He arched a brow, the corner of his mouth lifting up. "You were the one complaining about air."

"I've gotten my fill." *Now, I want more of you.* Ashley ignored the other, more practical voice in her head. The thought of confessing her purpose now, with his arms wrapped around her, felt absurd. Yes, if ever there was a time to slow the pace and have a conversation, this would be the moment. But she'd long since lost the thread of the original conversation she'd intended to have. Once he knew her true motives, he'd never look at her the same again—if at all.

This is not the time.

She wanted this moment for herself, a little longer. Looking into his intense eyes, she banished the impulse to confess, deciding to be a bit greedier.

"Should we move somewhere a bit more private?"

Later, she'd tell him later.

Chapter Twenty-One

S OMEWHERE MORE PRIVATE
He could arrange that.

"Don't these doors lock?" Ashley pointed to the stalls. "I don't mind the hay."

Minx!

"They're Dutch doors. They don't lock from the inside. Only the bottom has a latch."

Thomas stood up with Ashley in his arms, eliciting a startled yelp as he strode toward the carriage house. The woman truly had a talent to unnerve his very existence. He'd even missed the moment to announce the name of the foal. But that might be for the best. He didn't have his grandmother's ring with him.

There were too many people at the house. But the carriage house was the perfect place. Close. Secluded. Clean.

He set her down only when he reached a sleek carriage, opening the door with a flourish. Gently, he took her hand and helped her step inside. This counted as private, right? The interior enveloped them in luxury and warmth, with plush seats draped in soft woolen blankets and the faint scent of cedar lingering in the air.

The carriage house was quiet, save for the soft rustling of Ashley's dress as she settled onto the shiny leather seats. Thomas followed her in, the air thick with a palpable energy that hummed between them. It was as if the very space they occupied had come alive, each heartbeat resonating with the weight of the pace they had chosen to ride. He could feel the spellbinding pull from Ashley, a magnetic force that tugged at him, drawing him closer, igniting a fire in the pit of his stomach.

"There's so much room," she marveled, stroking the soft leather.

"The cabins were bigger a few decades ago. My grandfather once said my grandmother's dress would take up the entire seat when she dressed for the Ascot."

"I can just imagine." Ashley sprawled on the seat, leaning back with an inviting smile. "This space is just perfect."

Something stirred in Thomas's chest—a sense of achievement. He'd not told her yet about his booth at the Royal Ascot, but he couldn't wait to show off not only his horses but also the pride of his life: Ashley.

With a decisive thud, he shut the door behind them, the sound echoing his anticipation of sharing this part of himself with her. He settled in close next to her, the cabin feeling even more intimate than its size suggested.

Yes, it was just perfect.

His eyes traced the elegant curve of her neck, the way her hair cascaded over her shoulders, and the subtle rise and fall of her chest as she breathed. "Ashley," he whispered, his voice low and rough. He reached up to brush a stray lock of hair from her face, his fingers lingering against her skin. Her lips parted slightly, and he caught the flicker of desire in her eyes that mirrored his own. "Is this comfortable enough?"

"Very."

He leaned in, his breath warm against her cheek as he brought his lips close to her ear. "I've wanted to do this for so long," he confessed, the words a mere murmur. She shivered at his touch, swaying closer to him as if pulled by an invisible thread.

Without another word, he closed the gap between them, capturing her lips in a kiss that was both tender and undeniably urgent. Her response was immediate, arms winding around his neck as she pulled him closer. Thomas deepened the kiss, every movement igniting a fire that spread through his blood.

One of his hands slid down her back, pulling her against him while the other cradled her face. Ashley's fingers tangled in his hair, pressing closer as the kiss grew more frantic. Resting a knee on the cushioned seat, Thomas hovered over her, the carriage rocking slightly with their movements. His lips trailed down her neck, and she gasped. Her hands clutched his shoulders, pulling him closer, as if she couldn't bear even an inch of distance between them.

"Thomas," she breathed, her voice a whisper filled with need. Her hands roamed, exploring his torso and trailing over the ridges of his muscles. Her touch felt like a cool breeze on a hot summer day—welcome and tender. With a low moan, his mouth found hers again in a kiss that was both searing and consuming. Every touch, every caress, spoke of the passion that had been building, finally unleashed in this stolen moment.

Not enough.

Would it ever be?

"I want you to know that I have fallen in love with you, too!"

"Ashl—"

She put her finger on his lips. "Please hear me out. No matter what happens, please know that this is real. All of me. And I love you."

A flicker of worry seemed to darken her gaze but then she squeezed her eyes shut and pressed her lips onto his.

Thomas lost himself in her kiss, pushing all doubt aside until there was nothing but the heat of their bodies, the taste of her sweetness, and the undeniable connection that weaved through them with each touch.

They kissed for a while and Thomas forgot the time. But when he pulled away again, the glint in her gaze sparked brighter than before.

When her fingers brushed against his stomach, he inhaled sharply. She hooked her fingers into his waistband, a provocative move that sent a jolt through him.

"What are you doing?" he managed, his voice thick with desire.

"I want to see," she replied, gently tightening her grip.

Thomas swallowed hard, unsure how to respond. Yet again. But then, driven by an instinct he couldn't control, he lifted his hips, granting her access. In one swift motion, she slipped her hand around his erection.

This was going to be harder than he thought. The sensation of her hand gripping him felt so good, yet he'd vowed to himself not to go all the way. How he wanted to plunge into her and satisfy the aching need throbbing in him.

No.

He couldn't do that.

He had too much respect for her, for her station, and for the sanctity of her virginity. The pleasure pounding in his imagination was reserved for their wedding night, and he'd get a special license to ensure that day came sooner rather than later. Or he could just beg her to elope.

Her fingers squeezed around him. "It's much harder than I thought it would be."

"Take it, Ashley," he bit out, torn between wanting to yank her hand away to guide it for his pleasure and allowing her to continue. "Explore at your leisure."

"What? Weren't you the one who said to be greedy? That you would follow my pace?"

Yes, he had, damn it.

Why had he said that again?

He certainly hadn't meant *this*. He seemed to be the only one in splendid agony here. How had the tables turned so dramatically?

Gentleman though he was, he couldn't claim to be a saint. She wanted such a pace, he would not deny her.

With one hand, he supported his weight above her, so that she was sprawled on the seat beneath him, and with the other, he unfastened the laces of his breeches. She looked down when his erection sprang free, but she didn't say anything. Her smile, however, was telling; she wasn't intimidated by his size or the throbbing veins that pulsed with their own wicked mind. In fact, she seemed eager to explore.

Thomas kicked off his boots and let his breeches fall, trampling the fabric on the cabin floor. Naked, he settled one leg on the bench with the other kneeling beside Ashley. If he hadn't proposed already, this would be the perfect position. Except this was more than a proposal; it was an offering—of his body as much as his heart and soul.

She bit her lower lip, staring at him intently, and Thomas shifted under her gaze.

"I'm at your pleasure," he rasped, unsure whether to go fast or slow from here. But her stare was driving him wild.

Her gaze dropped, using both hands to touch him. She started at his chest, moving down to his upper arms, then to his elbows and wrists. When she reached his hand, he lifted her right hand, placing a gentle kiss on her palm before guiding it to his aching member.

"Isn't this what you wanted?"

Her lips lifted. And she explored. Oh, how she explored. "It's hard, but it's soft on the surface, too." She furrowed her brow when she cupped his balls, and he nearly roared with pleasure. But he sucked in his lips, nodding instead.

"Is this part of your body a bone?"

He cursed. "More like a rod," he rasped.

"A rod, you say?" she said, sliding down the seat for a closer look. "Truly?"

Oh no! Don't go down, oh!

Thomas held his breath as she continued to study him, her finger tracing the tip before enveloping him again. "It's not a bone. No bones inside."

He was losing his ability to form coherent sentences.

She squeezed again—too gently. He placed a hand over hers, showing her how hard she could press and glide. Rubbing was good—oh so good.

He flinched when her nail lightly scraped his shaft.

She paused, concern flickering in her gaze. "Are you all right?"

"Yes," Thomas rasped, almost beyond desperate. "Don't stop."

"I didn't mean to scratch you. I'm sorry," she said, bowing to place a tender kiss on his length.

Thomas looked down, his breath hitching.

This was awful. Absolutely terrible. And no way in hell he was pushing her away. His vision blurred for an instant, and his head nearly dropped backward from the sheer pleasure of her kiss.

"You don't mind if I kiss you here, right?" she asked, and kissed him there again, looking up at him with wide, innocent eyes.

Little wench!

"Ashley," he all but groaned in a plight. *Stop. Don't stop. Yes. No.* His mind couldn't rest on one singular answer.

She took the tip of his member in her mouth, swirling her tongue around it, and Thomas forgot to breathe. He forgot everything. Ashley was all-consuming for him, his everything. She kissed his cock like she kissed his mouth.

Wait.

Surely, he shouldn't be the only one enjoying this. What sort of gentleman was he to have a lady pleasure him without reciprocating? Thomas wrapped an arm around her, lifting her back onto the seat. The slight coolness on his cock reminded him just how deeply she'd taken him. She was magnificent.

Her brows furrowed.

"I don't mind that, love, but only if I may return the favor."

"What?"

"Lie back," he instructed, and she did, her brows smoothing out to give way for curiosity. He guided one of her legs onto the settee, then removed her slippers. He trailed his hands along her stockings, moving toward the center between her legs. To his indescribable surprise, she helped him by lifting her petticoat out of the way, bunching it under her middle.

That was all the permission he needed to move forward with a renewed pace. Thomas climbed over her as her hands wandered to his hips, her fingers tracing over the taut muscles at his lower back.

"You're so hard everywhere," she murmured.

"Do you like it?" He looked down at her, his own desire mirrored in her expression.

She nodded, hands drifting lower to caress his member. He groaned, reaching up to carefully slide her unmentionables down—and off—her long, graceful legs. The garters and lace edging of her stockings added a sweet allure, a hint of innocence woven into her tempting form. His heart raced.

When he parted her folds and leaned down for a lingering kiss, her body tensed slightly before she arched toward him, granting full access. And he took it, gently aiding his access with his fingers. He began with gentle licks, nibbled the sensitive bud, and slowly pressed a finger into her warmth, his breath catching at her softness.

She gasped at first. Down there, however, she was twitching around his finger. Then she mirrored him. She took him—he nearly choked when he looked down, for he'd never seen anything more erotic—in her mouth with delicate kisses and small, exploratory licks along his length. He had to remember to breathe and closed his eyes for just a second. When he looked down again, he found her cupping his balls, and he had to will himself to keep from fainting on the spot.

"Ashley..." he managed, voice hoarse with restraint.

"Tell me if you like it," she whispered.

He had to shake his head against the surge of pleasure. No woman had ever…and she'd somehow just known. He gave in, deepening his own kisses, letting her guide him as they explored one another in a rhythm that felt natural, a shared exploration of pleasure.

Thomas found himself lost in the rhythm of her lips tracing his length as he returned to her own delicate center. The world faded as he dove deeper, her moans feeding his urgency. With her hips rising to meet him, he dared to slip three fingers inside, feeling her tighten around him, her pulse in sync with his own.

Finally, he lifted himself to face her, meeting her flushed, parted lips in a searing kiss. She melted into him, her own passion blending with his. His fingers moved faster, drawing a heady response from her as she arched beneath him, her hands gripping onto the brass lantern nearby for support.

Instead, he let go of her and grabbed his cock in the other hand. He needed the release; there was just too much pent-up heat raging through him. And for the first time in what he hoped would be a lifetime with the passionate beauty in his arms, they climaxed together.

WHAT HAVE I done? What have I done? What have I done?

Ashley collapsed into his arms, her body melting against his warmth as the enormity of what just happened settled over her.

This had to be the boldest, most scandalous thing she'd ever done. She wasn't just ruined, she was wanton. She glanced around the carriage, reassured by the thick velvet curtains, drawn closed, preserving their privacy. A breath escaped her in relief. Not that she worried about prying eyes, but some part of her realized she'd crossed a line she could never uncross.

But why did he feel so wonderfully and amazingly good? She laid her cheek against his chest, listening to the strong, unruly beat of his heart. His breath rose and fell beneath her, grounding her in this shared moment, reminding her she was not alone. Gently, he ran his fingers through her hair, his touch so soft, as if he, too, wanted to cherish every bit of this closeness.

"You look like a satisfied cat," he said with a lazy chuckle.

"Shouldn't you have some metaphor about a horse at the ready?" she teased, not quite able to stifle her smile.

"Not everything in my life is about horses, you know."

"Oh? I'll believe that when I see it."

"You already saw it—or weren't you looking?" he quipped, a glint of mischief in his eyes. An expression she loved on him.

She let out a soft laugh. "Well, since you asked, I do feel a bit like a satisfied cat. I might not move for hours. It's not every day a lady finds herself such a…cozy pillow."

"Comfortable, are you?" He arched a brow, his tone carrying an amused challenge. "I'd have thought a man needed a bit more than comfort to keep a lady's attention."

"You're more than comfortable, Thomas," she murmured, a playful purr in her voice. "But don't let it go to your head. A gentleman should always maintain some humility."

"Humility?" He tilted his head, pretending to ponder. "Not sure that's within my skill set."

"Then it's never too late to learn," she countered. "You've proven plenty of times how adaptable you can be."

"True," he conceded, leaning back with a contented sigh. "Though I must confess, I've never quite mastered matters of the heart."

"That might not be such a terrible thing," she replied, a thoughtful edge creeping into her voice.

After a pause, he murmured, "But I do know how to treat a lady."

She let out a warm, soft laugh. There was no denying that, after today. "Though now that you mention it, I am curious about something."

"And what curiosity is that?" he asked, watching her with a faint smile.

"Well," she began, her voice softening as she pondered her question, "you have such a profound love for horses. Where did that begin?"

A thoughtful silence fell between them before he answered. "No one's ever asked me that."

"Well, I'm hardly 'no one,' now, am I?" She gave him a cheeky grin.

"Minx," he said with a soft laugh, his eyes twinkling. "My father, as well as my grandfather, were avid horsemen." A hint of nostalgia crept into his tone. "They passed that love on to me. I still remember the first time Father let me ride on my own. I couldn't have been more than three, but I felt like I was on top of the world."

"Three?" Her eyes widened with surprise. "That's so young! Weren't you afraid?"

"Afraid?" He shook his head, smiling at the memory. "Not in the least. Back then, I thought I was invincible. Of course, I had no idea what I was doing, but it didn't matter. All I knew was I loved the freedom—the idea that I could go wherever I wanted."

Ashley smiled at the image of a young, fearless Thomas, brimming with confidence. "I can just see it now—this little boy with a wild grin, holding on for dear life." She nudged him. "What happened to that fearless boy?"

He pinched her waist with a mock glare. "Oh, he's still here. Just, perhaps, a bit more realistic."

"More realistic, yes," she agreed. "But still fearless in many ways."

"Well, then, don't we make quite the pair?" he murmured, his gaze never leaving hers.

"We do, don't we?"

"My father taught me all I know about horses," he continued, his voice softer now. "He always said they were the most honest creatures. They never lie, never pretend."

Ashley stilled, his words blowing straight into her chest. "Unlike people," she murmured, almost to herself. "People do lie and pretend."

"Exactly." He rested his chin atop her head, drawing her closer. "That's why I trust horses far more easily than people."

A bittersweet ache rose within her, a chill she couldn't quite shake. "Well, I may be a bit outspoken, even prone to holding a grudge, but I'm afraid I'm not quite as noble as your thoroughbreds." She tried to keep her tone light, but how could she when she still harbored a secret. A secret that would further validate this very belief of his.

"Your parents must have had a rather interesting time raising you, impeccable breeding and all," he said cupping her right breast.

She smiled ruefully. "Quite right. I've always been this way. Even as a child, I never could keep quiet when I thought something needed to be said. My poor mother despaired of ever making a proper lady of me. I've had more than my fair share of scoldings for being too bold, too opinionated. But I couldn't help it—I've always believed that if something is worth saying, it's worth saying loudly."

"I wouldn't change a thing about you," he murmured, his gaze softening. "Your fire, your willingness to speak your mind... It's one of the things I love most about you."

If only he knew. If only he knew the things she couldn't say yet, the words that stayed locked inside. Her gaze flickered downward, lips parting as though to speak, but no words came.

I am not as good as you imagine, Thomas.

And yet, somewhere in the back of her mind, she wondered if she could be that person he saw. Were her friends right? Could she undo the damage and marry him because they both wanted it and not because he had to?

"So," he said after a pause, drawing her from her thoughts, "what else should I know about the formidable Lady Ashley?"

"Oh, there are plenty of things, but I'm afraid I'm not going to make it easy for you. Many you'll have to discover on your own."

"Is that a challenge?"

"Perhaps."

Or perhaps, she thought, it was a plea for just a bit more time—just one more moment, before reality set in. Just until tomorrow.

Chapter Twenty-Two

How he managed to bathe and dress for dinner, he didn't remember. Only that it was as fast as possible so he could get back to his Ashley. There were guests at his table and yet Thomas snuck a glance at her, still in a daze.

The crystal chandeliers cast a warm, honeyed glow over the dining room, illuminating the finest—if slightly outdated—china that adorned the long mahogany table, one of the many family heirlooms. His heart thrummed with a wishful intensity. He wanted to reach across the table, take Ashley's hand, and lead her through every part of his world: the castle, its heirlooms, the history within its walls. If she would be his wife, he wanted her to have free rein over it all—his household, his fortune, his heart.

His body...

From where he sat at the head of the table, Ashley to his right, if he inched his leg forward a bit, he might touch her slipper. His composure was a thin mask barely holding back the storm inside. He could still feel her lips, taste her passion, and the softness of her skin beneath his fingertips. Every breath drew him back to that moment, the memory of it throbbing through him like a rhythm he couldn't escape. He dared not look at her too closely, yet he was painfully aware of her presence beside him, her gaze fixed firmly on her plate, her cheeks touched with a damning shade of crimson.

He suppressed another sigh and willed his member to stay hidden under the napkin on his lap as the first course was served.

The first course, a velvety cream of mushroom soup, was placed in front of him. He stared at it blankly, unable to muster an appetite for anything that wasn't Ashley. Every flicker of her hand, every shift of her posture stirred a need in him, one that clung stubbornly to the quiet yet consuming wish she might share the same hunger for him.

He tugged at his cravat.

He glanced at her again, yet all her attention was trained on her soup. Her friends, Charlene and Sera, kept exchanging glances, their expressions sharp and vigilant, as though they could decode all the unspoken nuances between him and Ashley. It was the kind of silent looks only women seemed capable of, one that always left men feeling slightly adrift.

Sebastian, who sat at the other end of the table, glanced between him and Lady Ashley, arching a brow. "The Ascot is upon us soon," he said, drawing all eyes to him.

Thomas sent a silent thanks to his friend.

"Prinny himself will be there, along with Baron Gregory Stone and many other illustrious figures," Sebastian declared, his voice rich with enthusiasm. "The carriages are being prepared as we speak, and the entire staff is bustling about."

The word "carriage" seemed to strike a nerve in Ashley. She blinked rapidly, her lashes fluttering as though to cool the crimson that had crept up to her cheeks.

He bit back a grin, half-tempted to let her know that he was thinking exactly the same thing. How was he supposed to concentrate on small talk when every breath he took was filled with her scent? Beneath the table, his hand hovered near hers, fingers inching forward. The anticipation was almost unbearable, and when his fingers finally brushed hers, she withdrew quickly with a heated look that could have melted iron.

He chuckled, and when all eyes turned to him, he cleared his throat. "Indeed, the Royal Ascot promises to be quite the spectacle."

"You're uncharacteristically subdued tonight, Thomas," Sebastian noted, lounging at the opposite end of the table. "Normally you'd be chattering on about the Ascot uninterrupted."

Thomas's gaze flicked to Ashley, whose color deepened under the scrutiny. "Just…not very talkative tonight," he murmured, his voice trailing off as he sent a brief glance to Ashley, sipping her soup.

"Lord Cambridge," Charlene said suddenly, eyeing the marquess with mock suspicion. "Is the Ascot really the pinnacle of British tradition or just an excuse for everyone to gather and make fools of themselves over hats?"

"Oh, it's both, my lady." Sebastian grinned, sweeping his arm out as if explaining something grand. "Picture it: the pageantry, the prestige, the unspeakable hats. It's like every good story—a bit of honor, a bit of embarrassment, and a lot of horse smell."

Ashley, quietly setting her spoon down, mumbled, "And bets, lots and lots of bets."

Miss Sera cleared her throat. "Let us ladies stick to hats."

Lady Charlene nodded. "Do I need something positively daring? Or do I go for understated charm?"

Sera grinned. "The Ascot is all about standing out. If your outfit is too understated, no one will remember a thing about you." She caught Thomas's eye, adding with a playful wink, "And if there's one thing our Ashley knows, it's how to make an impression."

Sebastian chuckled, casting a fond glance at Ashley. "Ah, yes, she certainly does. She'll fit right in, no doubt."

Ashley returned his smile. "You mentioned the carriages were being readied?"

Sebastian nodded. "Yes, we leave in two days." He turned to Thomas with an arched brow. "I thought you'd have been informed."

Thomas cleared his throat, his voice a touch gruff. He offered a sheepish smile. "My apologies. It slipped my mind." *Like so many damn other things.*

But he could still make it right, in his own way. If his luck held and he won at Ascot, he could return not just with the thrill of victory, but with something real to offer her. An actual ring and a name for the new foal—*her* foal.

He would gift her Lady Ash.

Sebastian's voice broke through his thoughts. "Well, it's only natural for one's thoughts to scatter in the face of marriage, I suppose. Have you set a date? Your birthday is in a month, no?"

Thomas glanced a warning look at his friend. "We'll set a date after the Ascot. Hopefully, I'll have word of our special license by then as well."

Thomas resisted a smile, glancing at Ashley as she politely fended off Sera's questions about dresses and hats, her cheeks flushed and eyes bright. *More than a grand affair,* he thought, his heart thudding. This was about more than tradition or titles. This was about the future he was ready to build—a future he could almost taste, and one he wasn't about to let slip through his fingers.

After their moment in the carriage, he sensed she wanted it as much as he did.

So, why did a sliver of unease settle right in the pit of his stomach?

⇶⫷

AFTER DINNER HAD been cleared and Ashley had managed to not even drink the wine, so uneasy was her stomach, Ashley ushered her friends into the drawing room with an urgency she hadn't felt since the day she'd heard the Earl of Linsey had come to London in search of a wife. Her heart pounded against her ribcage as she shut the door firmly behind them. The men's casual chatter about the Royal Ascot had unearthed a plan she'd all but forgotten: the scheme to sabotage his victory, a scheme left in Maddie's daring hands.

"The race!" Ashley blurted, her voice barely contained.

Sera's brow crept upward. "Yes, what of it?"

Ashley leaned closer, her tone dropping to a whisper. "Maddie! Have you *forgotten*? She's going to slip Linsey's jockey some sort of sedative or other to keep him off the track!"

"Oh," Sera murmured, appearing utterly unfazed as she adjusted her skirts and glided toward the cherrywood table. "That."

Charlene crossed her arms, her brow creased. "Why are you so frantic? Don't tell me…" Her eyes widened. "Dear heavens, Ashley, you have grown *that* soft on him?"

"I knew it," Sera said. "I knew it was much deeper than you expressed when we arrived."

Ashley's cheeks flushed. "We have to call it off," she insisted, ignoring the insinuation.

"Call it off?" Sera shook her head, pouring herself a glass of port. "Impossible. Like your Lord Cambridge said, the race is only two days away, and Maddie is heaven knows where by now. We can't reach her in time."

"She's right, Ashley," Charlene added, though her voice was tinged with regret. "The only way to prevent it now is to track Maddie down ourselves."

Dear Heavens! What happens if they fail?

No.

You can't think that way, Ashley.

They wouldn't fail. They would attend the race, stop the plan, and Thomas would never be the wiser. If he didn't win, it wouldn't be because of her. They'd find Maddie before any damage was done.

Ashley exhaled sharply, pacing the room. "We'll have to go to the Ascot and deal with it then. We can intercept Maddie there and put a stop to this madness before anyone's the wiser."

Charlene touched her shoulder reassuringly. "You're in deep with this man, aren't you?"

Her heart panged at the question, and she swallowed. He'd not gotten as deep as she longed and yet the feelings for him had spread wider than she'd admit. "It's not about that—at least not entirely," she replied, though her voice lacked its usual conviction. "There are too many things that are not as they seem."

Her own feelings included.

Sera handed her a glass of port. "Nothing we can do tonight. We might as well enjoy ourselves."

Ashley took the glass and downed it in one go, earning two raised brows from her friends. She poured herself another, hoping it might ease the knot of guilt twisting inside her. How was she supposed to enjoy a dark cloud hovering over her head? "This whole ordeal, this thing with Jordan," she muttered. "It's brought me nothing but trouble."

"And yet, it brought you to the earl, too," Sera observed, watching her closely. "Tell us, how *did* he win you over?"

Ashley started, caught off guard. "Does it matter?"

Charlene's eyes sparkled with curiosity. "Only that you've gone from determined revenge to something else entirely. It must have been quite a shift."

Ashley hesitated, searching for the right words. How had he won her over? She couldn't isolate a single thing. It was everything, all at once. Their conversations, his quick wit, the ease between them, even the small sarcastic jabs. It was his smile, the warmth in his eyes when he spoke of his horses, and his maddening, impossible way of thinking.

Just him. Simply...*him*.

"Ashley, speechless?" Charlene teased. "Now, that's truly remarkable."

Ashley threw her friend a look, lips quirking. "I'm not speechless. I'm thinking."

Sera tilted her head with a knowing smile. "Isn't that precisely what 'speechless' means?"

"Thinking in silence," Charlene chimed in with a grin.

"Exactly," Sera said, barely hiding her amusement. "But please, don't let us interrupt. We're fascinated to hear about the man who unraveled our Ashley."

Ashley rolled her eyes. "Well, since you seem so eager...he just, well, he just feels right."

Everywhere. In her heart and body.

Sera chuckled, swirling her port. "That's rather sweet for someone who once declared revenge was her sole purpose in life."

"Don't remind me."

This was what a person got who set out for revenge it seemed. She didn't even want to imagine what Thomas might think if he ever learned why she approached him. Would he resent her? His reaction made her grasp at anything other than confessing. But, the fact remained, the Duke of Richmond already knew, so it was just a matter of time before the earl discovered the truth.

She had to beat the duke to an admission.

And what better time than after averting this current crisis with the races. Once his horse took to the tracks, she would confess to why she approached him, Jordan, and ask him about the wager. And then to hope against all hopes their chances weren't ruined.

Because, despite all odds, she had fallen in love with the man.

Deeply, and dangerously so.

"In any event," Charlene murmured. "We'll just have to ensure Maddie doesn't succeed in ruining your beau's race and that will be that."

"Save the day in silly big hats."

"Perhaps mine should be large enough to conceal a catapult for emergency measures," Sera suggested, feigning seriousness.

"Or maybe a feather stole for dramatic flair!" Charlene chimed in, waving her hands theatrically.

"Just remember," Sera said with a grin, "if we need to make a hasty escape, hats off to the fastest runner!"

Ashley smiled gratefully, her determination rekindling. "Ascot it is, then. Linsey will never know a thing if we have anything to say about it." She looked between her friends, a spark of renewed purpose lighting in her breast. "We'll find Maddie, set things right, and maybe—just maybe—I'll find the courage to tell him the truth."

The words echoed in her mind, mingling with the thrill of the plan. Whatever happened, she would face it all, consequences be damned.

Chapter Twenty-Three

THOMAS STRODE THROUGH the dimly lit hall, his footsteps echoing off the ancient stone walls. The scent of beeswax polish and a faint hint of roasted game from dinner lingered in the air, though his mind was elsewhere. He couldn't shake their encounter in the carriage; it replayed in his mind like a melody he couldn't stop humming. Her sparkling eyes as she smiled up at him, flushed and captivating in his arms—a memory that had him prowling the corridors for the fifth time tonight.

By his sixth pass, the portraits lining the hall seemed to watch him with mild disapproval. Scowling, he muttered to his great-great-grandfather's frowning likeness, "Yes, yes, I know—I'm a love-struck fool. Never felt like this yourself, hmm?"

A chill trickled down his spine as he imagined those painted eyes shifting toward him.

He shook off the feeling of being silently judged. He needed to see her. It was like an urge that became an obsession. Sending a pointed look back at the portraits, he turned the corner toward her room, his fingers brushing the cold stone wall as he went. When he reached her door, he stopped, resting his forehead against the solid wood.

Thomas took a steadying breath, an absurd little debate kicking up in his mind. Should he enter? Should he wait? Why was he so rattled?

The scent of jasmine and roses drifted from her room, tugging him forward. Finally, he pushed the door open, finding her deep in thought by the window, her silhouette framed by the moonlight streaming in. She looked ethereal, like a painting come to life.

"Ashley," he murmured, his voice low, but it carried everything he felt.

She turned, her eyes wide with surprise. "Linsey, what are you doing here?"

He arched a brow, smiling. "May I come in?"

"*Thomas*," she corrected, playfully, leaning back against the window. "To what do I owe this inappropriate visit?"

"I had to find you," he said, stepping closer. "You left abruptly after dinner, and I didn't see you after."

Her fingers picked at her dress as she regarded him. "I didn't mean to worry you. I just had things on my mind."

Closing the door behind him, he leaned against it. "Care to share? I'm known to be an exceptional listener."

She laughed, a short, guarded sound. "Maybe after the race."

He lifted a brow. "Why after?"

A flicker of something—caution, perhaps—crossed her features. "Let's just say, it would be better if I share my mind after a victory on the tracks."

"Victory is not guaranteed."

"Victory is racing," she countered.

He chuckled. "Very well, I can't claim to understand, but should I be worried? Is this good or bad?"

"Well," she replied, eyes sparkling. "It's not good; it's not bad either."

He pushed away from the door, crossing to her. "You and your contradictions." He traced her cheek with his thumb, enjoying the warmth beneath his finger.

Her lips parted, but no words came. Instead, she leaned into his touch, her eyes fluttering shut for a fleeting moment. When they opened again, he saw in her gaze the same fierce longing that burned in him. Without hesitation, he pulled her close, capturing her mouth in a kiss that was both tender and fierce.

When they broke apart, he let out a soft breath, voice rough with emotion. "I'll have something to say after the race, too." He had a lot. There was his surprise, but also the ominous note from Paisley and the matter regarding her brother. The last two, he hadn't wanted to ruin the mood between them when they were together, but she had the right to at least know.

"Good or bad?" she asked, her eyes dancing with curiosity.

"Not good," he replied, a smirk tugging at his lips. "Not bad, either."

"Stealing my lines now?"

"Borrowing them."

She reached up, brushing her fingers over his chest. "Why are you here? Are you planning to be greedy again?"

Instead of answering, he gently pressed his thumb to her lips, slipping past the barrier to explore the warmth within. The sensation was thrilling, a direct line to his very core, igniting that fire he struggled to contain when they were alone. An endless fight he always lost. She closed her lips around his thumb, her tongue brushing against his finger in a way that sent a bolt of heat through him.

"Can I be greedy all my life?" he asked, voice rough.

She smiled up at him, a glint lighting her gaze. Slowly, she drew his thumb away and, with quiet confidence, unbuttoned his shirt, her fingers grazing the bare skin beneath. "Ashley," he murmured, his back pressing against the bookshelf.

"You'll be the end of me," he muttered, a half-hearted jest that masked the depth of his arousal.

"That's exactly my plan."

"You're trying to kill me?"

"You or me."

"What about both of us?"

Ashley raised her brows and nodded with a hint of resignation. But she was so close that his heart started racing anew. Her hand, steady and sure, reached for the hem of his shirt and pulled it from his breeches. Then she unbuttoned his breeches, and the bookshelf blocked him from taking a step back and escaping her wandering hands, the hard edge pressing into the muscles of his back. So wonderfully bold this beauty. He didn't want to escape anyway.

"I want to touch you as you did me in the carriage."

"But you did," he found himself saying, even as every fiber of his being screamed in protest. It had been different in the landau even though he couldn't recall the reason.

"So?" she challenged and slid down and knelt before him. "You enjoyed it earlier this morning, and I want to give you pleasure."

Then, with a movement as fluid as it was deliberate, Ashley tossed her head, her blonde curls cascading like a golden waterfall over her shoulders. The sight of her, so bold and unashamed, struck Thomas like a punch to the gut. And as she began her slow descent from his tip along the length of him, her gaze locked on his, he knew he was witnessing something profound.

Thomas was at the brink of losing himself. Her motions were so swift, so adorable, so clumsy, so precious. He bucked when her tongue swirled around his tip and let his head fall backward.

His heart skipped a beat, and he forgot to breathe.

Looking down at the carefully piled curls on her head and the pretty pink dress sprawled around her made him wonder why *he* felt like a gift *she* was unwrapping. Or was unraveling the better word? He certainly wasn't himself.

"You feel so good," he croaked.

"I'm glad. Teach me all you like," she said, her mouth surrounding him. The vibration from her words nearly pushed him over the edge but the meaning, her desire to please him, reverberated to his heart.

"You can always teach me what you need."

"You." He groaned. "I just need you."

Just the mere thought of her lips, her mouth, taking him in was nearly enough to undo him completely, never mind her actually doing it. But then, amid the fire her tongue stroked, a flicker of conscience stirred within him.

At that moment, Thomas realized the truth of their connection. A meeting of minds and souls, a dance of equals drawn together by an undeniable force. And as he surrendered to the moment completely, to the exquisite promise of Ashley's touch, he knew he would risk anything for her.

His very life.

Her approach was unhurried, every inch she moved filled with intention, with the silent promise of pleasures that would drive him insane. Thomas watched, transfixed, as the distance between them shrank, his heart pounding a frantic rhythm against his ribcage.

Ah, hell.

Her lips embarked on a journey down the taut line of his arousal. The softness of her tongue, paired with the gentle, yet insistent caress of her fingers, drew patterns of pleasure across his skin, igniting a blaze that threatened to consume him whole.

His body responded instinctively, a reflexive arch into the air, a whispered curse that mingled with the charged silence between them, and he arched his hips toward her. When she paused, pulling back, he felt the sting of her absence like a physical blow, leaving him exposed, pulsing with an urgency that bordered on pain.

Yet, she didn't retreat fully.

Instead, she shifted her approach, her lips pressing against him in a series of butterfly kisses. Somehow, she managed to do even this with an air of elegance and innocence that made it seem just right, so very good. Each brush of her tongue was a delicate exploration that erased his ability to hold back. Thomas closed his eyes, surrendering to the cascade of sensations, each kiss a promise, each touch a revelation.

When she welcomed him once more, taking him deeper, the world narrowed to the point of her tongue on his shaft. Restraint shattered, giving way to a primal need that coursed through his veins with the force of a wild stallion.

Thomas reached for her, his hands finding the silkiness of her hair, guiding her movements with desperation. "Yes," he breathed out, the intensity of the sensation so damn sharp. "Ashley, you are incredible," he managed, each word punctuated by the rhythm they set together. "I need you, Ashley, I love you."

She gave the briefest of pauses before sucking his member in with a burst of renewed purpose, and he jerked and…bloody hell!

He yanked at his cravat, nearly choking himself in his rush to get it off. Just as the first surge spilled against her lips, he pulled back, catching the rest with a steadying breath. His hand slid to the back of her head, guiding her up to him.

Panting, still regaining his composure, he noted the blush that swept over her face, coloring her ears and trailing down her neckline.

Oh boy.

He needed that special license.

Tomorrow.

A WOMAN POSSESSED was a dangerous thing indeed.

And Ashley was possessed.

Just as she couldn't say what had possessed her to be so bold in her private chamber with her friends close by, only that the bold that had been lacking when it came to admitting secrets burst forth when taking action. Actions, after all, spoke louder than any words ever could. And how could she resist him with her mind if every bit of her body wanted him so wholly?

She slowly rose to her feet, tasting the words, the admission, the secret that still couldn't leave her lips even as his scent, his flavor, his very essence clung to them.

Pleasure came in many ways and forms, but most often, it was pleasure taken. This—giving pleasure—felt richer, fuller, more intoxicating than anything she'd ever experienced.

Pleasure in its purest form.

The pleasure of his raspy groans.

The pleasure of his hands gripping her hair.

The pleasure of his pure abandonment.

But it was his whispered "I love you" that sent a shiver down to the very heart of her. The confession was much more raw than the words let on.

She watched as he quickly readjusted his clothing as she readjusted her wits. She'd acted daring, too daring, to sidestep a much larger issue. And Thomas was nothing if not perceptive; he wouldn't press her tonight, but eventually, if she didn't make do on her promise to share her thoughts after the Ascot, he would probe again.

Her time was running out.

"I'm going to London the day after the Ascot," he suddenly said, circling her with his arms and resting his forehead against hers.

Her brows furrowed. "Why?"

"For the special license." He sighed, kissing her cheek tenderly. "I can't wait any longer."

Ashley froze. Could she truly run away now?

No, that would make her no different from Jordan, or even, in some ways, her mother. Whatever needed to be done, she would face it with the same brazenness she faced everything else.

"Are you all right?" he asked.

She glanced at him, quirking her lips. "I should be asking you that. It almost sounded as though you were in pain."

"I'm always in pain when I'm with you."

"Not very encouraging," she replied, raising a brow.

"It means you drive me to the brink of my sanity, then pull me back, only to drive me straight there again."

Ashley couldn't help but laugh. "That does sound painful."

"Your spirits seem somewhat revived now that your friends are here."

"They were never low."

He studied her for a moment, then nodded. "I'm glad they'll be with you at the race. I fear it might have been dreadfully tedious otherwise."

She tilted her head. *That will be the last thing it would be!* "Oh, I don't know about that. Honestly, I've never attended a race before," she continued. "It should be thrilling." *Or terrifying, if she couldn't stop Maddie.*

What if they couldn't stop her? What if—

She realized she'd been backing away from him, and his frown brought her to a halt. What was she doing?

Yes, Ashley. What now?

"I'm not running away," she blurted, more to herself than him.

The furrow between his brows deepened. "Ashley, if I did something wrong, tell me. I'm not a complete fool. Or maybe I am, because around you, I'm never sure how to act. You make me feel reckless—like I've never done this before."

"I know the feeling," she murmured. His presence made her feel both alive and utterly undone.

She looked away and then back at him. "You should rest. We leave for the race the day after tomorrow, and I imagine you have many arrangements to make." And she had a catastrophe to prevent.

"I don't want to leave."

She raised an eyebrow. "You wish to stay?"

"If I'm given half a chance, I'll leap into that bed right now."

"A leap, you say? And here I thought you were all charm and

grace."

He grinned, undeterred. "For you, I'll be whatever you wish. Even a rogue who dares invade your bedchamber."

"Well, you've certainly invaded this bedchamber. But you're the master of this castle. What do you think our friends will say if they find you here?"

"What can they say? They couldn't pry me away even if they tried."

"They can say why did I not send you on your merry way!" She moved toward the bed, her steps not quite keeping pace with her heartbeat. She clutched at her neck. *I can't breathe.* How can he be so charming at the most unexpected times?

"Stay if you want, then. I won't send you on your merry way." She promptly sat down on the bed before she realized her legs could no more hold the weight of her body than her heart could hold the burden of what she kept at bay. So yes, she would allow him to sleep with her tonight.

She wanted his warmth.

Needed it.

But she'd made a mess of the situation and didn't think any of her friends could get her out of it.

What would Papa do in this situation? His advice was always sage. Though, he would surely question the independence he'd provided her over the years should he catch wind of why she'd accepted this engagement with Linsey. What did he always say? The truth will come out even if it breezes in on the back of a leaf.

Yet again, her father would be right.

So long as it's a breeze and not a storm. A spring breeze was a good idea, not a storm.

She glanced at Thomas as he plopped down beside her on the bed, wrapping his arms around her and pulling her down with him. Her breaths came in rapid bursts. Leave it to him to not only rob her of her breath but to claim it entirely. Not even Jordan had managed that.

She inwardly scowled. Whatever she had felt for Jordan was nothing compared to this. It was time to let him go. Completely.

This wasn't Thomas's fault.

It was hers.

But soon, she would set everything right.

He settled into her bed as though he'd always belonged there.

"But be warned," Ashley suddenly said, narrowing her eyes at him. He had tossed his robe aside, his broad chest and muscled arms bare, with only his unmentionables preserving a semblance of modesty. He looked up, surprise flickering in his eyes as he met her gaze. "If you stay, you might be devoured."

"Devoured? That sounds intriguing."

"Does it?"

How about one night of love before he finds out the truth?

Just this once.

If she was going to be ruined anyway, she'd rather do it this way than retreat to a loft in London, ruined, jilted, and forever alone. Surely that would be the punishment if she couldn't stop Maddie, and he decided to cut all ties after discovering the truth.

She crawled to the center of the bed, the mattress creaking softly under her weight. Her hands trembled as she reached for the ties on her shoulders, the fabric of her shift whispering as it slipped down her arms and pooled around her waist. She reached up to her hair and pulled out the pins that held her hair in a loose bun. When her hair fell over her shoulders, she curled her lips. "Nothing to say?"

She gasped when his arms suddenly shot out and wrapped her, his touch firm and electrifying as he pulled her into his body. His voice, low and ragged, held a warning. "If you continue this, I won't be able to stop myself."

Ashley looked up at him, her pulse quickening. The glint in his eyes mirrored her own hidden longing. She knew this was about more than mere desire. She wanted to feel love, to be cherished, if only for a fleeting moment. *His* love. *His* cherishment. So, she leaned into his embrace, tossing caution into the country wind.

"I won't stop you," she said.

Chapter Twenty-Four

THOMAS LOVED CHRISTMAS. It had always been a happy time, and he usually woke up to a new saddle or some other treat when his grandfather and parents were alive. But this wasn't Christmas; it was spring. And yet, he felt like a child waking up to the best present ever. He certainly hadn't meant to seduce Ashley when he shamelessly hinted at sleeping in her room. And he most certainly hadn't ever imagined she would seduce him!

She was his spring awakening.

He knew it wasn't a dream, for nothing he could concoct in his mind could ever be so alluring.

Thomas's strength melted away when she smiled up at him.

I won't stop you.

Four words that robbed him of his damn breath.

He had pulled her into a searing kiss, his lips capturing hers with a hunger that had been dormant but suddenly roared to life. When her tongue darted into his mouth, he opened up, baring his heart and soul for her pleasure. He was at her pleasure and would always be, whether they were married yet or not. Her body had pressed against his, warm and inviting, as he guided her gently onto the bed, the satin sheets cool beneath them.

To his utter shock, and male delight, she did something that sent a thrill through him. She straddled him. Her confidence was intoxicating, and the sight of her above him, framed by the shadows and candlelight blazed into his memory.

Bloody hell.

So precious.

Their connection was tangible, each breath and heartbeat weaving them closer together. He understood that this was more than passion; it was an unspoken vow of trust.

Though she hadn't yet learned to ride a horse, she needed no saddle. Her hands rested on his chest, an unbelievably magical feeling. A fierce protectiveness surged within him—he wouldn't let her fall, not now, not ever. Their connection was a living, breathing pulse, each breath and heartbeat weaving them closer together. He understood now that this was more than passion; it was the rawest form of trust.

And love.

"Let me show you how I feel, all right?" he rasped, barely breaking the kiss. She gave a faint nod but clung to his mouth in the most delightful way possible. He cradled the back of her head, his fingers threading through her hair as she leaned back, eyes filled with a spark of roguery. No, not just a spark. A well.

A deep well.

He grinned, his lips tracing a deliberate path down her cheek, savoring the softness of her skin. He lingered at her ear, whispering "so delicious" before continuing his journey down her neck. As he reached her shoulder, he could feel her tension build, her breath soft against his cheek.

He cupped her breasts, and she gasped. His heart skipped when he caught her biting her lip as she looked at his hand on her breast.

So. Erotic.

So. Hot.

Her eyes met his. "So experienced. How many times have you engaged in such activities, hmmm?"

What? Was this a tease? "This is hardly the moment for such inquiries."

"It is quite the opposite. It holds greater significance for me; this is my first time."

Thomas inclined his head slightly. "I cannot claim a number."

"Is that so?" She cupped his face, relying on her strength to remain reclined against his lap. The sight of her flat front, accentuated in this position, was utterly captivating, and a surge of pleasure erupted at the mere view. How could he focus when she seduced him like this?

"I don't have a number. There was a girl once, the daughter of a neighboring estate, but we did nothing that came close to this."

"You mean to say you have never…"

"Never," he replied, leaning forward as he reached around her, deftly unfastening the back of her corset before casting it aside.

"Thomas!" She laughed.

He grinned as he dipped his mouth to her hardened nipples, cradling her back while teasing her delicate breast with gentle nibbles. Her head fell back in a shimmering blanket of golden curls as she groaned.

Oh, that sound.

His heart swelled with tenderness. He reached down with one hand, shifting to accommodate his movement, and he parted her folds.

His forehead fell on hers. "This can have consequences."

She smiled. "Like what? Loss of chastity."

"Children?"

"Well, being the man that you are, there are ways, are there not?"

He chuckled. "You really know how to test a man."

"You're so tight, but so wet," he added.

"Yes, I'm ready," she breathed. Her eyes sparkled. "I've only been waiting for you."

"Minx."

I CAN'T BELIEVE I'm doing this.

But, oh, yes, she could.

When Thomas shifted their position, rolling her beneath him, Ashley wanted to stop thinking altogether. If this was to be the irrevocable deed, she wanted to savor every second for as long as she could.

The weight of his body pressed against hers, a comforting presence that enveloped her in dreams and stars. The heat burned between them, making her deeply aware of every single touch. Her hands found his chest, the firm muscles beneath her palms protecting a heart that beat just as loudly as hers.

Tilting her head, she let her lips brush against his skin, tasting the saltiness of his flesh. In that moment, she sensed the essence of him, each shared breath weaving a promise she didn't know if she could ever accept. Her lips traveled to his shoulders, blocking out anything and everything but him.

This.

And then he positioned himself between her legs, the firm evidence of his desire replacing the gentle pressure of his hands.

"Stop me now," he rasped.

"Never."

His exhalation sent a thrill through her, and she dug her fingers into his back when he pressed his body against hers. A sense of wonder bloomed within her, mingling with the excitement of the moment. This was more than she had ever dared to dream—an intimacy she hadn't realized she craved so desperately until now. He hovered above her, and their eyes locked. The unspoken understanding deepened the connection that words could never capture.

With him, she felt safe, cherished, and, for the first time, completely herself.

He thrust forward, and Ashley held her breath, anticipation making her heart race. It felt as though he had breached the very fabric of their world. The initial pinch startled her, a sensation of being stretched in ways she hadn't expected, and her body tensed momentarily, every nerve alight with sensation. But to her surprise, she found herself yielding, adjusting to him with a natural ease she hadn't anticipated, and the chamber around them faded, narrowing their reality to just the two of them.

"Does this hurt?" he asked, his gaze lingering where their bodies began to meld.

"No." It might have burned a little, but she craved more.

He thrust into her then, and a soft gasp blew past her lips. *Yes.*

Thomas paused, kissing her forehead and stroking her hair. "You feel so good."

"You feel good, feeling good inside me," she murmured back, arching into him.

"Bloody hell," he breathed.

He didn't hold back after that. He didn't move with care anymore, and she didn't want him to. She wanted every single thrust of him the way he gave it. She dug her fingers deeper into his back, clamping her legs around his waist, as if she could hold onto that moment forever.

His hand found her center again, his thumb stroking her with what she could only describe as a magical touch that sent her spiraling over the edge, and a wave of pleasure rippled through every nerve of her body. Just when the moment had ended, Thomas showed her it had just begun.

May tomorrow never come.

⟫⟪

SHE WAS EVERYTHING Thomas had ever hoped for and more than he could have imagined. Saving this for the right woman had been worth every moment.

An electric charge seemed to fill the air as they moved in unison, a silent understanding passing between them with each touch. Every nerve in his body was attuned to her—her warmth, the softness of her skin, the cadence of her breath mingling with his. His senses absorbed each subtle movement, every sigh and gasp she offered feeding his need to hold her closer.

His hands traced the delicate curve of her waist, each touch, each kiss as natural as breathing, but he was driven by one goal—to bring her pleasure. As their movements built toward the crest, and all that existed were her wild, soft cries, his pulse thundering in time with hers, like the rhythm of hooves across open fields. He felt himself swept into a rush of emotion, the surge as powerful and exhilarating as leaning into a gallop, the world blurring around him as he met her at the peak. They moved like horse and rider, in perfect stride, a wild harmony that went beyond words.

A spark of tension rippled through him, like the coiled power of a horse at full run. And then, as he reached that pinnacle, the world shattered into ecstasy, his release so fierce it seemed to consume him. He pushed deep, feeling her gasp, a faint cry muffled as he covered her mouth with his, the house far too full for her unrestrained voice. She opened to him, drawing him in, trembling as she clung to him, and he knew he'd never felt anything like this.

When the last waves subsided, he held her close, devouring the steady, quiet murmur of her breath against his skin, like a breeze rustling the leaves. Satisfaction washed over him—a calm contentment, like the peace after a hard ride, promising endless horizons and an unspoken certainty that this was where he was meant to be.

He couldn't wait for tomorrow to come.

Chapter Twenty-Five

The morning of the Royal Ascot

THOMAS STOOD BESIDE the open carriage, the polished wood and brass fixtures gleaming in the morning sun. Flowers and bells adorned the carriages from the estate, a sight so splendid it seemed to belong to a fairy tale. The air was filled with the scent of fresh blooms, a sign that it would be a wonderful day.

Sebastian sidled up to him, glancing over the showy carriages. "You look rather chipper this morning. Something special about these races I don't know about? Something like taking Mrs. White's advice?"

"Something like that," Thomas replied, adjusting his top hat. After all, how could he not feel chipper after spending the past two nights in Ashley's arms?

"Oh?" Sebastian's eyebrow shot up, a sly grin playing on his lips. "And here I thought you'd spent the night topping over the races."

"It is a day of tradition," Thomas deflected, glancing at all the staff standing about. His fingers brushed the brim of his top hat—the same one his grandfather had worn at these races years ago, when he'd courted Thomas's grandmother. It was more than fabric and formality; it was a reminder of love woven into legacy, family, and honor.

Sebastian snorted. "Ah, I see. Tradition. So that glow on your face is strictly thanks to family pride, not to a certain woman who seems to have stolen your heart."

"Well, since you're so keen to probe, why not tell me what a proper romantic should look like, seeing as you're an expert?"

Sebastian gave an exaggerated shudder. "I'd be of no help at all, as you know." He looked around, eyeing the approaching staff with an approving nod. "Besides, with everything ready, you're set to make the grandest entrance the Ascot's seen." He nudged Thomas's arm. "What if it's the last time the Linsey thoroughbreds make an appearance?"

"Why would that be?"

"You read Paisley's note, didn't you? He's coming with some sort of trump card to ensure he wins the wager."

And then, as if summoned by his thoughts, Ashley emerged from the castle's wide doors. Everything else seemed to fade—the carriages, the sounds of gathering servants, even Sebastian's prattling. His world narrowed to just Ashley, in a sky-blue silk gown that caught the light that seemed to draw the very morning sun to her. Her face, framed by soft golden curls beneath her spring-flower-trimmed hat, was simply radiant. She looked so beautiful that he found himself unable to look away.

She looked absolutely breathtaking.

Sebastian followed his gaze, giving a low nod. "I'd say the day just improved tenfold. Though don't be a fool and tell her that directly."

"I don't have to." *She already knows.* Thomas watched her approach, mesmerized. "Today is going to be…well, memorable."

Ah, yes, today was going to be a great day.

※※※

ASHLEY STEPPED FROM the castle, her gaze instantly finding Thomas. He looked so handsome in his buff breeches, a crisp white shirt, and a tightly fitting tailcoat, white gloves, and a black top hat. But it was his smile when their gazes locked that truly stole the air from her lungs.

Today was the day—perhaps her last happy one.

She took a steadying breath.

Beside her, Charlene nudged her shoulder. "Oh, you are done for, my friend. You'd better find your footing quickly because he's already watching you as if you've set the sun in the sky."

"We should have insisted on sleeping with you in your chamber," Sera chimed in.

"Oh, stop it," Ashley muttered. They'd been teasing her all morning after they discovered the other half of her bed had been slept in, too.

"Focus," Ashley said, glancing at her friends. "We have an important mission today."

"Yes," Charlene said. "This day will require every bit of poise I possess."

Ashley straightened, steeling her expression. "Agreed, we are here with a purpose." She threw her shoulders back. "We must stop Maddie today. Try to look a bit more war-ready, if you can manage."

"Oh, 'war-ready' she says. Why do I get the sense that you've just dropped your pistol at the mere sight of your beau." Sera laughed, winking. "But do not worry, we are here, too."

Ashley swallowed, nerves fluttering as she met Thomas's eyes once more.

Yes, today would be memorable to be sure.

Tryingly so.

Chapter Twenty-Six

THE ATMOSPHERE AT the racetrack was lively with the excited chatter of people from all classes and sizes when Ashley exited the carriage.

The grandeur of the Ascot was undeniable. Expansive grounds and open air contrasted sharply with the stifling ballrooms of London, and the scent of freshly cut grass mingled with delicate spring blooms. The entire Ton seemed to be assembled, dressed to the nines and creating an undercurrent of excitement. Each box along the track was decorated with vibrant flowers—roses, peonies, and lilacs arranged to perfection.

In one of those boxes, she noticed the elevated presence of Prinny himself. Her gaze strayed to Thomas and Sebastian, exchanging easy conversation. They both looked at ease amidst the throng, seeming almost oblivious to the bustle around them. She could stare at Thomas all day if it weren't completely improper. She'd kiss him all day, too. And do more.

Since when do I have such a one-track mind?

Her lips twitched—perhaps, *always*? And given that her plan for revenge had recently derailed, her mind had wandered to other, more pleasurable things.

But she reminded herself of her true purpose here.

She had one focus.

Well, two.

Stop Maddie.

Confess her sins.

In that order.

"What do we do now?" Charlene murmured from her side.

"We wait and see what the men plan to do," Ashley replied. "Then we find an excuse to explore and search for Maddie." They didn't have that much time. Maddie could strike with her plan at any given moment.

"Perhaps start by the stables where they keep the horses before the race?" suggested Sera.

A fair guess.

"Ladies," Thomas interrupted with a polite smile. "Shall we head over to our box and then take a turn around the grounds?"

Ashley nodded, linking her arm with his. "Will you not visit your horses first?" She hoped he might allow her to tag along, hoping for a chance encounter with Maddie.

Thomas shook his head. "Bad luck."

"Bad luck?" Ashley echoed, brows raised. "Are you a sailor?"

Sebastian laughed. "Only for *him*, I assure you," he said. "Superstitious as they come, Thomas is."

Ashley chuckled, a bit of tension ebbing away. "Do you gamble on the races as well?" she asked Thomas.

"No," he replied, shaking his head again.

She arched an eyebrow. "Another bad luck thing?"

Sebastian snorted. "Thomas doesn't gamble. I, on the other hand, will happily wager a few quid."

Charlene's eyes lit up. "I want to place a wager as well!"

"Then follow me," Sebastian said, offering his arm to Charlene. He glanced at Sera, who merely shook her head.

"Do go on without me," Sera said dryly. Once they left, she turned to Ashley with a sigh. "Do keep all this *love talk* to a minimum. I beg of you, for my own sanity."

Ashley grinned, but before she could say anything, a voice behind her called, *"Ashley? Is that you?"*

She stiffened, the blood curdling in her veins.

What on earth was *he* doing here? How was he even here?

She didn't want to turn, but with her arm hooked through Thomas's, she couldn't avoid it.

Slowly, she faced the man she'd once thought she loved, who supposedly ran away, her gaze locking with dark, familiar eyes. "Jordan," she whispered, acutely aware of Thomas next to her. She felt his eyes on her but couldn't bring herself to look at him.

"What are you doing here?" they asked in unison.

She heard Sera mutter a foul word.

Jordan cleared his throat, his eyes narrowing as they flicked between her and Thomas. "Imagine my surprise when Richard gave me *The Times*. I didn't think I'd ever run into you here. Especially not with him!"

He gave you The Times *and now you come to find me?*

"You are friends with the Duke of Paisley?"

Jordan nodded with a smug smile. One she wished to slap if she weren't on display for the entire Ton.

Thomas's arm tightened around hers as if he'd felt the tension within her. "Why wouldn't my fiancée join me when I have a spectacular race of my horses?"

Ashley's jaw nearly dropped. She shared a wide-eyed glance with Sera.

"Fiancée?" Jordan's eyes darted back to Ashley. "Is this a jest? Ashley, surely this is some scheme to punish me for not sending word sooner. You can't possibly be serious." Jordan stepped right toward her and eyed her arm in Thomas's.

"What are you talking about?" Thomas demanded, his voice dropping to a dangerously low timbre.

Jordan's mouth set into a thin line. "Ashley is *my* betrothed," he declared as he pushed his hand over Ashley's and tried to tug her away.

"No!" *Oh that was articulate, Ashley, well done.*

"What?" The word left Thomas's lips like a hiss, his body taut with fury.

Ashley's jaw slacked then. This knave! What was he talking about? "That's not true, Jordan. You never asked me to marry you."

"You said you'd marry me," he shot back, eyes widening.

"Yes—*if you asked*," she snapped, glaring at the man. "Hypothetically." She'd once thought seeing him again would fill her with joy, but now there was only a hollow nothingness, as if he were a stranger she disliked. He was of no consequence anymore.

"I asked you to wait for me."

Ashley's face hardened. "Your precise words were, *do not wait for me*. And you didn't even say them, you sent a note after the fact." No promises. No commitment. And especially no love had existed between them.

"That..." Jordan's voice rose. "I just didn't want you to worry over me! We loved each other."

Her heart twisted—not for him, but for the man she truly loved. She turned to Thomas, silently pleading for understanding, hoping he could see how little this past entanglement meant to her now.

"No!"

"Ashley..." came Thomas's low voice.

Sera's voice cut off any further response. "Loved her? You left her with barely a word. Is that love?" It was good to have a friend by her side.

Jordan's frown deepened "This is between Ashley and myself."

Ashley straightened, her voice strong. "There's nothing between us, Jordan. Not anymore." She had vowed revenge for this man, but she'd picked the wrong target. "Perhaps not ever." Ashley turned to Thomas and wanted to explain. Jordan had never gotten permission from her father. He'd never kissed her as Thomas did. She'd never loved him like...the man whose mien had fallen and who looked as pale as his white cravat. "Thomas?!"

Jordan cursed under his breath. "Then at least return my brooch."

Brooch? Oh, that wretched knave.

Her mind pieced together the truth.

Of course.

He was here for a trinket, not her heart. She searched his eyes, looking for the man she'd once known and finding only a stranger. The man didn't look heartbroken at all. He wanted the brooch? He could go fish it out of the Thames!

But just as she thought this encounter could end, Ashley spotted another figure approaching. The Duke of Paisley.

Drat.

Why now?

"Thomas, old fellow!" he called out, a knowing smile spreading across his face. "I see you've finally met your lady's first love."

Ashley's cheeks flushed. Jordan had been her suitor. To deny it would do more harm than good, and though she feared the pain it might cause Thomas, she wouldn't pretend. She wasn't a coward like Jordan. And yet, Jordan was not a threat to Thomas. Then did he tense even further when Paisley arrived?

She turned to Thomas, her voice almost a whisper. "Thomas..."

He didn't look at her, his attention fixed on Jordan. "Miss Sera, perhaps you and Lady Ashley might join Lord Cambridge and Lady Charlene for a while. I'd like a private word with Mr. Critton."

She'd rather not, but one look at his rigid posture left her with no choice. Would he call off the engagement?

He probably wouldn't.

Even if his affections cooled, there was still the wager.

Ashley wanted to stay.

Sera nudged her gently, urging her on, mouthing, *"Maddie."*

Ashley nodded.

Right.

She still had a mission.

She only hoped that after all was said and done, she wouldn't lose the man she had fallen madly in love with, for at that moment, he resembled more a wild stallion than the refined earl she'd met at Almack's.

And it was her fault.

THOMAS'S CHEST FELT as if it were filled with lead, weighing him down as he forced himself to stare at anything but Ashley retreating with Sera. He couldn't look. He wouldn't look. If he saw even the faintest glimmer of affection in her eyes directed toward Jordan, he knew without a doubt he'd falter. And he couldn't falter.

Not now. Not with everything riding on him holding firm.

The two men stood in silence, the crisp sounds of the Ascot mingling with the tension that sparked in the air between them. Thomas clenched his fists, his knuckles white, and took a slow, measured breath.

Jordan was the first to break the silence. "You should know," he started, his tone smug, "Ashley and I had an understanding. A history you know nothing about. Whatever you think you have with her, it's nothing compared to what we shared."

Thomas's jaw tightened, the muscles pulsing beneath his skin. He met Jordan's gaze with a cool, steady stare. Did the man think he could be so easily ruffled?

"Whatever you were before, you are not now. She is with me. That's all that matters."

Jordan chuckled, a hollow sound that grated against Thomas's nerves. "How would you know? Did she tell you about me?"

"Only about how poorly you performed, if it was you at all." How many men she'd kissed she hadn't said. Only that she'd never kissed anyone like him.

"So, you've claimed her, have you? Tell me, is this some wager you made?"

Thomas snorted. Knowing what Jordan had been to Ashley, he couldn't shake the thought that she'd been far too generous in letting Jordan off. "You speak of wagers when you already lost against me? I let you off the hook that time; I won't let you off again. Don't misinterpret my charity. When it comes to the woman that I love, I won't show any mercy. Stay away from her."

Jordan scoffed. "Love? Don't be absurd, Linsey. You don't know her well enough to love her. Not the way I do. Not the way I did."

"Your love is rather fickle, isn't it. And if she loved you, why is she with me?"

Paisley's familiar, vexing drawl cut through the thickening tension. "You're still going through with this, Linsey? I imagine there are easier ways to lose horses than wagering them on a mere woman."

Thomas stiffened, refusing to look away from Jordan even as Paisley's words sank in. *Was this what she'd wanted to share with him after the Ascot? The truth about her and this jest of a man? This unfinished mess with a man she'd clearly once cared for?*

He steeled himself, breathing deeply. He couldn't waver—not now, not when so much was on the line. "Paisley," he said, keeping his voice level, "you've made your wager. Let's not lose our nerves now, shall we?"

"Oh, I haven't. But if it turns out she prefers another..." Paisley trailed off, casting a wicked glance at Jordan. "It would be a shame for you to lose both your wager *and* the lady, wouldn't it?"

"Don't bloody count on it."

"Has it never occurred to you why she approached *you* of all men right after old Jordan here ran off? He lost a wager to you..."

"What the devil are you getting at, Paisley?"

"Oh, I shall leave that to you to reflect on."

Thomas ground his teeth, suppressing a sharp retort as Paisley chuckled to himself and sauntered a few paces away, undoubtedly staying close enough to enjoy the show. Bloody arse. Taking a step closer to Jordan, Thomas lowered his voice. "Ashley's mine. I don't care what your connection was before, but it's done. Over."

"She might deny it, but she doesn't look at me like it's over," Jordan sneered. "I saw her face when she saw me again. There's still something there, no matter how much you want to deny it. We had an understanding. She was supposed to wait."

"Supposed to?" Thomas's brow rose, his face hardening. "Then why didn't you ask her properly if you felt so strongly? Or perhaps she knew you weren't worth it? But just so that we are clear, she is my betrothed. How we proceed with our engagement, that is up to us and us alone. And it seems to me like you're the one who stepped away."

"You understand nothing," Jordan growled.

"What I understand," Thomas said, his voice dangerous and low, "is that you left her. And now you think you can just waltz back in and pick up where you left off? Do you even know her? Really know her? I doubt you ever had a clue about how wonderful she is!"

Jordan's face darkened, and he took a step closer, just enough to force Thomas to look up at him slightly. "I know her better than you ever will. We made promises. She's just using you to get over me, and you're too blind to see it."

"Tell me then, can she ride a horse?" Thomas asked.

"Just as well as any woman."

Aha! "And does she like the countryside?"

"Of course, she loves the flowers and all that womanly stuff."

Hm! "And what does her hair smell like in the morning when she slept in and took a long bath, hm?"

"Violets. Roses." Jordan came uncomfortably close. "Daffodils these days. Perhaps horse dung from tumbling around your stables, Linsey."

A cold rage filled Thomas, his chest feeling ready to burst with the effort to hold back. Every word Jordan spoke seemed tailored to push him, to make him question what he knew in his heart to be true. But he couldn't let himself rise to the bait. Not with Paisley watching from the sidelines, not with Ashley's reputation tangled in the outcome.

"She may have waited once, Jordan, but not anymore. She's with me now. Whatever you think she felt for you, it's in the past. I don't care if it was love, infatuation, or pity—it's done. She's mine."

Jordan's smirk faded, his eyes narrowing as he scanned Thomas's face. "You're deluded. The first chance she gets, she'll leave you. That is, if she even loves you at all. And let me guess, she hasn't set a date."

Thomas flinched.

No, she hadn't.

But that didn't mean anything.

"Ah, she's waiting to see if there'll still be anything to your name once I get the horses?" Paisley called from the sidelines but Thomas's vision had blurred with rage.

"There's more to me than my horses. And there's more honor to my line than you'll ever fathom."

When Jordan smirked with a rude shrug, he clenched his fists, the cords in his neck straining as he reined in his temper. His voice was rough, brimming with conviction. "She loves me. You think she'd look at you now and see anything worth holding onto? She's stronger than that. Better."

Jordan let out a cold laugh, shaking his head as though pitying Thomas's naivete. "Believe whatever you want, but don't act so high and mighty. You think she's some perfect creature? Please. I doubt you even know the truth of why she's here at all. But maybe you'll realize soon enough that you've tied yourself to nothing more than a pretty face and false pretenses."

Thomas's vision blurred as his rage erupted, all restraint snapping in a heartbeat. "How dare you?"

Before he knew it, he swung, his fist connecting with enough force to snap Jordan's head to the side. But the bastard recovered fast, retaliating with a hard punch that landed squarely on Thomas's jaw, pain sparking hot and sharp. Ignoring it, he lunged forward, shoving Jordan back as they tumbled to the ground in a tangle of fists and fury.

Dust filled the air around them as fists flew, each man a blur of tightly coiled rage. They grappled, grunts and snarls spilling out between them, as though every buried resentment was suddenly dragged to the surface.

Thomas could hear Paisley laughing somewhere in the background, a sick thrill in his tone as he watched the spectacle. But none of it mattered. All he saw was Jordan, the man who'd abandoned her—and now, dared to insult her, to undermine the depth of their bond.

"Enough!" Sebastian's voice rang out over the melee as he charged forward, grabbing Thomas by the collar and pulling him back with all his might. "What the devil are you doing? Both of you, stop this nonsense!"

Jordan lay on the ground, blood trickling from his nose and a furious glare in his eyes. Thomas felt a bruise forming on his cheek, his hand throbbing from the impact. But he didn't care.

"Stay away from her," he bit out, his voice like steel. "Or you'll deal with me."

Jordan sneered, brushing the dirt from his coat as he stood. "Then you've got my sympathies, for you'll never truly have her."

Sebastian tightened his grip on Thomas's arm, his voice firm but quiet. "Enough. You've made your point."

But Thomas's point was far from done. And as he turned, the fury in his chest still raging, he knew one thing for certain: Ashley was his, and nothing, not even the arrogant bastard who once abandoned her, would change that.

Chapter Twenty-Seven

A THOUSAND BREATHS couldn't fill Ashley's lungs with air. She swallowed, trying to calm her heart once they'd arrived in Thomas's box. It was splendid, adorned with flowers, positioned with a perfect view—and none of it mattered right now.

"What on earth just happened? I thought that man had fled England." Sera's voice cut through the fog of Ashley's panic.

So had Ashley. She was certain Jordan had left, but his contemptuous glare at Thomas... No, something didn't sit right. Thomas hadn't been alarmed, hadn't even appeared wary, just coldly resolved. He hadn't demanded *why* Jordan was still in London. Not how one would react if faced with a nemesis—or a threat.

Focus, Ashley. There's more at stake than Jordan's return.

"Maddie, potion, the horse," she muttered under her breath, pushing herself to think past the knot in her stomach. This was all her fault, and if Thomas figured out the truth from anyone other than her, if she lost his trust...

She couldn't let his horse not run in his race.

Sera nodded, then stopped short. "First, are you all right? You look pale as death."

Ashley forced a steadying breath. "I'm fine. Let's focus on what we can control."

Sera pointed to a line of stables in the distance. "They're just there."

Ashley nodded and strode purposefully in that direction. Fortunately, they didn't meet anyone along the way except for that tall blond man who seemed to watch her. All she wanted to do was stop the mad plan, go to their box, and reassure herself that she hadn't made the biggest mistake of her life with this plot she had set into motion.

With each step, her determination grew, battling the wave of dread coursing through her. The choices that had brought her here—could she truly regret them? They'd brought her closer to him, and yet…regret didn't understand the latter.

"Oh my!" Sera's gasp brought her back.

"What?" Ashley's eyes swept over the crowd.

"Is that your mother? In the ostrich-feathered hat?"

"*What?*" Her head whipped in the direction that Sera pointed. Sure enough! Her mother laughed at something another woman said, her gaze darting over the grounds, searching. Ashley froze, heart pounding, then grabbed Sera's arm. "Run! If she finds me, I'll never escape!"

They dashed toward the stables, weaving between bystanders. What a close call! Ashley forced her focus back, but as they approached the stalls, a fresh wave of uncertainty swept over her. Which one was Thomas's horse?

Sera voiced her exact thoughts. "How will we know which stable?"

"I don't know."

"What's the name of his horse? Or are there several?" Sera asked again.

"I…I don't know."

"What do you know about him?"

That he loves me. And I love him. "Let's make haste. Over there."

Ashley glanced around. A new predicament presented itself. Still, how were they going to find Linsey's stall among all the others?

"I didn't see Maddie on the way. She must be here somewhere or still on her way."

"So, we wait?" Sera's expression was uncertain.

Ashley shook her head, scanning for any sign of their friend. Not ideal. Once Thomas had finished with Jordan and the duke—another shiver trickled down her spine—he would come in search of her to finish business with *her*. His joy that morning as he prepared the horses filled her thoughts, and a pang of dread gnawed at her. The race, Thomas's trust, her own future—this couldn't be the moment it all unraveled.

Just then, a jockey exited one of the stables with a horse in tow. Ashley waved him down. "Excuse me, can you tell us where to find the Earl of Linsey's stall?"

The man frowned, pointing down the line. "Eight stalls down, miss. Though, I doubt he'll race today."

Ashley's heart sank. "Why not?"

"Sick rider. Some lady went to fetch a doctor."

A chill spread through her.

They were too late.

"Thank you," she managed, pulling Sera toward Linsey's stall. Her heart hammered louder with each step, fear entwining with guilt.

They reached the stable, and sure enough, a man lay on a bed of hay, clutching his belly in pain. A heavy sense of failure weighed down on her, pressing the breath from her lungs. Thomas, her own heart—they were all on the line here.

Ashley's thoughts were racing when a familiar voice interrupted. "Ashley? Sera?"

She turned to find Maddie, the doctor at her side.

"Dr. Andre Fernando, here for the sick jockey." The man with wavy black hair and a large leather bag inclined his head and stepped into the stall, heading directly to the patient.

Ashley's pulse quickened. Too many eyes were on her. Thomas's steely composure, Jordan's cryptic contempt—it all threatened to pull the ground from under her. Could the jockey recover in time? Or would everything she'd hoped to salvage now shatter before her eyes?

"What are you doing here?" Maddie asked, her voice low with concern.

"We came to stop you," Sera replied, gesturing to Ashley. "She had a change of heart."

"A change of heart?" Maddie's gaze darted to the injured jockey. "There's no changing any heart now."

"Can he race?" Ashley asked the doctor but all she received was a faint shaking of his head.

"Not today. Perhaps tomorrow." The doctor helped the jockey out of his coat with the number 2 on it and the embroidered crest of the House of Linsey. Ashley recognized it from the elegantly adorned carriage they'd taken to the Ascot.

And also from the carriage house.

Her breath hitched.

Breeches. She needed breeches.

Ashley pulled the pins from her hair that secured the hat and set it aside as soon as the doctor and the jockey were out of sight. She pinned her hair up. "There! White breeches!"

"He won't come back from the outhouse for a while." Maddie flattened her lips. "I gave him senna. It's a mild laxative."

"Mild?" Ashley asked as she grabbed the breeches and the jockey's coat.

"In a single dose, yes. I tripled it," Maddie said. "That's what you wanted, right? I just poisoned a stranger to save your life, didn't I?"

This was a mess, and she'd dragged everyone into it. Thomas, and now Sera, Maddie, and the poor jockey. She was a plague to all who knew her. Perhaps Mother had been right all this time.

"This is what you wanted, right, Ashley?"

Wrong.

The finality in Maddie's tone tightened the noose of worry around Ashley's neck. This wasn't how things were supposed to turn out.

Jordan's return was a complication, but she could only hope that Thomas would understand the lengths she'd gone to, to protect them both.

Her jaw set in determination, and she pulled them to an empty stall, shutting the bottom part of the door, then pushing the top closed and holding it shut with both hands. Sera and Maddie gave her a bewildered look.

"It's a Dutch door. They lock from the outside only," Ashley explained.

Now bewilderment was an understatement. Sera and Maddie eyed her as if she'd sprouted horns or neighed. "What do you expect? Horses can't lock their own stables."

Ashley turned her back to her friends. "Untie my dress."

Sera gaped at her. "How is getting undressed going to solve anything? What is running through your head right now?"

"Not something smart, I imagine," Maddie said.

Smart? Many would say nothing she'd done had been smart up until now. But...

She had made mistakes.

She had to correct them. "I'll race in his place."

Maddie's brow furrowed. "You're terrible at riding."

"Linsey's jockey can't ride," Ashley shot back. "So, there's only one thing left to do. I shall race in his stead. Help me dress in his uniform."

"Why don't you tell Linsey to ride?" Sera asked. "He doesn't need to know about," she cleared her throat, "what happened here today."

"Have you seen him? He's not built like a jockey. More like a stallion."

"This is preposterous!" Maddie exclaimed. "You will die on that track."

"I won't die," Ashley denied. She was ready. Yes, it was preposterous, and yes, she was a terrible rider, but she would hold onto that horse for dear life and prove to Thomas that she was sorry. For everything. And sure, she'd almost fallen off a horse a few days ago, but she'd do better this time around.

A grand gesture as evidence of her repentance? Making up for her misguided vendetta?

She just needed to do *something*.

"We won't be able to change your mind, will we?" Sera asked.

"No."

"You'll never win," Sera went on. "You can't compete with all these other jockeys."

Winning the race wasn't the point here. She would probably come in last. Thomas didn't wager on his horses anyway. But she, however, was gambling everything.

"I don't need to win," Ashley said grimly. "I just need to win him back, not the race."

AFTER HE UNDUSTED himself and washed his hands from his scuffle with Mr. Critton, Thomas entered the box, scanning the crowd. Sebastian trailed in his wake. His gaze swept over each face, but Ashley was nowhere to be seen. Lady Charlene, reclining on a velvet-cushioned seat and fanning herself idly, raised her chin in mild amusement when she caught his eye, but a furrow appeared between her brows when she took in his disheveled state.

"Where is Lady Ashley?" Thomas asked, fighting to keep his voice steady, though tension coiled within him.

Lady Charlene raised a brow. "I haven't the faintest idea. Lord Sebastian escorted me to the box after we placed our bet." She shrugged, her fan snapping shut. "Perhaps they lost track of time—Ascot can be a bit overwhelming to those unaccustomed."

A bead of unease dripped into his thoughts.

Hadn't they come straight to the box? Then they had been gone longer than expected, and the knot tightening in his chest warned him this wasn't a simple delay. The likelihood of Ashley missing his race was low. However, they'd encountered a variable no one could have foreseen. Had Paisley perhaps found her since he'd gone off with Jordan in shame?

A cold whisper of doubt took root.

Had he, or had Jordan, frightened her off? His chest tightened. It was maddening to think she might be avoiding him, retreating from him when he'd barely begun to understand how deep his own feelings had gone.

Hell and damnation.

Another voice cut through his spiraling thoughts as a steward's call rang out across the racetrack. The horses were assembling at the starting line, and the growing murmur of the crowd rippled around him, infectious and electric. Thomas glanced back at the track, his gaze homing in on his own horse, Lord Midnight—a dark, gleaming thoroughbred, the pride of his stables. The other horses, equally grand, shifted and pawed the ground, each rider adjusting reins, readying for the thunderous start. Thomas's pulse quickened.

Sebastian cast him a concerned look, then leaned in with a low voice, "Thomas, you look as though you're waiting for the gallows."

Thomas barely registered him, eyes moving to sweep the scene for any hint of Ashley. "Where could she be?"

"She's bound to make an appearance soon," Sebastian reminded him, following his gaze. "She won't stray too far away. This is the Ascot after all. Where would a lady be?"

He wasn't so sure, but forced himself to turn his gaze back to the racetrack, tightening his jaw as he adjusted his gloves. The sound of the horn blasted, and the crowd stilled in anticipation. A gunshot cracked through the air, signaling the start of the race. The horses surged forward, an explosive burst of raw power and speed, their hooves pounding against the earth in a rhythmic thunder that vibrated through the stands.

His gaze locked onto Lord Midnight. But as the horses stormed around the first bend, he noticed something strange. His horse was struggling, falling behind, jostling with a lack of finesse and balance that clashed against his usual grace.

"What on earth?" he muttered, narrowing his eyes. It was almost as if the jockey had forgotten the technique they'd drilled into him. Was he clutching the horse's neck? But this jockey was seasoned, hand-picked and trusted for his expertise with Lord Midnight. That posture...

It looked troublingly familiar.

And with a sinking dread, Thomas noticed something odd: beneath the riding helmet and silks, stray curls—golden-blonde, distinctly feminine.

Shock sent his pulse skittering.

No.

Impossible.

"Ashley?" He spoke the name aloud in disbelief, his voice barely more than a whisper. But no. It couldn't be. She wasn't reckless enough to attempt something so foolish, so dangerous. Fear swelled within him, becoming something sharper, slicing through the thin guise of control he'd been holding onto since they arrived. *Why?*

Beside him, Lady Charlene's fan clattered to the floor, her attention fixed on a new commotion at the entrance to their box. Thomas's attention whipped to the doorway as a flustered man stumbled in clutching his belly, disheveled, in pain, and unmistakably garbed in Thomas's team colors.

The real jockey.

The jockey's frantic gaze scanned the box until he spotted Thomas. "My lord," he gasped, panting as though he'd run a marathon. "A woman...a woman took my place! She...she took my coat when the doctor..."

Thomas didn't hear the rest.

The world shifted on its axis.

Beside him, Sebastian cursed, and Lady Charlene slowly rose to her feet, eyes wide in shock.

His eyes found his horse again, lagging, but still racing.

She was on the track. She was out there, racing against seasoned riders, pushing Lord Midnight without any of the experience needed to keep control. All he could see was disaster—a misstep, a jostling rider, a single mistake that could send her flying from the saddle and trampled to death. At breakneck speed. "Bloody hell," he muttered, his voice rough with disbelief and rising terror. "What was she thinking?"

Thomas was on the verge of barreling out of his box track when another figure appeared in the doorway—a gaudy woman with a monstrous feathered hat, swathed in layers of lace and color, and the ugliest dog he'd ever seen in her arms. Her bright rouge seemed to glow against her skin as she scanned the box with a haughty scowl, her voice shrill and imperious. "Where is Lady Ashley? Where is my daughter? I demand to see her this instant!"

Trailing behind her was a familiar face: Jordan. Dusty and battered, with eyes filled with equal parts rage and bitterness, he glared at Thomas.

Did the man bloody wish to die today?

Thomas ignored the urge to react, his mind singularly focused on Ashley and the peril she now faced. "I haven't the time for this—" he snapped at the woman, his voice harsher than intended.

"Steady," Sebastian murmured. "There is nothing you can do while she's atop the horse."

Lady Charlene stepped up to Ashley's mother, blocking the woman's view from the track. "Let us get you a glass of punch while we wait for Ashley to come."

Thomas sent Lady Charlene a grateful nod and stalked from the box, breaking into a run the moment he cleared the exit. The horses were halfway through the first circuit, the earth kicking up in thick clouds around them as Lord Midnight fought his way forward, a dark streak among the others. Ashley clung to the reins, her posture rigid with inexperience, her blonde curls flying out from beneath the helmet. She appeared barely in control, swaying with each powerful stride of the thoroughbred beneath her.

The woman was a riding scandal.

He pushed through the thickening mass of spectators, each step more agonizingly slow than the last. His shoulder slammed into bystanders, elbows jarring into his ribs; but he barely noticed the discomfort. "Move, please!" he shouted, his voice cracking with urgency. Ashley was fumbling with the reins, her movements erratic and unsteady. He could see her lips moving, perhaps whispering words of comfort to the horse, but the stallion was skittish, sensing his rider's lack of rhythm.

Every nerve in Thomas's body screamed at him to do something, to get her off that track and to safety. But all he could do was watch, helpless, as the crowd erupted around him, enraptured by the intensity of the race while he was consumed by dread. Ashley's movements were erratic, and she was struggling to hold Lord Midnight in check, her grip on the reins visibly faltering.

"She's going to bloody fall," he muttered, his fists clenched tight enough to turn his knuckles white as he waded through the crowd.

"Look on the bright side," Sebastian offered, keeping up with him. "She won't be trampled if she's last."

"In this round," Thomas mumbled.

His friend's words were swallowed by the crowd's collective gasps and cheers as the horses thundered past the stands. Ashley was clinging to Lord Midnight, but the horse's instincts were kicking in, pushing him forward even as her inexperience held him back.

He was bred to win. With or without a jockey, Lord Midnight would gain speed toward the end. Nobody knew his horses as well as Thomas.

"Damn it," he cursed, voice raw, lost in the cacophony. "Just hold on." The seconds stretched into eternities as he waded through the human sea, with one thought burning in his mind: Get to her. Save her.

In that instant, everything blurred—the racetrack, the roaring crowd. He was no longer at the Ascot, no longer surrounded by society's finest; his world had narrowed to one singular point of focus: Ashley. He cared for the horses, yes, but she was *everything*. He had to reach her. There'd be other races but never another woman for him.

Ignoring the bewildered stares around him and whispered gossip, Thomas surged forward, his only thought to rescue the woman he couldn't bear to lose.

They reached the final stretch. Lord Midnight, as predicted, began surging forward, sensing the nearing finish line, and for a moment, Thomas dared to hope. But his breath hitched as he watched her struggle to maintain balance, the strain evident on her face even from his distant vantage point.

The horses flew past the finish line, a blur of motion and color.

Thomas barely registered the outcome. All he cared about was his love—where she was, if she was safe.

His heart pounded, drowning out the roar of the crowd as he watched her struggle to slow the spirited horse, her movements growing weaker, less controlled. Then, to his horror, she slipped, her body sliding from the saddle as her grip gave way.

"Ashley!" he roared. Pushing past startled onlookers and breaking through the barricade, he raced to where she'd fallen, his heart a relentless drumbeat of panic.

She lay still.

He called her name again as he dashed over to her, falling on his knees beside her.

But she still didn't move.

Chapter Twenty-Eight

Ashley didn't know how to let go of the reins and slid along the turf with her boot skidding along for a moment before the pain that shot through her shoulder forced her to let go. As she hit the ground, the impact jarred through Ashley's entire body, the world around her blurring in a shroud of red dust and bright light. The breath was knocked out of her lungs, leaving her gasping in disorientation. Her vision darkened, little purple and green flecks dancing before her eyes, and for a moment everything went still and silent, the roaring of the crowd a distant echo in some other world.

I made it past the finish line, did I not?

For a few endless seconds, she knew only the heavy ache spreading through her limbs, pulsing from her shoulder down to her fingertips, her mind swimming in and out of awareness. She tried to blink, but the simple effort felt monumental, her eyelids slow to obey.

However, her body protested every attempt to move. Somewhere in the back of her mind, a wry thought surfaced—*Well, it could have been worse. At least I'm not dead.*

Yes, she was still alive.

The shouts and footsteps grew louder, urgent voices piercing the fog. She forced her eyes open again, catching the hazy outline of a figure above her, his hands gentle but firm as they cradled her head.

"Ashley!" Thomas's voice, rough with worry, sounded like it was coming from far away. "Ashley, look at me."

Someone's arm propped her head up.

Thomas's crisp scent made her flutter her eyes open.

She focused on his face, the raw intensity in his eyes bringing her back, grounding her amidst the swirl of pain and dizziness. Thomas hovered over her, his gaze darting across her face as though searching for any sign of lasting harm. Her head throbbed, but the sight of him there, so uncharacteristically panicked, managed to draw the ghost of a smile from her.

Her gaze drifted over his dust-filled appearance, and she furrowed her brows when she spotted the bruise forming on his jaw. "You look worse than I do."

"Damn it, that's all you have to say! You shaved a decade from my life!" His voice broke with both relief, exasperation, and a bit of fury. "Are you mad? Absolutely mad?"

Ashley let out a weak laugh, though it turned into a cough as her lungs struggled to catch up. "Possibly," she whispered, her voice shaky. "But it seems I'm not entirely dead yet."

"Not dead? Not dead yet? You nearly frightened *me* to death!" He brushed a stray curl from her face, his thumb lingering for a moment, gentle and warm.

"What happened to you?" she asked him. "Did the horses trample *you*?" His elegant attire had been ruined, the sleeves ripped, and there was more dust in his hair at the Royal Ascot than even after he trained the horses.

Before he could answer, the world suddenly erupted around them as familiar faces pressed closer, their voices blending into a clamor of concern.

"Ashley! Oh, my dear Ashley! How could you do this to your mother!" A voice cried out above the rest, followed by a thump.

"Oh, my!" Charlene called. "Bring the smelling salts! Quickly, someone! And catch that dog!"

Ashley turned her head to see her mother had fainted and lay sprawled out a few feet away from her. Well, drat, the gossip rags would be plastered with caricatures of mother and daughter lying on the racetrack at the Ascot.

Even Lord Cambridge wore a look of genuine worry. He leaned over Thomas. "I must say, Ashley, you are quite daring. That was an impressive tumble."

"This is not the time for teasing," Maddie scolded, her hands clasped over her mouth as she leaned in, eyes wide with worry. "Ashley, are you all right?"

Ashley gave a slow nod. "I think so."

Thomas cursed again.

Jordan, dusted and slightly battered himself, kneeled off to the side of her mother. Her gaze moved back to Thomas. They'd fought?

Her mother's voice rang out again, shrill and horrified. "Oh, how will I survive this scandal! This is simply..." She fainted again.

Charlene rolled her eyes and sighed.

"Here." Sera came around to hand Charlene a small bottle. "But I vote to leave the countess be."

Ashley moved to sit up and winced, attempting to move her leg before a sharp pain shot up her calf. Instantly an arm cradled her. "My leg hurts," she breathed, squeezing Thomas's hand, and he immediately shifted closer.

"We need a doctor," Thomas called out.

"No," Ashley said. She didn't want a doctor. She wanted to go...home. His home. The castle.

"Yes." He cursed again. "Whatever possessed you to take such a reckless risk?"

"I had something to prove."

"To whom?" he asked, brows furrowing. "Because it certainly wasn't to yourself. Is this about what you wish to share with me?"

She hesitated, shifted uncomfortably.

"Easy now," Thomas murmured. "You don't need to prove anything else today."

Her eyes flitted to him, her heart twisting as she caught the rawness in his gaze. She sighed. "I wanted to make things right. But I've done everything wrong. Can we leave now, if that is all right?" Sitting on the ground, with people hovering, made her feel like a circus animal that didn't perform as wished.

He nodded, sweeping the track with a look. The crowd around them had quieted a little, but murmurs and shocked whispers still rippled through.

Her mother woke again, and once more the scene teetered on the edge of chaos. Through it all, Ashley kept her gaze locked on Thomas. The anger in his eyes was unmistakable, but she could see relief there too—a vulnerable openness that made her heart twist. She wanted to ask him about Jordan, but with the man a few feet away, she didn't want to take a chance. This might be the last time she'd be in his arms if he found out…what exactly did he know?

"Are you angry with me?" she whispered, needing to hear the answer even if she already knew.

His jaw tightened as he stared down at her, brows furrowed. "How could I not be furious?" he said quietly. "You are hurt. You could have been hurt much worse. Dead even." His voice softened.

Ashley's heart swelled, and she smiled weakly, placing her hand over his. "Then I suppose you'll have to keep a closer watch on me. If you still want me?"

Thomas let out a breath that was almost a laugh, his anger softening as he shook his head. "If that's what it takes."

The arm on her back firmed while another slipped beneath her legs. He lifted her up and strode from the track. Her arms circled around his neck.

Did that mean the worst was over?

THOMAS STRODE TOWARD the carriage with a furious determination, every muscle in his body taut. His heart was still hammering, the rush of adrenaline only beginning to ebb away, leaving a dreadful, hollow ache in its place. She'd been one slip away from catastrophe, and now, with every step he took, the fear he had tamped down boiled to the surface, nearly blinding him.

He felt as though he'd lost the youth in his life in those final, terrifying seconds of the race. It wouldn't have surprised him if he'd gone entirely gray from it. One thing was clear: like she'd lost grip of the horse, he hadn't been in control of holding the proverbial reins, either.

Bloody, bloody hell and damnation.

"Are you certain you're not hurt anywhere else?" he asked, his voice still gruff as he glanced down at her. Her face was still pale, her brow faintly creased as if even now she was debating whether she should apologize or argue or complain of hurt.

Her fingers clutched his jacket. "Just my pride—and maybe a few bruises here and there," she murmured, though her voice wavered enough to betray her own uncertainty.

"So, you are hurt everywhere."

He'd fallen from a horse before. There was no way she only felt a small ache here and there. He exhaled sharply, a faint laugh escaping him. "I could throttle you," he muttered, tightening his hold around her. "I still cannot begin to understand what you were thinking. You know you are not a seasoned rider."

Her smile was faint, almost sheepish. "I'm not entirely sure, now that I've had a moment to reflect on it."

So, she was still hesitant to tell him. "We need to talk, love. Really have a good talk." He pulled her a little closer as he reached the carriage, realizing belatedly he didn't intend to let her out of his sight for the foreseeable future. As gently as he could, he climbed in, cradling her on his lap as he sank into the seat and drew her securely against him. She melted against him, leaning her head into the crook of his neck, and he exhaled fully, finally able to breathe again. Somewhat.

But as soon as the door shut, it was wrenched open once more, and he blinked in surprise as Sebastian's head appeared, his expression urgent. Without waiting for a word, Sebastian stepped up into the carriage, and before Thomas could question him, Maddie, Charlene, and Sera scrambled in behind him, each of them shuffling to fit into the carriage's cramped interior.

"Go!" Sebastian called to the driver, rapping on the roof as the wheels began to roll.

"What the—" Thomas started, but Sebastian only shot him a look of mild panic.

"Your almost mother-in-law," he said grimly, jerking his thumb over his shoulder. "She's on her way over with renewed vigor and enough indignation to fuel the rest of London for the season."

Ashley groaned softly, her head sinking against his chest. "Is she—oh no, not again."

"Oh yes," Maddie said with a serious look. "And from the look on her face, I'd say we barely escaped unscathed. I wouldn't be surprised if she's rallying all the old dragons of her acquaintance to lay siege to the castle."

Sera leaned in from her cramped corner. "And Lord Linsey, I wouldn't rule out that throttling you mentioned."

Charlene gave a prim sniff. "You may want to watch yourself, my lord. She's not thrilled about your role in all this."

"My role?" Thomas repeated, looking at Ashley in bewilderment. "And what role would that be?"

"Allowing me to race."

"But I did no such thing," he all but growled.

"Tell her that," Ashley said simply.

Sebastian grunted, but he kept his voice low, glancing back through the rear window. "She's still coming, you know. And with remarkable robustness."

Thomas shook his head, barely able to muster more than disbelief at this point. "Remarkable indeed."

The carriage jostled as they picked up speed.

"I have half a mind to ride ahead and warn your staff to close the castle gates," Sebastian said.

Thomas swallowed a sigh. He wanted time alone with Ashley. They had things to discuss, but that didn't seem to be in their immediate future. He let out an inward groan.

"That might be a good idea," Sera said, shaking her head. "Once she enters, she may never leave until she sees you both wed."

Ashley groaned.

"True," Maddie murmured. "Your father will learn of this soon, too."

Ashley sighed. "There is no helping it now."

Thomas nodded. "This is going to cause a scandal, but nothing too wild, I think."

"Ah, well, what is the point of life if you can't have a little scandal attached to your name?" Sera murmured.

Charlene nodded. "You may have just secured a lifetime of notoriety. But don't worry—we'll make sure it's the *good* kind."

Thomas shook his head, his eyes meeting Sebastian's. With four women in the carriage and an almost mother-in-law with her feathers ruffled so badly that the Ton had seen it, he wouldn't get out of this one unscathed.

Chapter Twenty-Nine

Back at Fort Balmore

EVERYONE HAD COME.
 Everyone.

Thomas shut the door behind the doctor with a click that felt far more significant than it should have. The entire ordeal had nearly made him lose his head of hair. He'd barely breathed until the doctor—the only person Thomas had welcomed from the Countess Chaswick's following—gave his verdict. Ashley wasn't badly hurt—just a few bruises here and there, as she had said. Except for her shoulder, which she needed to rest for the next week. He reluctantly turned back to the occupants of the room. The discord of voices that filled the room was unwelcome, and he found himself wishing he could kick out every single one who didn't belong.

How was he supposed to talk with Ashley when no one would give them a second alone? She should rest, but every bit of her energy seemed reserved for placating the very people who should have been comforting her. *We should have eloped.* Then, at least, he'd have the authority to clear the room and be alone with his wife. How exactly had he lost authority in his castle, anyway?

Pondering the matter half-heartedly, he strode back to her, where she lay propped up against the pillows on the bed, while the Earl of Chaswick perched on the edge, concern etched into the lines of his brow. He cast a quick glance at her mother, who stood at the window with that ugly dog still clutched in her arms, her face contorted in distress. On the settee, her friends whispered furiously to one another, glancing between Ashley and himself.

"Thank the heavens you will live," her mother exclaimed, and Thomas nearly rolled his eyes, taking a seat at the head of the bed. Did the countess not hear the doctor? "Riding on a horse, of all things!"

"What else would I ride, Mother?" Ashley replied, her tone clipped. "It's just a small fall."

"Small?" the countess exploded. "You were thrown off a horse at a public event! Royal and public! The entire royal family *and* the Ton saw it! What will the gossip sheets say? This will be the talk of the season!"

Saints, save him.

Did they not understand what mattered here? Did her mother's concern only stretch as far as her reputation? Her fall had shattered him in a way he'd never admit aloud. Gossip was the last damn thing on his mind.

"Gather yourself, Lady Chaswick," Ashley's father said. "That is not what's important here."

Thank you.

"I beg your pardon? Just what is important, then?"

"Our daughter's well-being."

"Her reputation is her well-being! How could she do something so foolish as this?"

Thomas felt a flash of irritation flare within him. Couldn't they see that Ashley wanted to be anywhere but amid their bickering? She didn't need to be subjected to a verbal inquisition the moment they stepped through the door.

"I am right here," Ashley muttered. "And I say, what is life without a little scandal attached to my name?"

She threw a wink at her friends, and he couldn't help but feel a slight smile tug at his lips. Her resilience never ceased to amaze him. Ever the plucky optimist, Lady Ashley.

Chaswick rubbed his temples. "Your mother is right to worry," he said gently. "You gave us all a terrible scare."

"And for that I am sorry. I didn't throw myself off the horse on purpose."

Ah, she fell off a horse, but it is her reputation and her mother's feelings at stake. That explained everything.

I see why she is confused about her own feelings.

Lady Chaswick sighed deeply, a hand pressed to her forehead as if she were trying to ward off a headache. Thomas almost let out a wry laugh. Did he need to send for smelling salts? However, she wasn't the only one who'd felt on the verge of collapse tonight. But at least he had the grace not to make a spectacle of it. He clenched and unclenched a fist, inwardly counting the seconds until they'd all leave. "Perhaps this is not the moment for arguments," she said, her voice softer now. "We all just want to ensure you're safe, my dear."

Thomas blinked. That must be the calmest he'd heard the countess up until now. "I agree. The doctor said all she needed was rest."

"All's well that ends well," Sera chimed in, nudging her friends, who bobbed their heads up and down.

Just then, the door swung open, and Sebastian strode in, his face grim. He shook his head, and Thomas stiffened. It seemed Jordan Critton refused to leave. Hadn't he already made it clear that the riffraff wasn't welcome? But it seemed Critton was as determined as a cockroach. And to make things worse, Sebastian whispered in his ear, "Chaswick's son arrived as well."

He glanced at Ashley before his eyes caught Chaswick's.

Chaswick must have caught their glance, for he suddenly said, "I saw Critton lurking outside. I hope he's not welcome here."

All eyes swiveled to the earl.

Ashley frowned. "Why?"

Her question made Thomas halt.

Chaswick sighed. "The man is a gambling rogue." He sighed again. "That's why I used my connections to run him out of town, but it didn't seem to work."

"What?" Ashley breathed.

Thomas felt his heart drop to his shoes with that one breathless whisper, a sense of dread clawing at him.

Had Paisley been right?

⇶✦⇷

ASHLEY'S HEART SANK, her pulse hammering in her chest as her father's words caught her like a blow to the chest. *The man is a gambling rogue. I used my connections to run him out of town, but it didn't seem to work.*

It was her father? Not Thomas?

Her mind spun as she tried to make sense of it.

How could she not have known? All this time, she'd believed it had been Thomas's hand in Jordan's sudden disappearance. That single assumption had been the cornerstone of everything she'd done since—her anger, her schemes, even her engagement.

She had orchestrated an entire campaign of vengeance. She had accused him of cruelty, letting it fester until she convinced herself he deserved to pay for what Jordan had suffered. She had suffered. She'd crafted this relationship with a man she hardly knew, simply because it suited her purpose to be close to him, to dismantle some part of his world. Yet, it turned out it was the wrong man all along.

The realization hit her like a blow.

She had taken her ire, her fury over Jordan's alleged exile, and aimed it squarely at Thomas without a second thought. How could she have gotten it so wrong?

But she knew...

Of course, her father wouldn't mention anything. But in his note, Jordan had made it sound like it was Linsey.

Bile rose in her throat.

"Ashley?" Thomas suddenly said, concerned.

She glanced up, only to see him watching her, his gaze filled with worry. The look in his eyes said he wanted to reach out, perhaps to hold her. But so many eyes were in the chamber. She averted her gaze, inhaling a shaky breath. She couldn't look him in the eye—how could she, after her entire reasoning for being with him had crumbled in one moment of revelation?

Space.

She needed to think, to untangle the mess inside her head, for she could certainly not untangle the mess she'd already made. The best thing she could do for him was to remove herself from his life. He deserved much better than what he got.

"Why didn't you tell me, Papa?" she asked her father, who cleared his throat.

"You seemed quite..." He glanced at Thomas before returning his gaze to her. "Taken with him. I didn't want to disappoint you any further."

She stiffened, but before she could respond, her mother's voice rang out. "What's he doing here? How dare your by-blow show his face here?"

Ashley's eyes widened. "Whose what?"

Ashley turned to Thomas, but he shook his head. *Not mine.*

Her father cursed. "This is not the time."

Her head whipped to her father. "Don't tell me... I have a brother?"

"This isn't how I wanted you to find out, darling."

Her friends jumped up at that moment. "I think we should give you some space," Maddie murmured.

"Good idea," Sebastian muttered.

A pressing need for space throbbed within her.

"I...I think I need a moment," she murmured, barely a whisper.

"Alone."

She met Thomas's eyes again, his gaze probing her. Then he rose, nodding. "Then you shall have it."

"How can we leave you alone at a time like this?" her mother said. "I shall stay."

Ashley briefly shut her eyes. "Why must you always question my choices? I want to be alone. Alone means alone."

"Give your daughter some space." Thomas's tone was soft but firm.

She shot him a grateful glance.

"But—"

"No buts, my dear." Her father rose to his feet. "Let's go."

Ashley waited until the door shut before she rose from the bed and wobbled to the window, her eyes instantly falling on a man below. He was in conversation with Jordan, of all people. She shook her head.

She donned her riding habit, eager to get out of the sullied outfit she'd worn at the Ascot. Everything about it—the Ton, the scandals, the expectations, and the hushed gossip—appeared just as dirty to her as those clothes. How her perspective had changed. What had been sparkling and elegant in the morning was nothing to her now. The estate, the country, and everything about Thomas and what he held dear had become her everything.

Plus, she had a brother.

A half-brother, as it appeared. But a whole person she'd never known.

And her family had kept it from her.

Just as her father had kept from her his role in Jordan vanishing from her life, setting her on a path she couldn't even bring herself to regret. What a wonderfully bittersweet contradiction. How was she supposed to feel about all this? How was she—

The door suddenly opened, and Sera's head popped in. "Are you all right?" her friend asked. "Do you need help to escape?"

Ashley suddenly laughed. "No, just help to the stables."

She glanced back out the window, squaring her shoulders. She had a brooch to return.

And a brother to meet.

Chapter Thirty

"Ashley."

Ashley's head whipped toward the barn door, her heart dropping at the sight of the last man she ever wanted to see. But she had known that this confrontation was inevitable. "Jordan."

"What are you doing?" he asked, striding over, but coming to a stop when her eyes narrowed on him.

"Me?" She twirled the brooch between her fingers before tossing it over to him. She thought she'd lost it but found it stuck between one of her shawls. "This is what you came for, is it not?"

He caught it with one hand, staring at her broodingly. "What if I'm here for you, too?"

"There is no 'me' for you anymore." She turned to face him. "I was told that it was my father who tried to run you off. Why did you mention Linsey in your note?"

He sighed, averting his gaze. "Well, I couldn't very well blame your father."

He could, but that was probably the most redeemable thing about him at this point. Funnily enough, she felt no regret. Not even an ounce. "There's nothing further, is there?"

"Paisley," he suddenly said. "Be careful of him. He's the one who came to me. He might do more if you stay engaged to Linsey."

"Thank you for the warning, but you don't have to worry about me."

He nodded, then, with one last glance, inclined his head and left the stables.

It's finally over.

Ashley glanced back at the stall, where a baby horse lay, staring up at her with wide, curious eyes. Its mother was nowhere in sight. She knelt beside the little creature, gently patting its soft head.

Let's just hug it.

She just needed to hold something.

She sighed. The little foal rested lightly in her arms whereas her heart felt impossibly heavy.

"Where is your mother? Who is taking care of you?" she murmured, stroking its downy coat. Knowing Paisley, any horse that didn't turn a profit was likely bound for the stew pot.

Ashley cradled the foal closer against her chest, one hand resting on its tiny belly. She felt its heartbeat, a faint but steady rhythm against her fingers. The air was warm, thick with the earthy scent of hay and the subtle musk of horses. A scent she'd never expected to find soothing, let alone one that could calm her so completely.

Sunlight filtered through the open windows, casting soft patterns on the stable walls, and for the first time, she truly appreciated the haven the Linsey family had built here over generations. This was more than a place for horses; it was a sanctuary, a place that nurtured life.

No ballroom in London could rival the comfort she felt there. In town, it had all been about luxury, titles, and, of course, riches—exactly the sort of place where someone like Paisley thrived. It was no wonder, really, that Thomas felt out of place there. He may have the title, the castle, and the wealth—even handsomeness—yet his life was about something far greater than himself.

He would never drive a man off over a mere wager.

How could I have been so blind to what was right in front of me?

The hay pricked her through her dress, reminding her of the night she'd spent in the hayloft with the earl. The stables brought the memory back in vivid detail—heat and stolen kisses, a night that had left her breathless.

She should have known better back then.

She'd been foolish, caught up in the moment. Now, she wished she had admitted the truth. Her silence had woven a web of misunderstanding, each strand of it her own doing.

"You must be smarter with your life," Ashley murmured to the foal, but mostly to herself.

The foal nuzzled closer, its soft muzzle brushing her cheek, pulling her from her thoughts. She smiled, then let out a heavy breath. She couldn't hide here forever. She'd have to face the mess she had allowed Paisley to create—and that she had worsened.

She had to talk with Thomas.

Oh, the shame! The horror!

She suddenly laughed at herself.

You've been bold so far, Ashley. Don't stop now.

Maybe her mother was right. Perhaps she had been a mere empty shell—a pretty dress draped over nothing, a woman with neither heart nor soul. But not anymore. Thomas gave her purpose. Meaning. Or rather, in him, she had found herself. Found purpose. Found meaning.

"Ashley?" a voice broke through her thoughts.

The foal's ears pricked.

Thomas.

"Ashley?" Thomas called again, the hay crunching under his steps as he approached. "Are you here?"

Be brave, Ashley.

Yes, she was going to be brave! She scrambled to her feet and shut the stall door with a quick pull. Bravely *not* ready for this moment. "Don't let him find us," she whispered to the foal. She shut the bottom half, but as she tried to close the top, it swung back open.

"I already did!" his deep voice came.

Her hands gripped the rough wooden door as she realized, with a wave of embarrassment, that it was built with wide gaps between the planks.

"Why are you shutting yourself in the stalls?" Thomas asked with more bewilderment than anything else. He was a disheveled vision—crisp white shirt, tight breeches, and all the terrible combinations of irresistible manhood, alongside the devastating charm of a country lord.

Ashley gave the door another push, but it swung open again. "Why do you have doors that don't even lock?"

"They lock from the outside," he said with a smile. "Why would a horse need to lock its own stable?"

Ashley deflated, plopping back onto the straw as the foal sidled back into her arms. She didn't look up at the man, but she could feel his gaze resting on her.

How embarrassing!

She never seemed to make the right choices when it came to this man.

"You should be resting in bed," he said gently. "Or are you planning to run away?"

"If I planned to do that, I didn't manage it very well," she muttered, "or else you wouldn't have found me."

So much for being brave, Ashley!

Well, there was no putting it off anymore. "I think it's time for me to leave, don't you?"

⁂

THOMAS COULDN'T HELP but want to kiss those sweet lips of hers, especially with the little foal nestled in her lap. Funny how the tides had turned in the stables—now he envied the creature everyone had pitied only days ago.

That's until her words sank in. "What did you just say?"

"It's time for me to leave. Don't you think so?"

"Why the devil would you say something like that?" Thomas demanded, fists clenching.

"You still need to ask?" She swallowed visibly, brushing her hair out of her face. She sniffled and when she looked up at him, his heart shattered like a glass on the floor.

"Don't move," he commanded, bracing both hands on the door's smooth rim, feeling the worn grooves beneath his fingers. With a swift movement, he vaulted over it, his landing a soft thud against the packed earth. Ashley sat just a few feet away, wide-eyed, her breath catching in surprise.

"You leapt over the door?" Ashley's eyes were wide. "Just like that?"

"I told you before, I can navigate Almack's dance floor, but this…" He opened his arms. The early spring air drifted through the windows, carrying the scent of budding flowers and fresh grass. "This is where I'm at home."

He stepped closer, the crunch of straw underfoot filling the gap of the silence, and she set the foal down, rising to her feet. Their gazes locked, something unspoken passing between them, as if the stable had become a universe of its own. He reached for her face, trailing his thumb over the corner of her frown. "And what if I can't bear to let you go?"

"I'd call your sanity into question."

"It was always in question." He lifted the corner of his lips. "From the moment you approached me at Almack's. So, stay."

"I told myself to be brave," she suddenly said, shaking her head. "Yet I've found I can be quite cowardly when the moment calls for the exact opposite."

He cupped her cheek, and she inclined her head, nestling into his hand. He noticed the subtle shift in her weight, a small movement that spoke louder than words. He could hear the faint rustle of her skirt as she breathed, each detail sharpening this delicate moment. "You are not cowardly, love."

Then she withdrew, taking a step back, and he dropped his hand. "I didn't tell you the truth, even after...even after I realized that I might have misjudged you."

"That still doesn't make you a coward."

"Thomas. I approached you to get revenge because I believed you chased Jordan out of town and ruined my chances at love. Does that not bother you?"

He smiled at her. "Our start is our start."

She shook her head and laughed. "Is it honestly as simple as that?"

"It's a fact, so yes, it's as simple as that."

"And you don't feel an ounce of betrayal? I planned to ruin all you held dear."

"The only way you could do that is if you leave, love. The horses, the wager, Paisley, I can give it all up if it means I have you." And he meant it. He didn't need anything else but her. If he lost her... "So, yes, our start is our start. Fainting mother, secret brother, a revenge plot, I don't care."

She pinched the bridge of her nose. "You are a madman, you know that?"

"What about you? The Ashley who came here a short time ago would never have hugged a foal."

A hint of a smile touched her face. "I'm still the same Ashley."

"Converted to a country girl?"

She laughed for a moment, but tears suddenly welled in her eyes. "I'm so sorry."

Thomas froze, shocked. "Ashley?"

She covered her face with her hands. "Don't look at me!"

"I'm not." The response came instinctively.

"Liar."

He chuckled and pulled her in for a hug. "I forbid you to leave me because you approached me with vengeful thoughts." His arms tightened. "If it wasn't for that stroke of luck, I'd never have met you."

"Only you would call it a stroke of luck," she muttered. "And what is it with this stall door?"

He chuckled when she changed the subject. "It's called a Dutch—"

"I know, I know. A Dutch door," Ashley said. "How very impractical."

"Should I hold it shut from the inside?" He backed them both up until he could close it, leaning against the door with his back. She rubbed her face against his shirt. There wasn't anything at the stables that could surprise Thomas. He knew how to do everything, even cleaning up what his stable boys did. But a crying lady was a new challenge. "Apology accepted," he whispered into her ear. "I love you."

She suddenly gripped his shirt and stared up at him. "You're never allowed to take that back."

"I won't. Ever."

Her eyes narrowed, tears still clinging to her lashes, wringing his heart as if he'd been stabbed with a pitchfork right through the ribs. "You said it; our start is our start."

"Our start is our start."

Her tear-stained face split into a grin. "I love you, too."

Chapter Thirty-One

"SO YOU KNOW him?" Ashley asked as Thomas led her back to the house. Why on earth had he followed them from Ascot? Had the man not done enough?

"We went to Eton together, but I didn't know him well until Oxford. Seb knew him a little better," Thomas replied, placing his hand over Ashley's.

When they reached the drawing room, five solemn faces greeted them.

This was the entrance Ashley had been born to make—no ball gown, no fan to hide behind. She had Thomas by her side, and that was all that mattered.

"Shouldn't you change before dinner?" her mother asked, giving Ashley's attire a disapproving once-over.

"I'm not dining with Paisley or anyone he's brought along," Ashley said firmly. She glanced at the glass Paisley held, likely filled with cognac, and narrowed her gaze. "I want him gone."

Paisley chuckled and took a slow sip before setting his glass down. "Is that so, my dear? You may be betrothed to him, but Thomas here has other obligations to consider."

"Nothing is dissolved," Thomas said, meeting Ashley's gaze with a steady nod. "And my future countess has made her wishes clear. Leave now."

"Now, now, Thomas," Paisley began, his tone almost mocking, "no need to be rash."

"Enough," Thomas said sharply. "And if you have any lingering attachments to Linsey stock, you'd best let them go."

Paisley's face twisted with a scowl. But before he could respond, a tall blond man stepped forward from where he'd been quietly standing by the window.

"Thomas," he said, holding out a parchment, "I thought you might need this more than a traditional wedding present. It still needs your signature."

Thomas took the parchment, and the man turned to Ashley with a warm smile. "My heartfelt congratulations, Lady Ashley."

Ashley looked at him, her brow furrowing in recognition. So *this* was her brother. She couldn't take her eyes off him. "What is your name?"

"Clyde Sheffield," he said, bowing and extending his hand to her.

Ashley took it, her eyes studying his face. "We have the same blue eyes and curly blond hair."

Clyde smiled, a bit bashful, as their father came forward, clearly overwhelmed. "Clyde, my boy! How did you manage all of this?"

"I had some help," Clyde replied, glancing at Thomas and Ashley. "When I learned of Paisley's wager against Thomas, I took a gamble of my own."

Ashley's eyes widened. "You mean the Ascot?"

Clyde nodded. "I overheard Lady Maddie at the apothecary discussing a potential weakness, and I had to act. I knew that if Paisley lost, everything would revert to Thomas. So, I arranged for a little extra motivation."

"That's why you were at the stables?" Ashley's hand flew to her mouth. "I saw you there."

"Yes," Clyde said, looking to their father for confirmation. "I wasn't sure if Lady Maddie would go through with her plan, so I had a backup in place, ready to act if necessary."

Their father nodded, pride evident in his expression. "Clyde ensured Paisley couldn't take what belonged to the house of Linsey."

"Wait," Thomas said, scanning the parchment, his brow furrowing. "You mean Paisley never even had a true claim on my horses?"

"Exactly," Clyde replied. "He set the wager against me without realizing I'd preempted his move."

Paisley seethed, his face contorting in frustration. "This is outrageous!"

Thomas held up a hand, his tone calm but firm. "So let me understand—Paisley tried to sabotage my engagement to Ashley over something he'd already lost?"

Paisley's face darkened, but he remained silent, rage flickering in his eyes.

Clyde stepped in, turning to Thomas. "Consider the debt cleared with a handshake." He held out his hand.

Thomas took it, their grip firm, a silent agreement between them. "Your horses will stay at Elysian Fields, where they belong."

Clyde turned to Ashley with a warm smile. "And may I formally congratulate you, Lady Ashley—"

"No," Ashley said, stepping forward and embracing him in a heartfelt hug.

The first of many for her brother.

Epilogue

Thomas held the reins of his sturdy horse as a gentle spring breeze brushed his face, carrying whispers of the past. The mare neighed softly, trotting in a slow circle around him, the rope serving as the radius of her orbit. Thomas realized he'd been at the center not only of this circle but also of his family's legacy. He'd been the pivot point, nearly risking his family's estate, their horses, their legacy—everything the name Linsey stood for. And though Paisley got what he deserved, now that the ice had thawed, so had Thomas's heart. His fears had dried up like the mud left behind by winter's harshest days. The worst was over.

The icy grip of winter had long given way to the sun's warm touch, casting a golden glow over the meadow. It was a scene of rebirth: primroses revealed their golden hearts, daisies shone with innocence, and birds chirped cheerful wake-up songs. Like bejeweled dames at a grand ball, bluebells chimed in the wind while magenta corncockles dotted the lush English countryside. Thomas inhaled the crisp air and felt the familiar, grounding love he had for Fort Balmore and Elysian Fields. Now that he'd secured their future through the cherished horse breeds, he felt he'd finally earned his place in the portrait gallery of his ancestors. The house of Linsey would continue to grow and prosper because he'd ensured it. He, Thomas, the Earl of Linsey, had grown up to an extent he never believed was required.

And his heart had grown, too—it was ready to burst with love for Ashley.

The vibrant green grass brushed her knees as she approached him from the stables. The meadow had shaken off its winter slumber, and the morning dew sparkled brighter than the chandeliers at Almack's on the first day he'd seen her. Only a few months had passed, yet it felt like a lifetime.

His heart fluttered like the butterflies that flitted from bloom to bloom, drawn to the sweetness and array of colors surrounding her. As Ashley drew closer, she cast him that bone-melting smile. He yearned to be near his beautiful countess, his heart echoing the rhythm of the butterflies.

Suddenly, a yellow butterfly, as bright as Ashley's hair at their first dance, waltzed into his view. It danced in the wind before landing lightly on a purple flower, its vibrant colors standing out in contrast. Thomas knew life was fleeting and resolved to make the most of it. His love for Ashley was as certain as the dance of butterflies from blossom to blossom—brilliant, boundless, and steadfast. Watching the butterfly ascend, he felt their love, too, had taken flight, soaring to the heights of the infinite sky. Time had only deepened his affection, transforming it into a love as enduring and rich as the countryside stretching before him. And he hoped that, despite all he'd done wrong, their future as Earl and Countess of Linsey would be as bountiful as their estate.

Ashley ran toward him, and they kissed.

He pulled her into his arms, the world melting away around them, and kissed her with all the aching tenderness of a man who had found his salvation and refused to look back. It was a kiss that spoke of promises, of futures unknown yet certain, and of a love fierce and unyielding.

"I never thought I'd do more than tempt you this spring," Ashley said, her voice teasing though her eyes shimmered with sincerity.

Thomas laughed softly, his hand brushing against her cheek.

"Tempt me? You've undone me entirely, Ashley. One smile from you, one glance, and no force in this world could pull me from your side. You are my spring, my summer, every season I never knew I needed. I didn't just fall for you—I surrendered completely."

Ashley's breath caught, her fingers resting lightly on his chest.

"Thomas..." she began, but the rest of her words were lost as he gently took her face in his hands and kissed her again, pouring a lifetime of love into that one perfect moment. "I think I've caught wedding fever," Ashley confessed, her cheeks flushing as she leaned closer to Thomas. "Every time I dream of us, it's you waiting at the end of the aisle, looking at me like I'm your whole world."

Thomas's smile tugged at the corners of his lips, his fingers lacing with hers. "You *are* my whole world, Ashley. Every plan, every hope, it all begins and ends with you." He paused, his voice dropping to a tender whisper. "If I had my way, we'd already be married. I don't want to wait another moment to—"

"Then don't wait," Ashley whispered as she pressed her lips onto his.

The series continues with Sera's story in *How to Lose a Prince This Summer*. Find out how the next girl catches the wedding fever despite all odds and finds her happily ever after with a beloved character, Prince Alex, whom we know and love from Sara Adrien's *A Touch of Charm*.

About the Authors

Sara Adrien

Bestselling author Sara Adrien writes hot and heart-melting Regency romance with a Jewish twist. As a law professor-turned-author, she writes about clandestine identities, whims of fate, and sizzling seduction. If you like unique and intelligent characters, deliciously sexy scenes, and the nostalgia of afternoon tea, then you'll adore Sara Adrien's tender tear-jerkers.

For more information and exclusive sneak peeks, new releases, and more, sign up for Sara Adrien's newsletter at www.SaraAdrien.com.

Tanya Wilde

Award-winning and International Bestselling author Tanya Wilde developed a passion for reading when she had nothing better to do than lurk in the library during her lunch breaks. Her love affair with pen and paper soon followed after she devoured all of their historical romance books! When she's not meddling in the lives of her characters or pondering names for her imaginary big, white greyhound, she's off on adventures with her partner in crime.

Wilde lives in a town at the foot of the Outeniqua Mountains, South Africa.

Find out more at www.authortanyawilde.com.

Printed in Great Britain
by Amazon